The Resurrection Stone

George
Enjoy,

The Resurrection Stone

Frank Hertle

Writers Club Press
New York   Lincoln   Shanghai

The Resurrection Stone

Writers Club Press
an imprint of iUniverse, Inc.

For information address:
iUniverse
2021 Pine Lake Road, Suite 100
Lincoln, NE 68512
www.iuniverse.com

ISBN: 0-595-20808-8

Printed in the United States of America

"Our deepest fear is that we are powerful beyond measure. It is our light not our darkness that most frightens us."

Marianne Williamson

Monday

The August sun burned like the point of a white-hot spear thrust through the thin blue sky as the ferry boat *Traveler* out of Ft. Hamilton, Maryland, humped a trawler's wake. The boat jolted. Salt spray splashed, mixed with the suntan lotion on Jason's face. The breeze forced by the ferry's motion cooled him. Gulls shrieked.

Jason Eric Stern shook water out of his curly black hair. His eyes burned as lotion ran into them. His heart beat fast. He hated boats.

Jason looked over the mixed crowd of summer travelers. Fathers, mothers, grandparents, kids, teens, singles, couples, groups of friends, carrying and dragging luggage, groceries, boxes, television sets, radios, shopping bags, babies, strollers, backpacks, dogs, cats, talking, laughing, listening to Walkmans, chewing gum, drinking beer, soda, coffee, soup, sunning themselves on the upper deck of the *Traveler*, all heading out to the small barrier island called Cranberry four miles off the coast.

"Your nose is burned," his mother said, squinting as she used her Superman-like microscopic vision to scan his face. "Put something on it."

"Just did, ma." Jason rubbed his face for emphasis.

"The water's washed it off. You know how fair you are."

Jason knew how fair, how white, how like a ghost he looked compared to the beautiful suntanned people on the ferry. And how like a ghost he would stay during his time on Cranberry Island because he would never bare his zit-infested back to the world's gaze and because his mother

1

would make sure the exposed parts of him were larded with sun block each time he dared go outdoors.

"Now put something on or we're going down."

Down meant to the enclosed lower deck. Jason sighed and surrendered, glancing at the strap of his sandal, an old worn strap ready to break, before offering his hands to his mother. She squirted lotion onto his palms and he smoothed it over his face and arms while he watched a girl of fifteen or sixteen dressed in a bikini top and jeans shorts adjust her curves. She was with a well-muscled boy wearing a Bud tee-shirt.

The girl stood, the gentle tanned lines of her thighs melting into her shorts. She glanced in Jason's direction, carelessly tossing her streaked blond hair to one side. She was sexy, but not beautiful. Not like Carol. More like Aunt Lee. Or Bunny. He crossed his legs to cover the stirring of that part of him he called Snake.

Jason heard seagulls. He watched one dive, its sharp beak biting the bright water, coming away with a squirming silver prize. Other seagulls squawked after the lucky one. Poor fish, thought Jason. Lived to be eaten. A bird's snack.

"...to me?" His mother again.

"What?"

"I said, are you listening to me?"

"I was watching the seagulls."

"I don't want you wandering around getting lost. Pay attention to where we're going when we get off."

"It's not like I've never been here, ma." He had made the trip to Cranberry Island with his mother during the last week of August ever since his Aunt Lee had bought her beach house six years before.

"I don't care."

Jason flushed from remembered fantasies. His aunt was into fitness, always jogging or swimming or exercising. Before jogging, she liked doing her warmups on the tree-secluded deck that surrounded her house and liked doing them in the comfort of a tee-shirt and panties. White silk panties. Panties that Jason had noticed more and more with each passing year until the image of her being in them came at last to provide hours of imaginative delight.

The boat slowed and Jason realized they had reached the dock. He sighed in relief, glad to be leaving the ferry. He stood and picked up the bags, then moved with his mother and the bustling multitude toward the stairs that led to the lower deck and the exit. The girl in the shorts had disappeared with her boyfriend. Two dogs started growling, barking, going for each other. The owners pulled them back. Somebody dropped a beer bottle over the side and his buddies yelled at him. From the dock, people called to their arriving friends and relations.

Jason saw Aunt Lee waving to them. When she saw them wave back, she ran one hand through her mane of auburn hair and smiled. Aunt Lee wore tight black shorts and a green halter top that made her breasts protrude like tree-covered mountains. Sunlight glowed from a pearl choker that circled her neck. Next to her were two red Radio Flyer wagons that would hold the bags.

Jason and his mother descended with the tangle of people on the stairs and walked out onto the dock. As he did each summer, he read the welcoming sign. It had not changed.

Welcome to Cranberry Island

A Family Community

NO Loud Radios
NO Nude Sunbathing
NO Public Drinking
NO Unleashed Dogs

Jason and his mother bumped their way through the mob and greeted Aunt Lee. Jason inhaled her strawberry perfume like a man taking his first sweet breath after being confined in a deep cave for a long, dark time.

"It's so wonderful to see you," she cooed, giving her sister a hug and pecking Jason on the cheek. He burned with embarrassment, knowing her deep red lipstick would be on his face until he could wipe it off without seeming rude.

"How've you been, Jason?" Even though a year had passed, a year in which Jason knew he had grown, his aunt still stood a few inches taller than he did.

"Fi-ne." His voice cracked in the middle of the word, dropping half an octave in a breath. Jason cleared his throat to cover the change as best he could. His voice had started to break in June and had served to undermine any remaining confidence he had in his ability to navigate the world.

Aunt Lee helped them get their bags arranged in the Radio Flyers and they were on their way. They passed the Island Mart, where groceries and general supplies could be bought, the Pizza Palace, the liquor store, and the House of Ice Cream, all busy providing the summer throngs with their vacation-time needs. The soft warm air smelled of sunlight and honeysuckle. A man filled a rubber boat with air from a hose near the Island Mart. Kids on bikes threaded their way through the swarm while others screamed in the playground and splashed in the bay near the ferry dock.

When he was little, his mother had let Jason go wading only under her watchful eye, ever fearing he would drown. As Jason grew older, his mother had continued to hover over him until he eventually lost interest in the water. Now he feared it.

The wagons rattled over the wooden boardwalk as Jason hauled them behind the women, getting a good rear view of his aunt. The snug shorts accented her curves and Jason imagined the silk panties, imagined her taking them off, imagined slipping Snake into the crack between her cheeks.

He stumbled.

His mother's super-hearing kicked in. She turned. "You all right?"

"Yeah, ma."

"Be careful."

"Okay, ma."

"Let's go. I need to use the bathroom."

Aunt Lee's house stood on the dunes immediately adjacent to the beach. The dunes, sandy slopes populated with thick entwined grass, angled up from the beach and acted as a barrier against the tides.

The beach house stood on thick wooden stilts and was guarded by a growth of pine trees. A wooden deck with a railing wrapped around the house, whose weather-beaten white paint needed a new coat. Jason dragged the wagons up the ramp that connected the walkway to the deck and looked at the beach where sunbathers lay toasting on bright colored blankets or taking the shade under beach umbrellas that stood like tall mushrooms painted with watermelons, polka dots, rainbow stripes, or flowers.

White caps slapped at the shore and a strong sea breeze tugged at the taut fabric of the umbrellas, snapped the green lifeguard flags. Here and there kites flew, one a ribbed blue and yellow box, one a golden hawk, one a connected series of red birds that whirred as they skimmed the air. Couples played Kadema, hitting the hard black rubber ball endlessly back and forth between their wooden paddles. A bunch of jocks ran clumsy pass patterns with a bright yellow football, others batted a volleyball around. Children screamed at the waves. Dogs chased sticks and frisbees. Joggers ran. Girls laughed.

"Can you get those things inside?" Aunt Lee called to Jason as his mother hurried into the house.

"Sure," said Jason.

He unloaded the bags near the front door and rolled the empty wagons around back where he wiped his aunt's lipstick from his cheek. Then he took in the luggage.

The house seemed smaller than he remembered it from the year before. Most of the island's beach houses had a combined kitchen-dining-living room right off the front door and his aunt's was no exception. The actual kitchen area, with its refrigerator, sink, dishwasher, and stove, was separated from the dining area by a high counter. Four bar stools were arranged on the dining side of the counter along with the dining table and six chairs. The table, a leftover from the fifties, had a black and white speckled formica top and aluminum legs. The chairs were aluminum with thin stuffed plastic cushioning decorated with orange flowers.

The rest of the room was the living area, with two creaky couches, an old easy chair, the television with its VCR, a wooden coffee table stained with rings from countless glasses and cups, a complement of table and floor lamps, and the radio and CD/tape player.

The walls were decorated with carved wooden faces that resembled primitive African folk art, several faded photographs of island scenes, and a few paintings by local artists. Nothing in the room showed the skill he knew his aunt had as a sculptor. He had once asked her why she kept none of her work at the beach house. She told him the beach was a place to get away from everything, a place to escape Baltimore and the Bradford school where she taught tenth-, eleventh-, and twelfth-graders, and even her art.

A short corridor led from the kitchen-dining-living room to the three small bedrooms and the bathroom in back. The first bedroom on the left, smallest of the three, would be Jason's. It was directly across from the bathroom, which was really a double room consisting of the shower/bath and toilet area and a small attached powder room with a louvered door that led to the outside deck. The bedroom in the back on Jason's side belonged to Aunt Lee and the one in the back on the bathroom side would go to Jason's mother.

From the bathroom side of the house you could see through the trees to the ocean and from the bedrooms you could see the surrounding houses. Closest to it and facing Jason's room was Carol's house. The beautiful blond girl was a year older than Jason and she and her family had been in their house since he had started coming to Cranberry Island. As he had gotten older, Jason had taken to spying on her room at night but had never dared to do more than say hello to her during the day. Maybe this year would be different.

Jason closed the door to his room and unpacked, pulling out his jeans, two bathing suits, underwear, shorts, socks, old sneakers, half a dozen blue cotton tee-shirts, jacket, sweatshirt, toothbrush, toothpaste, deodorant, acne cream, laptop computer, binoculars, *The Martian Chronicles*, a book on yoga, his poetry notebook, and the worn copy of *Wide Open Legs* hidden inside his *PC* magazine. Jason was not old enough to buy skin mags like *Wide Open Legs* but from time to time he picked up a copy from the trash, discarded, he presumed, by the three guys in their twenties who lived on his floor in New York. He flipped through the magazine, keeping it between the covers of *PC*.

A knock jarred his door. Before he could answer, the door opened and Jason slap-closed his double magazine.

"Ma!"

"Sorry. We're going to the store. See you soon."

"Okay."

She shut the door. Jason waited until the house was empty, hanging his things in the closet or stacking them in drawers in the small bureau. He put the computer in one of the drawers as well, where it would stay until he used it. Thefts were rare on Cranberry Island but Jason felt more secure keeping his mother's 486 out of sight. Their financial situation did not allow for the loss of a computer.

When he heard his mother and aunt leave, Jason kicked off his sandals and slipped out of his tee-shirt and jeans, then lay down on the carefully made bed. He liked being at Aunt Lee's because she coddled him, making his bed and not bothering him if he didn't keep his room clean. The pastel sheets were thin and faded but felt smooth and cool against his hot skin. The bed was soft and comfortable with a big fluffy pillow that was great for sleeping.

Jason pulled off his shorts and looked at himself. He hated his skinniness, 97 pounds of 5'3" bean pole. And that which would have been the pride of most men, a fully functioning male organ of 6 and 3/4 inches in length when erect (at last reading, measured with a plastic Mickey Mouse ruler that he kept at home in a bottom drawer under his socks for that purpose only) served primarily to embarrass him, protruding at the worst times in the worst places, coming to life with a life of its own, a pink Snake lustingly curious about every female, ever straining to reach them. Jason always had to guard against its stiffening movements, crossing his legs or putting his hand or a newspaper or magazine over himself at just the right angle lest it betray him.

Now it was free.

Jason scratched his groin as Snake stiffened and rose, its single eye liquid with desire, a peniscope scanning the horizon for a target, Tyrannosaurus Rex searching for prey. He leafed through *Wide Open Legs*. A blond named Lynne, dressed in black garter belt and stockings, resembled Aunt Lee but with smaller breasts and fuller thighs. She posed for him on a bed covered in pink satin sheets, her legs open, breasts bare, cupped by her hands. She stood in front of a full-length mirror, bending over to show her cunt and ass at the same time, smiling, teasing. He thought of her sucking him, Aunt Lee sucking him.

Jason turned the page, holding himself. She had panties on now. White silk panties. Lynne. Being inside her, inside Aunt Lee *look at that ass lynne aunt lee how would she do it up and down so sweet squeeze smiling holding herself stuffing it in sliding up and down do it meet lynne she does it right 42d and looking for love cum with her who writes this stuff likes it from behind in the behind doggie style loves to love drivel love to stuff it in does lee smile like that when she does it bet she always wants it lynne is ready to please you wants your cock what a shot her ass panties off cunt smiling out tits belly button cunt looks like a face with a little beard wants it from you i bet she got it from the photographer squeeze her tits lynne those tits could i ever fuck her ram it home slam it in till it squirts out   out   out*

Jason opened the storage shed under the house and dug through the boxes of paper towels, canned goods, bottles of soda and seltzer, through the worn and broken gardening equipment that Aunt Lee never threw out, to find his prize steed, the rusted blue one-speed boy's Ross bike with pedal braking. A spider scuttled away and Jason brushed the beginnings of its web from the bike's frame.

Ever since he had been big enough to get on it, the Ross had been his favorite bike of all time. The clean design, with no mud guards or baskets to spoil its lines, was perfect for him. The lean, mean riding machine he called it. Touring on the Ross was one of Jason's chief pleasures on Cranberry Island.

Jason dragged the bike out of the rubble and inspected it. The newest thing about the Ross was the seat, a shiny black Crown cushion Aunt Lee had found at a rummage sale and installed the year before. Just for Jason. As usual, the tires were down and Jason had to search for the hand pump.

When the tires were inflated, Jason got on the bike, clenched his fingers hard around the cracked rubber handlebar grips, rang the old single-chime bell, and headed off to say hello to the island.

Cranberry Island was a six-mile long barrier reef named for the abundance of cranberries that grew in the bogs at its marshy northern end. South of the cranberries lay the community called Cranberry Island, home for some 250 houses used by vacationers, summer residents, and a few hardy year-round inhabitants.

The little community occupied an area about three-quarters of a mile wide by one and a half miles long. Immediately to its south was a narrow sandy two-mile strip upon which nothing could be built and which simply provided beach area for those who liked to sunbathe by themselves or in the nude. South of this section the island widened again, enough for an aggressive real-estate entrepreneur to ignore environmental considerations, such as the effects of erosion and the natural migration of barrier reefs, and construct The Colony, a 100-room resort condominium time-shared by

2,180 residents from mid-April through mid-October and reached only by private ferry.

The bike tires made a soft, rhythmic putta-putta-putta sound on the wooden boardwalk as Jason rode. He turned at the corner to go south, planning to ride the central boardwalk, named Midway, as far as he could, then make a right to the bay and come back along Bay Walk.

Cranberry Island, being near Annapolis and the Naval Academy, had always been a favorite of Navy personnel. After World War II, it became popular among returning veterans of the Pacific Theater. Houses went up quickly and the boardwalks that connected them were named for victories over the Japanese and for branches of the Armed Forces.

From the northern end, the boardwalks were called Marshall, Gilbert, Marine, Navy, Sailor, and Coral. All but Sailor crossed from east to west, connecting Midway to Bay Walk. Sailor ran from Midway only to the beach. Aunt Lee lived on Gilbert. Jason thought the naming was much too chauvinistic, but had decided it did not detract from the island's appeal.

The afternoon was bright and clear, with a pleasant breeze. Jason rode intently at first, both hands on the grips as he weaved in and out around walkers, joggers, and other bikers. When he reached a less crowded part of the walkway, he dropped his left hand to his side and rode casually, an easy rider on a lazy day.

The sun cast leafy shadows as Jason passed the broken wood fence that bordered part of the path, its two long horizontal wooden posts cracked and collapsed from a collision with a small construction truck years earlier, wooden posts that had never been repaired. There was no land route to Cranberry Island and only emergency and construction vehicles were permitted. The three fire trucks used by the volunteers were permanent fixtures on the island and the construction vehicles were brought in by ferry.

A lawn sprinkler sprayed the fresh cut grass in front of St. Paul's Church and Jason breathed in the damp green smell. He took a chance that the bike's old gear chain wouldn't slip and pedaled faster, making a wind blow past him. The tires buzzed as he raced several hundred feet past houses and gardens to the end of the walk.

Jason saw something hop in front of him and swerved to avoid hitting the frog that had come to rest in the middle of the road. He stopped and dismounted, resting the Ross against a tree, and gave the frog a little poke with his toe. The startled amphibian jumped into the safety of the bushes and Jason remounted his bike and looked to see where he was.

Coral Walk. He headed west, toward the bay.

Most of the houses along Coral were hidden behind the thick tall grass that crowded this part of the island. Now and then he could see up a walkway to the deck of a house and spot the trash cans or see the bikes resting in a wooden rack. Jason always envied the houses with lots of bikes. Lots of bikes meant lots of people, more than Jason's own small family, more than his extended family that included Aunt Lee. It meant a father, brothers, sisters, uncles, grandparents, cousins, all with their bikes and trikes lined up waiting for them in a wooden rack in front of the house.

As he rode, Jason wondered about the people who owned these houses, the people whose names were painted on their trash cans or adorned cute little wooden signs over their doors, the Burrs, Oakleys, Smiths, Russos, Andersons, Walters, Dunnocks, Hubbels, Harts, Cantors, Matthews, Careys, Davidsons, Browns, Barkleys, Bensons, Wellerbys, Grays, Carters. He imagined them swimming and sailing and surfing during the day, cooking on the grill in the evening, laughing at each other's jokes and playing Monopoly by the fireplace in the chill autumn nights that were coming. He imagined they were happy.

When he reached the end of Coral, Jason turned north to ride up Bay Walk, the only concrete walkway. He glanced at the stores, busy as ever, and at the kids hanging out by the Pizza Palace and the House of Ice Cream. He saw George Wensel, owner of the Island Mart, outside his store watching the flow of business. Jason thought he saw Carol carrying groceries but when he managed a closer look, saw that it was someone else.

Jason rode on past Navy, Marine, Gilbert, and Marshall to a quiet spot at the end of Bay Walk where he always stopped to look out over the water. The fishing boats, the sea gulls, the ferries, all seemed far away as if he were viewing them through a gossamer veil, far away and still, like a faded photograph in an antique frame.

Jason sat on his bike. The sun shone. The water lapped at the shore. The clouds drifted.

A light lunch of tuna on toast, chips, and carrot sticks was waiting when Jason got back. His mother, seated at the table, scanned him as he entered.

"Where were you?" she asked, as Aunt Lee poured iced tea for everyone.

"Riding my bike," said Jason, taking his place.

"I don't see a helmet," his mother said. "Lee, do you have a helmet?"

Jason groaned. His aunt replied.

"We go through this every year, Anna, and every year I say the same thing. Nobody wears helmets out here. There's no cars, most of the walkways are wooden, there's not a lot of accidents. It's okay."

"You can fall off anywhere," Jason's mother went on.

"Sure, and a sniper could get you, too," said Lee. "Or an earthquake. Let him be. It's okay."

"It really is, ma. I'd look like a fre-ak in a helmet. They're not cool." He flushed, wondering if his aunt had heard his voice break.

"Better a freak and alive than cool and brain dead."

"Ma."

"I just want you to be careful."

"Anna, He's almost fourteen. Nearly all grown up."

"Not quite," said Annabelle. "He's got high school and college to do yet. By the way, Jason, did you thank your Aunt for her birthday present?"

Jason had forgotten.

"I'm sorry, Aunt Lee. Thank you." She had mailed him a card the previous week with a fifty dollar gift certificate for books. *The Martian Chronicles* was one of the several he had bought.

"Don't apologize," said Aunt Lee. "You're welcome. Did you pick a high school?"

"Stuyvesant," said Jason.

"Why?" she asked.

"My CrossNet friend went there," Jason answered.

"CrossNet?" His aunt look quizzical.

"The Crossing Network. Like AOL."

Aunt Lee nodded. "Where you talk to each other on computers connected by phone lines?"

"Yeah," said Jason.

"That school's all the way downtown," his mother said, worried.

"I think he can make it," said Aunt Lee.

"And, it's a public school," Annabelle went on. Jason had spent the last eight years at the Townsend Academy, a private school on Manhattan's East Side. It was expensive, but Aunt Lee had helped with the tuition. Townsend went only to eighth grade.

"What about one of those schools closer to you. Dalton, that type?" Lee asked.

"No," said Jason.

Aunt Lee tousled Jason's hair. Her sweet perfume made Snake twitch.

"As far as money goes, you know I'm happy to contribute," she said. "Jason?"

"What, ma?"

"Did you hear what your aunt said?"

"I don't want to go to Dalton or any of those private schools. They're small and snobby. I want to go to Stuyvesant. Besides, I had to pass a test to get in. It's a great school."

"You're losing your little boy, Annabelle. He's ready to go out in the world on his own."

Jason's mother excused herself from the table and went to the bathroom.

"She still has her problem?" Aunt Lee asked.

Jason nodded. His mother had had a bowel problem for as long as he could remember, a problem that shifted from constipation to diarrhea on a cyclical basis, an interminable roller coaster ride for which she medicated herself alternately with Citrate of Magnesia, Milk of Magnesia, and prunes, prunes, prunes to make herself go or Kaopectate, Imodium, and rice, rice, rice to keep from going. Jason liked to think of his mother as Colonically Challenged.

He took a bite of his sandwich and watched as his aunt picked up a carrot stick and nibbled it. Jason could think of only one thing as he watched her and Snake stretched with the thought. Jason forced himself to look at his sandwich and eat.

"He ever show you around the school?" Lee asked. "Tell you about his courses?"

"Who?"

"Your friend, the one you said went to Stuyvesant."

"He doesn't live in the city anymore. His family moved to Pittsburgh at the end of his sophomore year."

Annabelle returned. "Who moved to Pittsburgh?"

"Phil," Jason said. "From CrossNet. You remember."

"I remember I've told you not to spend too much time online. Now did you thank your aunt for lunch?"

"Thank you, Aunt Lee," Jason said.

"You're welcome," she said, pushing her hair back. "Tuna's delicious, if I do say so myself. And the carrots are so firm and crunchy."

"They're not good for me," Annabelle said.

Jason finished. He made sure Snake had relaxed before he stood. "Thanks for lunch."

"Please help clear," his mother said.

"Forget it, Jason," said Aunt Lee. "This one's on me."

"Thanks," said Jason. He ran from the house.

Annabelle clucked her tongue. "You're too easy on him," she said to her sister. "You'd spoil him silly if he were yours."

"And why not?" said Lee. "He's a good kid."

The sisters were a study in contrast. Lee was robust, sexy, tanned, and sensuous, loving what she called the "good things in life" which meant men and food. At 41, she was four years younger than Annabelle and in excellent health, keeping in shape with regular exercise.

Unlike Lee, Annabelle looked her age. She had a round, owlish face, made even more birdlike by thick reading glasses, and she accentuated her avian appearance by looking down as she walked, like a chicken searching the ground for feed. While Lee dressed to feel good and attract men, Annabelle dressed to protect herself from the sun and from the world in general. She wore slacks and shirts and hats, and only the most conservative bathing suits.

Her recent attempt at looking young and lively had been to have a perm and dye her hair blond, a tactic that had left her topped with a yellow-streaked crest of brittle ringlets. She sat down at the table.

"How's work?" Lee asked.

"Okay, I guess," Anna replied. "Either hectic or boring. Sometimes I hate computers. You do any sculpting this summer?"

"No," said Lee. "Needed my yearly break. See mom lately?"

Their mother, Meredith Henderson, was 76 and a resident at the Belmar Nursing Home in the Bronx. She had Alzheimer's and had long since stopped making any sense of the world or to the world.

"Last week," said Anna.

"She know you this time?"

"Thought I was you."

"At least she remembered one of us."

"Why don't you go see her?"

Lee finished eating and took her plate to the sink. "I hate going there."

"So do I."

"It's like talking to a wall."

"She's your mother."

Lee rinsed her plate and put it in the dishwasher. "Is she? I think my mother died years ago. This is just a shell."

"Lee!"

"That's how I feel. I'm sorry."

"Why'd you ask about her if you don't care?"

"I didn't say I don't care." She came back to the table to finish clearing.

"Then why don't you visit? It might cheer her up."

"Do your visits cheer her up?"

Anna watched Lee taking things off the table. "Well?" Lee asked.

"I don't know."

"So what's the point?" Lee carried the dishes to the sink while Anna finished eating. "What's the point?" Lee repeated to the air.

"The point is she's your mother," said Anna. "And you could visit just to visit."

Lee sighed. "Maybe in the fall."

Anna nodded. "In the fall. We'll go together."

Outside, the afternoon sun ascended like a yellow helium balloon floating higher and higher until, as if losing buoyancy with the coming evening, it descended from its zenith toward the mainland in the west where it expanded into a reddish mass. Long, thin stratus sheets of pink, orange, and purple stretched across the horizon. Gulls came in from their hunting to rest on the heavy poles that anchored the wooden docks at the bay.

The air chilled, became damp. Porch lights turned on and in those houses with fire places, fires were lit with newspaper and dry twigs, then fed cord wood cut from dead pine trees or purchased for a good price from George Wensel's store. Flames crackled. Smoke puffed from chimneys.

A pungent burning smell scented the evening and the night insects, the moths, mosquitoes, crickets, and fireflies, fluttered and whined and buzzed and glowed in the twilight haze. Stars emerged from the darkening sky like images on a developing photograph. An incredible peace settled over the island.

Jason stood on the deck watching the beach lose its gentle summertime colors as the light dimished. He rested one foot on the deck railing and played with the broken strap of his sandal. The old shoe had finally given out, although its partner still held together. Funny, he thought, how two identical things could have different life spans. Different lives.

He slipped off the broken sandal and left it on the deck as he started for the beach. He'd show them. He'd wear one sandal. They'd know who they were dealing with. They'd know.

The sand, cooled from the day's heat, felt damp on his bare foot. Jason walked toward the ocean, its waves calm, splashing gentle on the shore. Here and there gulls stood, watching the water, watching each other, watching Jason. When he came too close, they trotted away on their thin legs, then flew off.

Jason saw Venus bright in the southwestern sky, a few wispy clouds near it. It made him think of his father, who had once, on Jason's eighth birthday, taken Jason to the Planetarium. The show had been about Venus.

His father, Frederick Stern. Korean War vet. Holder of the Purple Heart. Now lying in his perpetual bed in the VA hospital because of chronic alcoholism. Wet brain.

The name had not always been Stern. Jason's father had changed it from Stein when he got to America. God knows why, not much of a change. He used to say he wanted to be a star instead of a stone. He was neither. Just a drunk.

Jason continued on, scanning the darkening beach for sea glass or other interesting collectibles. For humans, it would be hard to see in the dim evening light. But he was the Terminator, equipped with IANV (Infrared-Assisted Night Vision) that allowed him to see in the dark. Object acquired at 50 meters. Catalogue and classify.

Frederick Stein/Stern born Berlin, 1931, fled to Montreal with his parents in 1939, emigrated with them to New York in 1948. He fought a war, went to college, found work as a draftsman, got married late in life, had a son he didn't want.

Frederick had worked for a little engineering firm on the West Side. Until they finally got computers, long after all the other engineering firms. Frederick never could get the computer part. Then his eyes started going. Macular degeneration they called it. Ate away at his vision until he couldn't read small print, couldn't see the details. So he drank more than usual, which already had been a lot. Drank and cursed the computers, cursed Annabelle, cursed Jason. They had all done it to him. He drank and cursed. Then just drank.

Jason heard distant shouts and laughter. Two boys and two girls wearing bathing suits ran from the boardwalk to the ocean.

Jason dropped to his knees and sifted through the treasure of stones washed onto the shore. Like precious jewels they glowed in the blue evening light, ruby, diamond, jade, emerald, opal, topaz, turquoise, amethyst, garnet, onyx caught in a net of seaweed and shells.

Catalogue and classify. A few were light and flat, skimmers. He gathered a handful and stood up, threw them sidearm across the water, watched them skip two or three times before going under. Like his father.

For most of Jason's life he barely knew Frederick. For most of his life, Jason's mother was his only real parent. For most of his life, Jason's father was a shadow slipping in and out of the house at odd hours going to bars or liquor stores. For most of his life, when he did see his father in a state approximating consciousness, Frederick raged against life, telling Jason how unfair it all was.

One of the girls screamed in mock terror as she played at fighting one of the boys while the other couple laughed. The girl's breasts were full under her bikini top.

Jason's mother had gone back to school to study the very thing that Frederick had let destroy him. Computers. She started doing programming for a large insurance company. Mother Annabelle. Always talked about having dreams and working to make them happen.

Aunt Lee's first husband, Carl, had been more of a father to Jason than Frederick. Carl had a moustache, played roughhouse, and would carry Jason up the short flight of steps to his aunt's house in New Jersey, a white cottage near the shore with window boxes and a garden. Carl left when Jason was five. A year later Aunt Lee married Ralph who ran off when Jason was seven.

Jason remembered the cottage, with the sun beaming through green window curtains, the pots and pans hanging from nails in the wall, burnt pot holders, an old kettle with a half melted handle. He remembered driving around in the Oranges, Perth Amboy, Secaucus, places over the bridge where it smelled of chemicals and where detergent clogged the streams with pillows of white suds.

The boy lifted the girl in the air and she screamed. He let her down and pulled off her bikini top, waving the top in the air while the girl jumped for it, her breasts jiggling. He ran to the ocean and she chased him.

Carl was a lawyer, a big man who had been a linebacker in his college days. He used to tell about ramming into people, slamming them down, stomping on them. He wanted a child but Lee couldn't give him one and he left. Ralph was a drunken car salesman who worked in Hoboken. He met Lee at a club and they married and divorced in a year. He drank like Frederick.

A light breeze came in off the ocean. The moon edged up over the water, orange and huge. Jason dropped the rest of his stones into the sand and headed back to the house.

By the time Jason came close to the four teens, they were skinny dipping. Jason walked past them rapidly, not wanting to seem like some degenerate who liked to watch, not wanting them to notice him wanting to be one of them.

Jason broke into a trot, his single sandal slapping against his heel.

The digital clock on the VCR read 10:47 PM. Jason's mother sat across from him, reading. Aunt Lee puttered in the kitchen area. Jason wondered whether or not to hook up his laptop's modem to Aunt Lee's telephone so he could connect with Phil. She had said it would be okay for the week. The phone rang.

"Can I get it?" he asked his aunt.

"Sure," she answered and Jason picked up the phone.

"Hello?"

"Greetings good buddy." Jason recognized Phil's raspy voice.

"Did I give you this number?" Jason asked, surprised.

"No, but you told me your aunt's name. Not many Hendersons on Cranberry Island."

"I guess not."

"How's it going?"

"Okay."

"Who is it, dear?" His mother.

"Phil."

"You're not alone?" Phil asked.

"No."

"I copy. Code four-oh-seven."

"Which one's that?"

"Communications Under Close Surveillance."

"That's the one, all right."

"You get it on with auntie yet?"

"Not yet."

"How's she look this year?"

"Excellent."

"Still have those great legs?"

"You bet."

"Wrap 'em around your head."

"Earmuffs."

"You're too scared to do anything except joff."

"What would I do?"

"Stuff it to her."

"Jesus. Not likely."

"Jason."

"Yeah, ma?"

"Don't curse."

"Ma."

"You sure are under surveillance."

"Yeah."

"What else is new?"

"Not much. You?"

"*Blade Runner* was on."

"Tell me about your mother."

"I'll tell you about my mother."

"Great flick."

"Always. Hit the beach yet, do any combing?"

"Combing?"

"Beach combing. Got to find the Resurrection Stone. Then you have the power."

"Yeah."

"Seriously. I promise. Did I tell you about the dinosaurs?"

"What about 'em?"

"What makes them popular?"

"I don't know. They're huge, powerful."

"That's the easy explanation."

"What's wrong with it?"

"Easy explanations can hide the truth."

"What's the truth?"

"Check out the anagram."

"Jason?"

"Yes, Aunt Lee?"

"I might be getting a call. Could you finish up?"

"Sure. Phil?"

"I heard."

"Talk to you tomorrow."

"On the net."

Jason hung up the phone and said goodnight to his mother and aunt, then brushed his teeth and went to his room. He retrieved his binoculars, turned out his lights and knelt on the bed, peeking out of his window at Carol's house. Her shade was up a few inches. He watched and waited like a sniper.

The old binoculars had been his father's. Jason hefted them, felt their weight, read the numbers 7 X 50, 372 FT AT 1000 YDS, knew they would make the thirty feet between houses seem like a mere few yards. He lifted them to his eyes, peered through, hoped he would see something.

Carol walked around the room, picking things up, putting things down, doing her endless bedtime chores. Jason loved her face with its light dotting of freckles, her small nose, green eyes, blond hair pulled back in a pony tail. She undid the pony tail and brushed her hair. Carol, *thy beauty is to me like those Nicean barks of yore, that gently, o'er a perfumed sea, the weary, way-worn wanderer bore.*

Jason waited. Carol brushed. She got up and went someplace. He wondered if she played with herself. He had heard that girls did it. Jerked off. Joffed, as Phil said. Carol was too beautiful to joff. On the right was the bureau with the lamp, on the left he didn't know, could be the edge of a desk.

She came back. Picked something up. Put it down. Examined her brush. Rubbed cream on her face. Got up again. Came back with tissues. Wiped her face. Got up.

The overhead light went off, leaving only the lamp to illuminate the scene like a single spotlight casting its beam on a solo performer.

Carol stood next to the bureau and took off her summer cotton shirt. Jason closed in with the binoculars, saw her white bra stuffed with burgeoning mammaries. Bigger than last year. He adjusted the eyepieces. Focus. Focus. Be ready.

She undid the bra and let it fall away from her, revealing in a moment briefer than a flash of summer lightning her twin mounds of delight, hills of passion, peaks of perfection, mountains of joy. Then she reached for the lamp and the room went dark. Jason's heart died along with the light.

Jason peered around the binoculars, watching her room in the moon-light, squinting until his eyes hurt. He finally gave up and put away the binoculars. He dug out *Wide Open Legs* and a small flashlight.

As he paged through the magazine, he remembered Phil's anagram. Dinosaurs. Jason considered it for a while, then got up and found paper and a pencil. He started scribbling letters, first separating vowels from consonants.

DNSRSIOAU

Nine letters. Not easy. He started making combinations. SAD popped out at him. DIN. SIN. RIND. ROUND. SOUND. IN. AN. DARN. AS. No help. They had to combine to mean something, something somehow related to dinosaurs if Phil was up to his usual tricks.

Jason puzzled over the word and its derivatives until, having made no progress, he tired of the game and went back to *Wide Open Legs* for a com-panion. He found Darcy. Brunette. Dressed in a French maid's outfit and posing in a hotel room. Bending over to dust a bureau, her black lace panties stretched tight over her glorious ass. Posing with the long hose of the vacuum cleaner, caressing it, holding it near her pouting red lips. Taking off her panties. Making the bed, then settling onto it, spreading her legs, fingering her cunt. Smiling. Always smiling.

In the late August night throbbing with cricket and sea sounds, under the fat moon and amidst the heavy fragrance of honeysuckle, Jason breathed hard in the thick air as he stared at glossy photographs and kneaded his sweet hot flesh.

Blue Shirt Files—2009.9.BG1

The night was sultry when I first met Bunny Glands. I lay on the sagging leather couch in my office in the old Graybar building above Grand Central Terminal, soothing my temples with a wet cloth to ease the pain of an early hangover, when there was a knock at the door. And another. I tried to ignore the sounds that slammed through my throbbing head like pistol shots, but to no avail.

I swung my legs off the couch and managed to croak out "Okay" which got the noise to stop. I threw the cloth on my desk and opened my eyes. The full moon provided the room's only illumination, shining through the window like a searchlight. I flipped the switch for the aging overhead fluorescents several times before they flickered into life and I grimaced as the bulbs filled the place with their harsh blue-white glare.

Now I could see the spots that hovered like black butterflies in front of my eyes and that had come to keep me company a few months earlier. Spots that made it hard to read, hard to see a computer screen, hard to fire an accurate shot at anything more than twenty feet away. Spots that were threatening to put me out of business. Nobody wants a private dick who can't shoot.

"Mr. Blue Shirt?"

The knocking started again and I made my way to the door, kicking the AC back into life as I passed the window. My watch said 9:40 PM and the month was September, but the temperature in New York City in the year 2009 must have been in the nineties.

"Mr. Blue Shirt!"

"It's just Blue Shirt, there's no mister," I said, annoyed, as I yanked open the door.

Then I saw her.

My heart nearly stopped, my headache vanished, even the spots seemed to disappear as I took in her beauty, absorbing it like a dry sponge dropped in a reservoir.

Her face was round and sweet as an angel's but she had the slutty polished look of a centerfold model. Her perfume, the scent of strawberries, exploded in my brain and all I could do was gawk at her lush blond hair, her skin tight green dress, and her curves.

"Do you always stare at women?" she asked.

I tried to breathe and found to my surprise that I could.

"Only beautiful ones," I said.

"Thank you," she said. "Now will you please invite me in."

I stepped back from the door and motioned her inside. The office was large, one of a suite I had on the tenth floor of the building that, like the rest of New York, was mostly abandoned. And I'd let the place go to seed. The furniture had gotten shabby, sections of the paint peeled, and there was a film of dust everywhere.

I got her a chair and sat down behind my desk, trying to act professional. I trashed the empty Soyfood containers that littered the desk and was about to put away the scotch bottle when she interrupted me.

"I wouldn't mind a taste of that."

"Scotch?" She nodded. I took a glass from a drawer and poured her a stiff drink. My stomach flipped as I looked at the booze and I passed. Rare for me.

"You're not having any?" she asked.

"I'm on duty now," I said, taking up a pad and pencil. "Let's start with your name."

"Bunny Glands," she said. I looked hard at her.

"You're doing it again," she said.

"What?"

"Staring."

"It's your name this time. The only Glands I know is Homer Glands."

"My husband," she said. "Inventor of the Glands Biochip."

The Glands Biochip! The most significant breakthrough in computer technology since the computer itself was invented. A carbon-silicon chip that was half biological, half electronic. A chip that could be suspended in a saline solution and injected by the hundreds of thousands into the bloodstream. A chip whose biological element would attach to a neural receptor in the cortex and whose electronic element acted as a computer component. Once all the injected chips had hooked into the brain, they formed a neural net capable of linking to any computer. It had made Homer Glands a billionaire.

Her voice reached me through my thoughts. "…trying to kill me."

I put down my pencil, not believing. "Why would Homer Glands want to kill you?" Why would anyone want to kill this babe, I thought.

She sipped her drink and crossed her legs. They curved like sculpted ivory and I followed the curves up her thighs to where they molded into the tight dress. My snake felt more alive than it had in years. She smiled, as if knowing.

"Because I had an affair."

I picked up the pencil again, trying to get back to my professional manner. "Who with?"

"Ranger Armstrong."

Ranger Armstrong! The hockey player turned actor who had starred just a few years ago as Bill Clinton in the movie "Whitewater Grafting," a complicated conspiracy story that I never bothered seeing. But it had made Armstrong famous. And gotten him laid with Bunny.

"Didn't he just buy it?" I said, with what I too late realized was my usual lack of tact.

"If you mean he was killed, yes. He died in a car accident in Reno. But it was no accident."

"How do you know?"

"I know my husband. I know what he's capable of."

"Then why hasn't he killed you already?"

"Because I have certain information that could ruin him."

"And what's that?"

She took a big swallow of scotch and pulled her chair closer to the desk. I leaned forward. Her strawberry perfume filled the air. I felt dizzy from wanting her.

"There's a flaw in the chip," she whispered, her voice low, husky. "One of the quality analysts found it and wrote a report. His name was Robbie Sera. He's dead, too, and the report is gone. Except for my copy."

"How did you get it?"

She leaned toward me, enveloping me with the rich scent of her perfume. "Robbie trusted me, gave me a copy, said if anything happened to him I should release it."

"Homer knows you have this?"

"Yes, but he knows I'm not dumb enough to leave it lying around. He knows I've got it someplace so that if I die it'll come out."

"Sounds like a standoff."

"It's never a standoff with Homer. He plays to win, all the time. I know he's up to something and I'm scared. I need your help."

"What do you want me to do?" I asked.

She reached into her purse and took out a wad of cash. Americash, not the mostly worthless GEC that passed for money now that the Global Economy was in place. Global Economic Currency wasn't worth the aluminum it was stamped on.

"Keep me safe. This is fifty thousand."

Fifty thousand! It was like what a million used to be! I picked up the phone. "Philip," I said to the voice-activated dialer.

"Why'd you come to me?" I asked Bunny as I waited for Phil to answer.

"Because you're the best, even with that nickname. Blue Shirt."

Blue Shirt! People had started calling me that because I wore blue tee-shirts with my year-round summer pants. Thin cotton tee-shirts, which were increasingly hard to find because of the cotton blight that had ruined crops world wide.

Blue Shirt. People called me that because I'd stopped using my own name years earlier. At first it was to give myself a little extra appeal in the Private Dick business, a catchy handle that clients could hang onto. Then, as the years passed, I realized that my own name didn't mean much to me anymore, that it had lost whatever significance it ever had. I stopped using it altogether and became, simply, Blue Shirt. That's who I was.

Phil picked up. "Hello?"

"I need a safe house." Phil knew my voice but took no chances and would verify it with his analyzer.

"Be right there," he replied in a few seconds. I hung up.

"Friend of mine," I told Bunny. "He'll tuck you in while I check out Homer."

Bunny sighed deeply, for which I was grateful as it made her breasts rise and fall sensuously. "How can I ever thank you," she said.

I thought of a few ways as I fingered the money, feeling the rich greenness of the worn bills. All I said was, "This is a good start."

She looked around, uncertainly. "Is there a bathroom I could use?"

"Sure," I said, pointing to the john. "That door."

She stood and walked over to it, her body moving like a porno star's, supple, lithe, animal-like. She closed the door behind her.

I poured myself a drink and stared at the overhead light for what seemed like a long time, stared at the hovering butterflies that Dr. Blinker hadn't yet diagnosed. I took his eye drops out of my drawer and put a drop in each eye, blinking away the excess. I wondered about Bunny's story. It all sounded so crazy. A flaw in the Glands Biochip! That would ruin him. Maybe he was serious about killing his beautiful wife. I'd seen greed before and knew it had no limits. None at all.

I heard Bunny come out of the john and looked in her direction. She sat down and returned to her scotch. I was staring at her legs when she spoke.

"Will he be long?"

"Phil? Should be here any minute." His office was in an adjoining building.

On cue, I heard a knock at the back door. I motioned for Bunny to follow me. Phil was there, wearing his usual Baltimore Orioles baseball cap, his oversize white shirt, and jeans. He was short, shorter than Bunny, but built like a fireplug, strong and a fierce fighter. I trusted him completely.

"Bunny Glands," I said by way of introduction. "Phil Crane. She's afraid her husband's trying to kill her."

"Homer Glands?" he said.

I nodded. "She'll tell you about it." I looked at Bunny. "He's okay," I said. "You can tell him anything."

She extended her hand to me and I shook it. Her grip was warm, exciting.

"I'll call soon with what I find out," I said.

"Thank you," she replied. Phil and I exchanged mock salutes and I shut the door as they left.

Back at my desk I poured another drink and tried to figure out my next step. The first one was always the hardest.

There was a knock at the door.

I sighed. Two clients in one night was a record. But when I opened the door I knew these weren't clients.

Three big men stood there. Standing 6'2" and weighing 190, I wasn't small myself, but these guys were big. I was an ex-cop, knew how to box, and had a black belt in karate. But all that was no match for the tranquilizer dart one of them fired into me.

The spots in front of my eyes disappeared into a dark, cool night.

Tuesday

        rock   *sway*   *fall*

no way out

closed off   *suffocat*

        close

water   *not able to breathe*

          hold   *clutch*

                          safety no safety

dizzy   *lost*

                  rock   *sway*   *slipp*

bump   *water water water water*

                          engines roar

stench   *choke*   *gaspe*

                          safety no safety

precaution

                    drown

wind   *scream scream SCREAM*

  waves boat rolling

        lurch   *stagger*

overload over board
floundering

                               water   *mouth nose throat stomach lungs*
                    dark cold salty
sinking sinking

                                          helpless
                 thrashing

what a life
                  not able to breathe not able to breathe

                                  drowning drowning
drowning

Jason woke in a start from the dream to his first full day on Cranberry Island. His body ached and the sheet, damp with his sweat, clung to him like a shroud. He threw it off and opened his eyes. There was always at least one drowning dream every time he came to the island. His mother had trained him well.

The digital clock on the bureau read 8:37 AM. He stretched, glad to be away from the city, glad to be done with the day camp his mother had put him in for the past eight weeks. Their poor finances along with Annabelle's overprotectiveness argued against sending Jason to a sleepaway camp, so he spent his summers in New York City at a neighborhood community organization called the Yorkville Youth Center. Most of the kids played basketball or swam in the city pool, but Jason hung out with the nerds in the chess or computer rooms. But even chess and computers got to be boring after two months. Now he would have the chance to ride a bike without being watched by his mother, go for long walks alone, and ogle girls in bikinis.

Snake poked out of him, hard. Jason needed to pee, so he got up, stuffing it between his legs like a stolen salami. He opened his door and met Aunt Lee in the hall, still wearing her nightie. He jerked back, trying not to stare, trying to hide Snake.

"Good morning," she said in a cheery voice. "Sleep well?" Jason thought she glanced at his crotch.

"Ye-es," he said. Snake squirmed.

"Glad you didn't sleep the day away like your mother seems to be doing. Want to go to the store for me?"

Jason would do anything for her. He nodded, not trusting his voice, and edged toward the bathroom.

"Sorry," said Aunt Lee. She stepped aside and went to the kitchen. Jason tried to see through her nightie as she walked away from him. He imagined her in high heels.

Jason closed the bathroom door behind him. He wondered if his aunt had really been looking at his crotch or if he had just imagined it. Snake was erect and Jason had to sit on the toilet to piss, pushing his stiff penis down so that the urine, whose passage through his constricted urethra made it shoot forth in spasmodic jets, would not squirt everywhere. As his piss squeezed out, the erection diminished and Jason decided his aunt's glance had been his imagination. He finished in the bathroom and went to his room for his bathing suit and tee-shirt.

Jason rode the blue Ross to the Island Mart, the only grocery store in the community. The Mart's high prices, which George Wensel justified by invoking the expense of shipping from the mainland, reflected the monopoly he held, a monopoly for which he was often cursed. On top of it, George was a mean sort, a squat man with a hawk-like face and a pinched expression. He was as likely to frown as to smile, to growl as to chuckle, and who never, ever laughed unless it was at somebody's expense. He kept track of everyone on the island, knew when they arrived and departed, where they stayed, and, of course, how much they could be

expected to buy, how much they owed, and how prompt they were in paying their bills.

For Jason, the best thing about the store was the girls who worked
there, all of them nubile young teens making pocket money for jewelry or
makeup or clothes or whatever else they needed to attract the lusting bun-
dles of hormones in Speedos that continually bustled around them. Jason
knew he had no chance with these suntanned damsels but Snake enjoyed
being near them for even the little space of a shopping trip. The girls provided endless fodder for fantasy.

His favorite was Cindy. He had heard them call her that the previous
summer and had started using her name himself whenever he was lucky
enough to have her working the checkout line when he went through.
Cindy was a short blond with a pageboy haircut who usually wore a man's
white shirt, tied at the waist, over a bikini. Wensel was a lecher himself,
which was why he allowed her to work that way. Cindy was guaranteed to
lift Snake from its lair.

Jason parked the Ross and went into the store. He saw Cindy wearing
her usual and said hello. She smiled vaguely and Jason's heart shifted into
second.

The store was enormous, with a front and back section on the ground
level and a huge upper floor. The ground level held the food and household
items, the produce, frozen foods, beverages, meat, fish, poultry, baked
goods, deli specialties, dairy goods, canned goods, coffee, tea, desserts,
spices and condiments, pastas, plastic wraps, cleansers, mops, sponges,
detergents, ant killers, cat and dog food and toys, paper products, burner
bibs, fireplace logs, suntan lotions, bug repellents, books and magazines.

The upper floor contained anything anyone might need to outfit themselves and their homes for the summer, from rubber boats and Radio Flyer
wagons to hardware and houseware to sweatshirts and bathing suits and
rain slickers to shorts and skirts and toys and games and beach umbrellas.

Jason used the list Aunt Lee had given him to pick up what they
needed. When he reached the checkout counter, Cindy was waiting for

him with that same vague smile. He put the eggs, milk, bread, juice and other items on the counter and smiled back.

"Hi," he said, forcing himself to speak and calculating that he could manage one short syllable without his voice breaking.

"Hi," said Cindy, looking away from him to ring up his purchases. Jason's head spun. His heart shifted to third. What to say?

"Nice day." Two syllables.

"Yeah," Cindy replied, pricing and ringing up, not looking at him. Jason moved his gaze to her ample breasts, breasts that pressed against her bikini top and shirt like grapefruit full with luscious sweet sharp juice.

Jason's mouth went dry.

"Get out much?" he managed to ask. Three.

"Naw. Come in early, leave late. That's twenty-four fifty-two." She looked at him and he moved his eyes to meet hers. He swallowed.

"My aunt has an account." A whole sentence!

She nodded as he signed his aunt's name on the bill. She bagged his purchases and tore off his receipt.

"Tha-anks," Jason said, flushing as he dropped into a register he had never before heard come out of him.

Cindy didn't look at him or answer. She was already busy with the next customer. Jason took a last look at her breasts and lifted the bag. He went out into the bright day, his heartbeat gradually returning to normal.

When Jason returned with the groceries, his mother was up. She made him a bagel with cream cheese and Jason ate while his mother had prunes and talked with Aunt Lee, who had already eaten. Afterwards, Jason decided to go for a walk on the beach.

The bright day burned and the sand pressed like soft fire against the tender undersides of Jason's feet. He jogged to the water, splashed in up to his ankles, felt the cool Atlantic wash away the heat. After refreshing himself, Jason walked along the water's edge until he spotted Carol on a blanket with three guys. They were surly-faced and tough-looking.

"Hi," said Carol.

He looked at her, surprised at her friendliness. Carol wore a light sea-green one-piece bathing suit with a slash opening down one side. Her lipstick was pale pink, like a girl he remembered from *Wide Open Legs*.

"Hi," said Jason. He slowed down, not knowing whether to stop.

"Jason, right?" she asked.

"Yeah." He stopped. Voice okay.

"Jason Jaybird," said one of the tough guys. The others laughed. Carol did not.

Jason's stomach knotted. He wished he were Blue Shirt. Then he'd show those guys.

"Gotta go." Jason's voice sounded to him like a squeak.

"You do that," said the tough guy.

"Yeah," said one of the others. "Go far." The three laughed again, mocking his impotence.

Jason went. He hated his name. His father's grandmother or great grandmother was half-Greek, a Greek Jew, so his mother thought let's name him Jason. Jason Jaybird. Fuck him. Jason thought of jumping on the guy who had called him that and pummeling the shit out of him. That would show him.

Jason saw some kids playing volleyball and watched from a distance as they hollered and laughed and jumped and slapped at the white ball. The girls were cute and Jason had the sudden desire to get in the game. Maybe he could get to know someone, get to know a girl, get laid for the first time. Was that a lot to ask?

He walked over to the game and stood, watching. There were eight on one side, seven on the other. The side with seven had four girls, including an especially sexy one in a peach-colored bikini who had tits that bounced higher than the ball.

"Can I get in?" Jason called to no one in particular.

Nobody answered him.

"Looks like you could use one more on this side," he said, moving to the group of seven, who were serving. "I got a pretty good serve." That wasn't true but he said it to get a reaction. A tall, wiry guy grinned at him.

"Okay, kid, You're up." He threw Jason the ball.

Jason moved to the service line from where the net seemed as high as Everest and as far away as the moon. Jason had served a volleyball twice before in his life, once during a game in the school gym where he put it into the net and once at a friend's birthday party where they played on the lawn and Jason served into the cake.

"Put it over, skinny," a curly-haired guy on Jason's team yelled. He had more muscles than the Hulk and looked like he ate weights for breakfast.

Jason served and the ball went under the net. He burned with embarrassment.

"Sor-ry," his voice cracked. "Guess I should've warmed up."

"Fuckin' cost us a serve," said Hulk. "Cost the fuckin' serve. Fuck us."

"Lay off," said the tall guy who'd invited Jason to play. "It's just a game."

"I play serious," said Hulk.

The other side served, a looping ball that Hulk punched but couldn't put away. The ball bounced high in Jason's direction and he panicked as his teammates shouted encouragement. He lost it in the sun and struck out blindly, slamming the ball into Hulk's groin. The Hulk grunted in painful surprise.

Everyone laughed. Except Hulk.

"Fuckin' asshole."

"I'm sorry," said Jason.

"Should break your face."

"I'm real-ly sorry," Jason croaked.

Hulk strode up to Jason and pushed him hard, knocking him down. Jason felt the air go out of him as he landed in the sand. Startled and stunned, he could do no more than lie there like a turtle on its back, unable to move.

"Fuck you, pretty good serve. Get the fuck off the court."

Hulk looked like he would blow an artery. Jason used his elbows and heels to edge backward across the sand and out of harm's way, afraid to apologize again for fear of further enraging the victim of his bad shot.

The tall guy came over. "Come on, lay off."

"Keep the fuck away," said Hulk, "or wind up like him."

"Can't you ever play a game without a hassle? Those steroids are poppin' your brain."

"Fuck you, wanna try me?"

"Ease up," someone yelled.

Jason recovered enough to get to his feet as the boys faced off.

"I don't want to hurt you," said the tall guy.

"Fuck you," said Hulk, lunging at him, grabbing him around the middle, pushing him to the sand. Jason could almost feel Hulk's burning fury, almost knew his thoughts *show this fuck a thing or two show them all fucking bastards* a firestorm of hate.

The girls screamed for the fighting to stop while the boys watched, eager to see who would win. Hulk and the tall guy rolled in the sand, then the tall guy slipped away and got to his feet. Hulk jumped up and they began trading punches. Hulk was stronger but the tall guy was faster.

From the distance Jason heard the wail of a police van speeding along the beach. The lifeguards must have reported the fight. The tall guy pushed away from Hulk.

"The cops. Let's forget it."

But Hulk couldn't forget. He came at the tall guy and tried to hammer him with a powerful hook. The tall guy dodged the blow then lashed out hard, tagging Hulk on the side of his head. Jason heard a loud crack that turned his stomach. Hulk went down like a dropped sandbag. The police van arrived, kicking up sand with its tires. Two cops jumped out.

Jason took several deep breaths to keep from throwing up. Everyone quieted as the cops surveyed the scene. One bent over the still form of

Hulk, who now appeared shriveled and small, and tried to rouse him. A trickle of blood from the boy's ear stained the sand.

"What was it about?" the second cop asked the tall guy, who was tending a cut on his mouth.

"Nothing," he said. "A bad shot."

"Bad shot?"

"Bad volleyball shot." He searched the crowd and found Jason. "That kid hit him by accident with the ball."

The cop studied Jason.

"That right?"

"Yes," said Jason.

The first cop put his ear to Hulk's chest.

"That what happened?" the second cop asked. Everyone agreed. The first cop shook his head. He stood and spoke into his radio.

"Anybody know this kid's name?" asked the second cop.

"Allie Grant," a girl said. "Lives on Bay Walk."

The cop on the radio finished. "Have one of the kids take you over there. Notify the parents their son's been hurt."

"How is he?" asked the tall guy.

The cops said nothing. By the time the emergency helicopter arrived, Allie's mother was there, clinging to her son's lifeless body like a drowning woman to a life preserver.

Jason gave the police a statement and left the scene an hour later, his mind a tumult of confusion and guilt. Allie was dead and all because of Jason. Jason's lie. If he hadn't said he could serve, he wouldn't have gotten into the game. If he hadn't gotten into the game, he wouldn't have hit Allie with the ball. If he hadn't hit Allie with the ball, the fight wouldn't have started. Allie would still be alive. Jason had killed him.

No. What would Phil say? Not because of Jason. Allie did it to himself. He was the crazy one, the one who wanted to fight. Over a stupid volleyball game. Hurt pride. He picked the wrong guy. The tall kid killed him. With one punch.

The tall guy had told the cops he was just defending himself, that Allie started punching and hitting as if his life depended on it. It turned out it did and he lost. Killed himself, Phil would say, did it to himself, nobody did it to him, not Jason, not the tall guy. They were just instruments, that's what Phil would say, instruments for Allie's karma.

Jason walked down the beach trying not to think about it, trying not to think at all and when that didn't work, decided to think of something altogether different. The Nude Beach near The Colony. A good mile and a half walk. He would go that way to see the people who came to undress and lie in the sun, to broil like steaks on a grill.

Jason looked at the lifeguards watching the ocean like King penguins staring out at the sea, waiting for something to happen. Imitating them, Jason stopped to inspect the vast Atlantic. He thought of what it would be like to be a lifeguard with the girls swooning all over him, cunts dripping with desire. He saw a tall brunette in a gold bathing suit and imagined rescuing her.

He would be at the top of the lifeguard tower wearing a tight Speedo and maybe a baseball cap on backwards, his tanned muscles rippling, Kool-Ray sunglasses shading his eyes, his nose coated with zinc sunblock. He chewed gum, scanned the horizon, occasionally blowing his whistle and waving at swimmers to get back between the flags.

He had his eye on the brunette in the gold suit as she swam out. She stroked cleanly and seemed confident of herself. Just the kind of swimmer who sometimes got in trouble, he would think, regarding her with his experienced lifeguard's eye.

Then it happened. Very far out, something went wrong. Her strokes seemed weak, ineffective. The current worked against her, pulling her away from shore. Jason tensed, picked up his binoculars, found her, saw her flailing at something.

He knew immediately what had happened. A jellyfish, likely a Man-O-War, had stung her, taken her strength. She would need help. Fast. Jason spit out his gum, threw off his hat, dropped the binoculars, and blew the alarm horn. He jumped from the tower, grabbed the rescue line, and raced into the ocean as his partners secured the line on the beach. He cut through the surf with the speed of a shark, his powerful strokes propelling him with machine-like efficiency to the woman. He reached her in no time and lifted her head out of the water. He held her tight and swam back to shore as his fellow lifeguards pulled in the rescue line.

Afterward, that evening, she would thank him. They would have dinner then go to her house to be alone. She would dress in a satin nightgown the color of ripe peaches and sit next to him on a soft couch. They would kiss. He would touch her. She would whisper in his ear.

"Hey, skinny! Give us the ball!"

Jason woke from his fantasy to see a volleyball at his feet and a dozen people waiting for him to return it to them. He picked up the ball and tossed it to the nearest player. Too bad he was afraid of the water.

He went down to the edge of the shore, letting the tide ripple in over his feet, crunching on stones and shells, stepping around the scraps of white jellyfish, looking for sea glass or for the Resurrection Stone.

The story of the Resurrection Stone, according to Phil, came from an obscure Christian text whose validity was a matter of some controversy. The text said that when Christ rose, the Holy Ray of Resurrection shattered the great boulder guarding His tomb and scattered the boulder's fragments across the earth. The Resurrection Stone, also called the Heart Stone because of its reputed shape and coloring, was said to be that part of the boulder through which the Ray had directly passed. The stone was supposed to possess immense power.

Jason saw a small piece of green sea glass and retrieved it, feeling its smooth dusty surface, worn down from years of abrasion by ocean and sand. He put it in the pocket of his bathing suit and moved on.

Jason didn't know if he believed in the Heart Stone or not. It was nice to think there might be such a miraculous thing in the world, but miraculous things were hard for him to accept. He had seen no miracles in his life. Only the common and dull.

As he passed the row of houses that marked the southern end of the community of Cranberry Island, Jason found himself mostly alone on the beach, seeing only an occasional jogger or, now and then, couples walking. He splashed sea water on his face to cool himself and continued walking.

In the distance, he saw the beige concrete slab of The Colony rising out of the sand, so totally out of place on this fragile barrier reef, so much an intrusion of industry, engineering, and finance into a delicate ecostructure, so much an abomination that it did not seem real but rather appeared as a mirage, a shimmering illusion of something that could not, should not be.

It loomed on the horizon like a Disney version of Camelot, its ten-story tower capped by an aquamarine cupola. As he headed toward it, Jason imagined himself on Mars, imagined the beach a desert, its dust cool under a distant sun, imagined tiny twin moons staring at the dead planet like the sad eyes of a God without worshippers, imagined the Colony an ancient Martian structure long ago constructed for a forgotten purpose by that obscure, extra-terrestrial race.

Later, closer to the Colony, Jason saw its first nude sentinel. And wished he hadn't.

The man, asleep, was fat, blubbery like a whale but without a whale's graceful beauty, slopped over with oil and beached disgustingly on a garish orange towel under an umbrella that compared poorly in diameter with his enormous girth and gave him little shade. Jason saw a scattering of empty beer cans around the man and heard him breathe great rumbling snores that matched the ocean for regularity and volume. The man had paid no attention to the intensity of the sun's rays and his entire body was the color of boiled lobster.

And as the whale-lobster man lay on his back with his bloated legs spread obscenely, Jason could not help but see his privates, now publics. Embarrassed and fascinated, Jason glanced and looked away, glanced and looked away, all the time continuing to walk, walk, walk casually down the beach as if merely strolling by with no interest in what was on display.

The man's penis was small in comparison to his overall bulk and, probably because of an erotic dream brought on by the beer, stood straight up in the air like a flagpole. Beneath the penis, the testicles sagged like deflated balloons in lifeless contradiction to the energy of the erect member. The entire genital collection was burned painfully, sorefully red.

Jason winced as he passed by, gulping hard at the horror. He thought of the man coming to and seeing his crisped body, like a roasted chicken waking up in the oven. A chicken with a blackened penis sticking out of it. Cajon Penis.

Further on Jason saw couples sunbathing together, young men and women not afraid of showing their bodies to each other and to the world. Jason wished he could be like that. But whenever he thought about his body he felt ashamed, ashamed of his skinniness, of his zits, of his cock that stood out and apart from him like an alien being.

Then he saw her. A slim brunette, maybe eighteen or nineteen, with long hair and wearing a black one-piece suit with revealing oval cutouts on the sides. She had just arrived on the beach and, with a quick motion, pulled the straps off her shoulders and stepped out of the suit to reveal a trim body and a shapely tanned ass.

Jason forced himself to look away, forced himself to keep walking, and, as he felt Snake stir, forced himself to think about the whale-lobster man, think about his fatty swollen cooked body and how it must smell from a day of sweating in the hot sun, oozing out the reek of a dozen beers.

But Jason couldn't get his mind off the brunette. He wanted to take her right there on the beach, wanted to roll in the sand and fuck her like a dog while everyone watched, wanted to slide Snake in and out of where it wanted to be until it spat its seed and withdrew, satisfied.

All Jason did was stop to watch the ocean. The waves had gotten stronger and in the distance he saw whitecaps. He watched them for a few minutes, hoping to look only like a stroller out for a walk on the beach and not like a pervert come to leer at the nudies.

Jason turned to begin the trip home. He scanned the brunette and saw that she had settled on her blanket, lying on her back. One curved leg was drawn up, arched at the knee, leaving the calf turned in an enchanting way. Her dark cunt hairs glistened in the afternoon light. Jason kept walking.

When he got back to the house, no one was there and Jason decided that instead of silently joffing he would play Pod Attack on his Omega Game System. The noise it generated made his mother crazy so he could play only when she was out. He hooked the game into the television and turned it on. The screen lit up with the three-dimensional image of a hooded figure. It spoke.

"SO, FOOL, YOU DARE CHALLENGE LORGO THE CONQUEROR? THEN KNOW THIS—I SHOW NO MERCY."

The game began. Jason started where he had last left off: on Level Four with eight lives remaining. He had never gotten that far before.

Jason held tight to his weapon and flight controls as Lorgo's pods darted around his fleet of battle cruisers. The pods' lasers blasted his ships with rainbow rays of color and screaming shrieks of sound. Jason fought back, shooting the pods down with loud whanging bursts from his own photon cannons. Jason lost two lives, then advanced to Level Five.

Here Lorgo's pods took on a different form. Instead of small fast moving ships they were diffuse clouds that formed out of nowhere in the middle of Jason's fleet. Their weapons were snake-like ropes of fire that tunneled through the space-time continuum in which the battle took place. Jason had warning detectors on his cruisers but their alarms sounded bare moments before the fire tunnels hit.

Jason had a new weapon, too. His cloud disperser dissolved the new pods but often not before they managed to launch several fire tunnels. Jason could shield his cruisers but that took immense energy and meant leaving some cruisers to be destroyed so others could be saved.

Jason lost a life, restarted the level, lost another life, restarted again, made headway in clearing out the cloud pods and pushed deeper into Lorgo's galaxy, got to a marker point, lost a life, restarted at the marker, wiped out another pod cloud, and avoided the black hole that materialized in front of his fleet. Jason's heart raced as Lorgo's home planet shimmered on his sensor displays. Level Six! A loud clanging issued from the television and Lorgo's face appeared.

"ARROGANT TOAD, DO YOU THREATEN THE SEAT OF MY EMPIRE? THEN DIE, AS MUST ALL WHO TEMPT THE POWER OF LORGO!"

Jason's fleet was down to three ships. Three lives remaining. He chose a close-in defensive formation. Then the pods came. By the hundreds.

Jason thought the TV would bounce off its stand as the sound effects blasted from it. The screen blazed as the pods attacked, this time firing bright white lasers that burned through shields and hulls almost instantly. Jason's only defense was to keep moving as fast as he could, deploying his own weapons in short bursts. He lost a ship. Then another. The pods swarmed around his remaining vessel. Their lasers fired again and again, tearing it apart, exploding it in a conflagration of light.

Lorgo spoke, his gloating laughter booming from the TV.

"HA, HA, HA! SO END ALL WHO DEFY LORGO! TOO BAD, WORM. WANT TO TRY AGAIN? HA, HA!"

Jason turned off the game and went to his room. He wished he'd been implanted with Biochips. Then he'd have beaten Lorgo.

That evening, during dinner preparations and much to Jason's discomfort, the fight on the beach became a topic of conversation.

"Did you hear what happened today?" Aunt Lee asked. "About that kid who was killed? Allie Grant?"

Dinner was cheese ravioli. Jason wasn't crazy about pasta. He preferred meat. But meat wasn't as healthy for you as pasta, that's what his mother said. And meat was more expensive. So at home they ate capellini on Monday, cheese ravioli on Tuesday, meatless lasagna on Wednesday, linguine with clam sauce on Thursday, and spaghetti on Friday. The weekends were fish on Saturday and chicken on Sunday. His mother was determined to keep to the home pattern even though they were on vacation.

"Somebody said it was over a missed shot," his mother said. "I can't believe they'd kill each other over a volleyball game. You can't be too careful these days."

"Were you there? Did you see anything?" Aunt Lee asked her nephew.

"Somebody missed a shot, like ma said," Jason answered, not wanting to worry his mother by saying that he had been part of it, that he in fact had been the catalyst for Allie's death. "Then a fight started. I guess it was an accident."

"Some accident," said Anna. "Excuse me." She went to the bathroom.

"I knew the kid," said Aunt Lee. "A real bad one."

"What do you mean?" Jason asked.

"Crazy for weightlifting. They say he took steroids. You know what they do to your brain." She lifted a spoon out of the tomato sauce she was preparing and let the thick redness of it plop back into the pot.

Jason heard his mother close the bathroom door. He whispered to his aunt.

"I didn't want to say before, but I, well, I kind of started it."

"What do you mean?" Aunt Lee asked. Jason quickly told her the story.

"Don't blame yourself, Jason. You wanted to play, so you puffed yourself up. People do it all the time and nobody gets killed. It wasn't your fault."

"That's what my friend Phil would say, but I still feel bad about it."

"It's okay to feel bad, just don't feel guilty. You didn't kill him."

"He was crazy," said Jason. "Wanted to fight real bad. Do you know the kid who he was fighting with? A tall kid?"

"Mike Sanders. Nice guy."

Annabelle returned from the bathroom. "Where were you all afternoon?" she asked Jason.

"Down the beach."

"Toward the Colony?" asked Aunt Lee.

"Yeah."

"See any nudies?"

Jason flushed, said nothing.

"Bet you did," his aunt said, grinning.

"That's a lifestyle I don't understand," said Anna. Jason silently thanked his mother for bailing him out of having to respond. But Lee wouldn't be put off.

"See the fat guy? Burned to a crisp?"

She'd been there too? "No," Jason lied, too embarrassed to admit he had seen the man.

Aunt Lee hooted a laugh, a loud raucous laugh at the jerk who had broiled himself on the beach. "He won't be getting close to anybody for a while."

"Could we talk about something besides death and sunstroke," said Annabelle. "After all, it is dinner time." To Jason, "Go wash up."

"Sure, ma," Jason said.

As Jason went to the bathroom he heard Lee snort another harsh laugh.

"He looked like a blister," she said to his mother, who groaned. "It's a miracle he didn't burst." Jason wondered about his aunt prowling the nude beach. He wondered what his mother thought about her younger sister.

When Jason returned to the table, his mother had found a new direction for the conversation.

"Tell Aunt Lee about your writing," she said, eager to display what she considered his budding literary genius to her sister.

"Ma," Jason whined, toying with his ravioli.

"What writing?" Lee asked.

"He's written a book," said Annabelle, unable to contain her pride. She nibbled on her salad like a rabbit testing the lettuce.

"It's not a book, ma," Jason said. "It's just a story."

"Wonderful," said Lee between mouthfuls of food. "What's it about?"

Jason hesitated but his mother would have none of that. "Go on, tell her," Annabelle said.

"Ma," Jason whined.

"C'mon, Jason," Lee demanded. Under the table she bumped her knee against his. "I want to hear."

The sudden touch of his Aunt's knee sent a shock through his body. He would talk.

"It's science fiction. Well, it's science fiction mystery, a detective story set in the future. But not too far in the future."

"How far?" his aunt asked. She took some bread and Jason tried not to stare as she popped a piece into her delicious mouth.

"Two thousand nine," he said, then ran out of words. He didn't really know how to describe the Blue Shirt Files.

"The hero is a detective," Annabelle said.

"Have you read it?" Lee asked.

"No," Annabelle replied. "I only found out about it when I came into his room one day and saw this file he was working on. But he hasn't let me read it. And now he keeps it stored on a floppy disk that he hides from me."

"Could I see it?" Lee asked.

Jason blushed. He didn't want his aunt to recognize herself in Bunny Glands. He didn't want her to read about Blue Shirt's lust, about getting laid.

"Well," he said, "it's not done yet."

"I think it is," said Annabelle, reaching for more salad.

"Ma, it's not done."

"Well," said Lee, "if it's not done, it's not done. Keep me posted, Jason. I'd like to read it when you're through."

Jason exhaled for the first time in what seemed to him like an hour. "Okay, yeah, sure," he said, happy to be off his mother's hook. He ate as the talk turned to less threatening matters.

After dinner, dessert, and a few TV shows, Jason connected his laptop to the telephone. It was just past ten-thirty. His mother had gone to bed and Aunt Lee was reading her latest Dean Koontz thriller. From time to time, Jason looked up from his labors to spy on her legs dangling over the side of her chair. Legs curved like those of the women in his magazines.

Outside a moth cloud surrounded the porch light and the crickets trilled without pause. The Atlantic provided a hissing, rhythmic background to the insect noise. At the laptop's keyboard, Jason tapped in his CrossNet sign on code. His screen name, the name by which he was known on the network, was *genzero*. In the year 2000, Jason would be twenty, class of '00. Generation Zero.

He typed his password *991980* and was in, ready to have his thoughts transformed into bit configurations and transmitted to the duplexed main frames in Houston where the Crossing Network was headquartered, ready for his ideas, hopes, fantasies to become pulses of ones and zeros surging across twisted pairs and fiber optic lines and microwave relays to join with the binary coded musings from an array of desktops, laptops, notebooks, Compaqs, IBMs, Macs, Dells, Toshibas, Digitals, Honeywells, NECs, Gateways, TIs, H-Ps, Compudynes, Leading Edges, Packard Bells, Epsons, ASTs, Canons, Sharps, and Homebuilt computers powered by millions of hearts and brains linked in an intangible space of instant communication, pure consciousness with multitudes of interests, desires, and whims all connected electronically. A virtually infinite consciousness. As Phil would say, the closest people have come to being in the mind of God.

Jason scanned the familiar Main Screen with its dozen major categories: Headline News, Financial Planning, Computers, Special Interests, CyberMarket, Conversations, Media Connection, Lifelong Learning, Reference, Internet Gateway, SportsNews, Kids Korner. He selected

Conversations and in a few seconds saw the next list of choices arranged in a table across his screen.

Alternate Lives	Art Forum	Astrology
Astronomy Club	AUTOWORLD	Baseball Digest
Cat Fanciers	Chatters	Dog Lovers
Friends of Bill W.	GameRoom	Gay Men Only
Ham Radioettes	Healthercise	HIV+ Helpnet
Hockey Talk	Hoopsters	LesbianLife
Love Connection	MilitaryMan	Mystery Lovers
New Members	NextGeneration	Open Forum
Public Rooms	Quilters	Religion & Ethics
RockNet	SeniorNet	SF&F
Skibums	Stereo Times	Talk Show Crazy
Teen Talk	The Pros	Trekkies
Trivia Times	Under Par	VietVets
Wine & Dine	Writer's Line	Youngbloods

He made his choice and watched as the system connected him.

CROSSNET: !!! Welcome to the Love Connection !!!

The screen spilled out yet another list of choices. These were the conversation rooms in which Jason could send and receive messages to and from other participants as if they all were on a single telephone, a computerized party line. Next to each room was a count of the number of people signed into it.

Men4men	23
Handmaidens	21
NYCM4M	23
Gropers	23

BOSingles	19
BiF4BiF	20
SWMSWF	19
Florida	22
CONNetc	18
NiceLadies	23
DofLesbos	20
Swell Times	21
Class Act	17

As he often did, Jason selected SWMSWF. The screen blinked and opened up a conversation window.

CROSSNET: !!! You are in SWMSWF !!!

Jason scanned the list of people in the room and found the one he wanted. LOVESlace was logged on. He watched the talk for a while.

Alone2Much:	that's a good one!
CAL213:	Sure I smoke dope. Play Pod Attack, too.
Bettyarms:	So why'd you move from such a great place?
STIFF1:	Alone, I'll send you a photo
Birdman6:	<——- into mountain biking, herbal tea and love
HCrone:	Can't stand those lines for stamps >:-<
NEWAGER:	Cal, dope's out, turkey. Live NATURAL!
ZAPPER76:	Cal, what level?
Swarmer:	Had to move, lost my job, no money, kept my MAC!
Alone2Much:	Not necessary.

LOVESlace was quiet. Jason brought up her profile, the little blurb that people used to describe themselves to others on the network. You could be yourself or anyone you wanted to be online, with any name, any sex, any age, occupation, interest, or desire.

CROSSNET Name:	LOVESlace
True Name:	Linda Kay
Address:	For me to know and u to find out
Sex:	Yes!
Interests:	Lingerie, silk stockings, high heels, LACE!
Occupation:	Performance Artist
Notes:	Loves to meet young guys.

Jason cleared the profile and checked the chatter. There she was!

LOVESlace:	Doesn't anyone have anything intelligent to say?
PAUL323:	Thank God you kept your MAC! It's all you need.
STIFF1:	Sure you'd be interested. I'm not modest.
CAL213:	Never do needles. All the way, Z.
Birdman6:	Anybody wanna play nude Jeopardy?
STIFF1:	FYI 7 1/2"
AmyBGood:	>:-> I like to wear boys' underwear, cozy!!

Jason typed a message and saw it come up on the screen, folded in with the thoughts of others.

genzero:	i do, lace. e = mc squared!
BettyArms:	Stiff, nobody cares.
Alone2Much:	Not as big as my massager.
DREAMR69:	Amy, I'll lend you mine!
PAUL323:	Nude Jeopardy? Tell me more.
LOVESlace:	Hi, Zero! How you keepin?

Jason typed in his reply.

genzero:	missed you there for awhile. can we talk?
AngelFace:	Bird, do you play it on mountain bike?
CAL213:	<————HAHAHA
Babylocks:	Hi, everyone. I'm new here. What's up?
STIFF1:	That's real sad.
LOVESlace:	Want 121, Zero?
Alone2Much:	Baby MORF?
Bettyarms:	Stiff, you're the only sad one.
DREAMR69:	Cal, laugh like this :-D
ZAPPER76:	Me, too, Cal. Want to team up?
genzero:	ubet

A message box appeared on his screen. It was a private message from LOVESlace that no one else could read.

Join me in BEDROOM?

Jason's heart beat faster. He typed a reply.

ubet

Next, Jason selected the private room LOVESlace had created. No one else could converse in this room unless she or Jason let them in. Something neither of them would do. Snake stirred. Jason typed.

genzero:	i'm here
LOVESlace:	What's cookin?
genzero:	i am honey
LOVESlace:	I am horny. Tell my your fantasy.
genzero:	to be with you watching you loving you

LOVESlace:	What should I wear?
genzero:	blue garter belt and stockings, blue bra
LOVESlace:	No panties?
genzero:	they get in the way
LOVESlace:	They add to the mystery. Sex is about mystery.
genzero:	ok, panties—blue
LOVESlace:	Of course. Now what.
genzero:	take them off
LOVESlace:	But I just put them on!
genzero:	please
LOVESlace:	Beg me, I like that. What will you do for me?
genzero:	kiss you
LOVESlace:	Where?
genzero:	where do you like?
LOVESlace:	My panties are split at the crotch. Will you kiss me there?
genzero:	yes
LOVESlace:	Beg me to open my legs :-)
genzero:	please please please i'm on my knees crawling

"Jason, what is that clicking sound? Are you on the computer?"

His mother's super-hearing. Even when he thought she was asleep, she was always on the alert. Always listening. Always. How could she hear from her room? It was incredible.

"Yes, ma."

"Shut my door."

LOVESlace:	Zero, where are you?
genzero:	back in a sec

Jason struggled to his feet, covering Snake as best he could, squashing it down. He shuffled to his mother's room and started to shut the door.

"Jason?"

"Yeah, ma?"

"Come here."

"Ma…"

"Come here, honey."

"Ma, I'm busy."

"Please."

Jason rolled his eyes and waited for Snake to relax.

"Jason?"

Ready at last, he went into the room.

"What is it, ma?"

"Give me a hug."

Jason bent over his mother and she put her arms around his neck, trying to pull him close. He held back.

"Jason."

"Yeah, ma?"

"Don't stay up too late."

"I won't ma. I've got to go."

She released him. Jason shut the door as he left. When he got back to the computer, he saw LOVESlace's last messages.

LOVESlace: If you come back I'll open my legs.

LOVESlace: Zero, oh Zero??? My legs are open!

LOVESlace: Couldn't wait, Zero. Play tag to find me.

She wanted him to search for her on the network, to jump from room to room looking for her CrossNet name and, if he found it, to tag her by sending a private message before she could leave the room. LOVESlace could be anywhere, sitting in on a conversation about movies or basketball or photography, playing in GameRoom, listening to one of the large group discussions that took place in the Open Forum, being anywhere she wanted to be in the nooks and crannies of cyberspace.

Jason sighed and shook his head. The search would be long and hard. It was 11:08 PM. He couldn't stand the thought of the frustration he would have to endure to find her. If he found her. Besides, there was Phil.

If they didn't talk on the phone, he and Phil tried to meet between eleven and twelve on the network. Their meeting place was the Mysticism Forum under Religion under Special Interests. Jason found the room and scanned the list of current users. Phil was already there, screen name JACKER69. Jacked in, as he loved saying.

Jason sent his friend a private message to make contact, then set up their private room JOFFER. Phil responded.

JACKER69:	Goodbuddy, whaddayu say???
genzero:	lost loveslace to my mother
JACKER69:	What's that mean?
genzero:	had to shut my mother's door, when I came back lace was gone
JACKER69:	Just like a woman. Say, the news said somebody got killed down there.
genzero:	it made the news?
JACKER69:	Allie somebody.
genzero:	i started it
JACKER69:	Yeah and I'm Bill Gates.
genzero:	true, no bs, it was over me. i hit this allie kid in the balls with a bad volleyball shot & he went nuts. started a fight with this other kid who got in a lucky punch
JACKER69:	Karate blow, they said.
genzero:	don't know. feel bad about it. guilty
JACKER69:	Why?
genzero:	i lied to get into the game, said i had a good serve, then when i messed up this kid got into a fight and got killed
JACKER69:	Who started the fight?
genzero:	allie

JACKER69:   So he did it to himself. You didn't.

genzero: if i hadn't lied it wouldn't have happened

JACKER69:   Sooner or later it would. His karma, you were an instrument, remember that. His karma demanded consequences for past actions.

genzero: then shouldn't we always let people suffer instead of helping them? they're only paying for their sins

JACKER69:   Do that and you generate your own bad karma. You must ALWAYS act out of love. Loving acts are the only ones that free us.

genzero: what's new out there?

JACKER69:   Lunatic shot 5 people in the post office. Said he couldn't wait on line anymore.

genzero: SHOULD HAVE BOUGHT HIS STAMPS BY MAIL

JACKER69:   Don't shout.

genzero: HIT CAPS LOCK BY MISTAKE

JACKER69:   What else is new?

genzero: YOU WERE TELLING ME

JACKER69:   Learned the secret of life this week.

genzero: WHAT IS IT?

JACKER69:   It's a secret.

genzero: HAHAHA…SO?

JACKER69:   Check it out, there's a web page.

genzero: URL?

JACKER69:   thesecretofliferevealed.com

genzero: WHAT'S IT COST?

JACKER69:   Nuttin'

genzero: I hope it's not about God.

JACKER69:   Why?

genzero: there is no God.

JACKER69:   Gotta be something bigger than the net.

genzero: you know my theory about God

JACKER69:	Do I?
genzero:	the early cavemen saw this lightning come down and kill one of them, or set fire to a tree, they got scared and made up some bullshit to try to protect themselves. made up gods
JACKER69:	That explains it all?
genzero:	look at the greeks. zeus, head god, throws lighting bolts
JACKER69:	Case closed. Forget about Christ, Buddha, etc…
genzero:	you got it
JACKER69:	What a philosopher!
genzero:	you take philosophy at stuy?
JACKER69:	Why do you ask?
genzero:	came up in conversation here. what you took at stuy. you never said
JACKER69:	Math, science, history, the usual stuff.
genzero:	maybe you could help me plan my curriculum sometime
JACKER69:	Not much of a planner.
genzero:	got any names for me, good advisors, that sort of thing?
JACKER69;	It's been a while since I was there. You work on DINOSAURS???
genzero:	what?
JACKER69:	The anagram.
genzero:	all i got was sad
JACKER69:	I'll give you a hint. ASTEROIDS made them this.
genzero:	and asteroids is another anagram
JACKER69:	You're getting smart.
genzero:	i'm signing off
JACKER69:	Don't joff too much. Makes you blind, can't see keyblfodlf board thoj jkey boad
genzero:	talk to you tomorrow
JACKER69:	Righto. Boot up. Jack in. Take off.
genzero:	bujito! part of the net
JACKER69:	Part of the Nineties.

Jason exited the Crossing Network and shut off the computer, then unhooked it from the telephone. Aunt Lee was still reading.

"Good night," Jason said as he got up from his chair. His aunt smiled at him. "Good night, Jason. Sleep tight."

Jason took the laptop to his room. He put the computer away then brushed his teeth and rubbed acne cream over his back. He put on a clean tee-shirt and turned out his light, then glanced out at Carol's house. It was dark. He lay back on his pillow and closed his eyes, drifted.

dont care what they say i had a lot to do with it shouldnt have lied about my serve he would be alive wouldnt he wouldnt have gotten into that fight
          who knows maybe into a different fight over something else gotten killed anyway   stupid   getting   so angry over a stupid volleyball must have hurt in the balls like that jesus how could i be so stupid ive got a good serve bullshit never made a good serve in my life what bullshit
          so now hes dead im alive what the fuck does that mean

just like bobby people die like in war these live those die who knows why god knows fuck him no god anyway just a bunch of natives saw lightning hit a tree start a fire kill somebody prayed to it leave them alone or bring them good crops some such bullshit there was your god lot of bullshit   wish i had seen carol tonight should have gotten off the computer earlier might have been able to see her oh carol so beautiful   ah love let us be true to one another   how does that go   for we are here as on a dark-ling plain   i like that

                                                                   swept   with   confu-sion and fright   where ignorant armies clash by

     night   terrific   ignorant armies clash by night wasnt that the name of a movie

i dont

remember

Blue Shirt
Files—2009.9.BG2

When I came to, my head felt full of rocks. I opened my eyes and lifted my chin off my chest to look around.

I'd been tied to a chair, hands behind my back, in a small windowless room lit by a bare bulb hanging from the ceiling. Across from me sat two of the thugs who had paid me the visit in my office. The third one leaned against the dirt-streaked wall, his eyes fixed on me like a snake gazing at its prey.

I'd never seen the three before. One of the seated men was very fat, but solid looking. He ate something that looked like a pastry from a small brown paper bag, dropping crumbs on himself and the floor. The other seated man was tall and thin, with a habit of digging his finger into his nose.

The standing man was big, muscular, like a linebacker, and his breathing made a wheezing, raspy noise. He was the toughest of the bunch, I could see that. He would have to be first. I tested the ropes that bit into my wrists. I'd learned a few tricks during my days in the Far East and knew I'd be able to slip out of the bindings soon enough. The question was, would it be soon enough?

"Welcome back, Blue Shirt," the standing man said. "I hope you're not too uncomfortable."

"You have me at a disadvantage," I said. "Who are you?"

The standing man pushed away from the wall and approached me. "I'm sorry," he said. "I've been impolite. The man eating is Mr. Scone. The other is Mr. Pickett. I'm Mr. Rattler."

Scone, Pickett, Rattler! I knew their names and faces from my days on the force but these weren't the faces I remembered. They'd had plastisurge done to give themselves a new look. Whoever hired them had lots of money to spend and didn't care about who got hurt. They were vicious killers, henchmen for hire, who would do anything to anybody for a price. I never understood men this evil or how they could do the things they did. I concentrated more intently on the ropes.

"Your reputation precedes you," I said. Rattler, Pickett, and Scone were usually employed by the big Corporations. The last I'd heard, they'd beaten an old woman to death who was suing United Media, the holding company for the five television networks. Seems her husband had been run down by a UniMed mobile news van. UniMed preferred to pay these three slimeballs than settle with her for a large sum.

"Thank you," said Rattler.

"Why am I here?" I asked.

"The obvious question, isn't it," he said, lighting a cigarette. I had the feeling it wasn't for smoking. "We have a few things to ask you about." He took a drag on the cigarette, making its tip glow like a red hot poker. "And we want answers."

I still had a way to go with my ropes so I decided to play along.

"What kind of questions?" I asked.

"What was Bunny Glands doing in your office tonight?"

Bunny Glands! So that's what this was about. They worked for Homer and he was already on her trail. I was glad I'd thought to get her to Phil's safe house.

"She's my client," I said. "Our conversation is privileged."

Rattler laughed, a sharp cracking laugh like the sound of a whip lashing the air. He turned to face the others and they laughed with him. I watched them laughing and I began to laugh, too, nervously at first, then harder as they laughed at my laughing. Scone dropped crumbs everywhere. Pickett took the finger out of his nose. And Rattler wheezed.

Then he pressed the cigarette's business end into my cheek. It felt like an ice pick going into my face, then I smelled my skin burning. I pulled away. He wasn't laughing anymore. Nobody was.

"That was amusing but we're not here to be amused." Pain radiated over my face like ripples of flame spreading out from the center of a fire. "Now tell me, why was she there?"

I'd made progress with the ropes. I just needed to keep the boys talking a little longer.

"You're quite persistent," I said. "How much is Homer paying you for this?"

Rattler sneered and crouched down in front of me, holding the cigarette near my eye.

"Enough banter," he said. "If you don't answer now, I'll have Mr. Scone hold your head while I burn out your eye. Would you like that?"

I could see Scone smiling as he licked crumbs off his fingers. "All right," I said. "She's afraid he's going to kill her. She came to me for protection."

"What else did she tell you?" He brought the cigarette closer. I could feel its awful heat.

"She was hysterical," I said. "Started talking about the Biochip. Highly technical, I couldn't understand most of it."

"Tell me the parts that you did understand."

"That it doesn't work right, that there's a flaw nobody knows about. That was it."

He puffed on the cigarette and blew the smoke in my face. I nearly had the ropes undone.

"Where is she?" I'd known that would be the next question. They wanted her and I'd be in big trouble if I didn't get my hands free. I needed only seconds.

"A safe house," I said.

"And where is this safe house?" Rattler asked, again moving the cigarette close.

"I don't know," I lied. "A friend took her. He'll contact me by phone."

"Are you quite sure you don't know?" said Rattler. "Mr. Scone, I need your assistance." Scone put down his eating bag and got out of his chair. Pickett forgot his nose and leaned forward to watch. This was it.

I slipped out of the ropes and brought my hands around in a lightning strike, smacking my open palms against Rattler's ears. The blows shocked and deafened him and I followed up with a head butt to his nose that knocked him halfway across the room into Scone. Pickett was on his feet, reaching inside his jacket. I stood up and threw the chair at him, aiming for the middle of his body. The chair was hard to evade and caught him squarely in the stomach. The pistol he was trying to draw fell to the floor.

I went for the gun, throwing a vicious kick into Scone's head and smashing my fist into Pickett's jaw. I grabbed the old Smith & Wesson .38 and used its butt to play a tattoo on Rattler's head. He was bloody but still conscious when I got through with him.

"Listen, Rattler," I said. "I'm only leaving you alive to take a message to Homer Glands. Tell him to lay off or this'll happen to him. Do you get it?"

Rattler nodded. I disarmed him, then found the cigarettes in his jacket. I opened the pack and put one in his mouth. Then another. Then another. Hie eyes pleaded with me. In the background I heard Scone and Pickett stirring.

"Eat," I said. "Now." I got up and revisited Scone and Pickett, giving each one a crack on the skull from my new friends Smith and Wesson. I looked down at Rattler, who was gagging on the tobacco tubes. I kicked him in the ribs, then bent down and held the barrel of the gun to his head. I cocked it.

"You know," I said. "Maybe Scone and Pickett can deliver my message to Glands. Maybe you don't have to do that after all. Maybe I should just finish you right here."

Rattler began to sweat.

"Eat," I said.

I made him eat the whole pack, then tied him and the others with their belts. I called my old friend Lt. Harper at the Central Precinct to come pick them up, then stuck a tracing button on Rattler's forehead. The button would send a signal that Harper and his men would use to find the place. "'Night, boys," I said, and left.

I walked to an all night pharmacy and picked up a tube of Healit-All, dabbing a few drops on my burn even before I reached the checkout counter. The burn would be better in a couple of hours. From the pharmacy I called Phil at the safe house.

There was no answer. I knew I'd better get over there. Fast.

Wednesday

Jason woke and checked the digital clock.

7:56 AM.

He listened for sounds of activity from the rest of the house.

All was quiet.

Besides Jason, only Snake was up, pressing at his shorts. Jason pushed it down, scratched, went to the bathroom. He used the toilet, brushed his teeth, checked the zits on his back, returned to his room, changed his tee-shirt, put on his bathing suit. Ready for anything.

Jason opened the front door. The incandescent sun promised another beautiful day and Jason decided to go for a walk on the beach. The only obstacle was a huge spider web strung waist-high across the wooden railing at the top of the ramp that led to the Gilbert boardwalk, a gossamer net to snare the unwary, its strands shimmering in the sunlight like a delicate silver brooch. Embedded in the net were three packaged meals, helpless, waiting to be eaten. The web's spinner, a fat brown arachnid, rested in one corner of its miraculous gravity-defying construction, no doubt pleased with the night's catch. Jason went back into the house and took a broom from a utility closet.

He swept the broom through the net, tearing it down, tossing its prisoners to the ground in their wrappings and sending the surprised spider scuttling for safety. Jason smacked at the spider but it eluded his blows and darted under the house. Jason considered the encounter a victory, returned the broom to the armory, grabbed his towel, and left for the beach.

He would eat later.

The beach, empty save for an occasional jogger or dog walker, spread out like a golden blanket next to the blue ocean. The lifeguard towers, pulled back to the dunes the evening before to keep the incoming tide from claiming them overnight, lay on their sides like the bleached skeletons of ancient beasts. The water shooshed in and whooshed out with metronomic regularity, pumped by a vast heart somewhere far away, a heart that had first beat long before life on earth had begun.

Jason headed north.

He hadn't gone more than a quarter of a mile when he saw a man with sunglasses and wearing a polo shirt and jeans sitting on a blanket and eating breakfast. As Jason approached, something odd happened.

From over the sea came gulls, first one, then another, then more and more until they shrieked and cried everywhere around the man. They swept down like the terrors of a Hitchcock movie and stole his food, snatching it from right in front of him. The man lifted a thin white cane and began swatting at the birds.

Jason couldn't believe the aggressiveness of the gulls. They usually didn't come within ten feet of people, but these swooped down right at the man himself, whose cane was proving ineffective against the predators. He could do nothing to save his food or to chase the gulls away as they flapped around him.

Jason ran to the man, shouting and waving and slapping his beach towel at the air to frighten the birds. The scavengers screamed at him but then pulled away, flying to a safe distance from where they watched as Jason stood guard.

"They were eating your food," Jason said, feeling he had to explain his sudden noisy appearance.

"I know," said the man. "They always do. They somehow seem to know I can't see them, so they've learned to sneak up and steal scraps." His voice was rough and scratchy, and when he spoke he tilted his head in an odd fashion. Jason realized that the man was blind.

"They weren't just sneaking up," said Jason. "They were coming by the dozens and grabbing things."

"They've gotten bolder."

The man cocked his head to listen.

"Where are they?"

"Around," said Jason. "Mostly about twenty feet back on the beach, watching us."

"But not coming close?"

"No."

The man picked up a piece of melon. "Will you join me?"

"Thanks. Not hungry." said Jason.

"Please," said the man. "I insist. How else can I show my gratitude?"

"All right," said Jason, taking a piece of the proffered melon. He bit into its tender sweetness.

"It's at its peak," said the man.

Jason ate hungrily, following the melon with a wedge of yellow cheese. The man laughed as he heard Jason wolf the food.

"I guess you were hungry after all."

"I guess so."

"Maybe you just needed the right thing to get your appetite going."

"Maybe."

"Where do you live?" the man asked.

"New York," said Jason. "Out here, I stay with my aunt on Gilbert."

"I know where that is," said the man. He chewed another piece of melon and said nothing. Jason became uncomfortable and spoke to break the silence.

"Where do you stay?"

"I have a sister on Marine. I visit from time to time. I like it here. It's quiet."

"Except for the gulls," said Jason.

The man gave a short laugh. "Yes. The gulls."

He continued eating and Jason watched the ocean. It swelled in and out, pushing gentle waves over the small shells and pebbles that had accumulated on the shore since the tide had ebbed, moving them, making them tinkle like tiny bells.

"The water's calm," said the man, as if reading Jason's mind.

"Yeah," said Jason.

"Do much beach combing?"

"I like to walk and look for things. Sea glass, shells, odd stones."

"I used to do that," said the man. "Do you know about the Resurrection Stone?"

"That's weird," Jason said, surprised. "My friend told me about it."

"What did he say?"

"That it's from Christ's tomb. That it looks like a human heart."

"It has unspeakable power."

"You mean, it's real?"

"Oh, yes."

"What does it do? Grant wishes?"

The man laughed. "No. It works miracles."

"I think it's a fairy tale."

"Don't be so sure," said the man. "Strange things can happen. I bet you've been looking for it."

"Not really."

"They say it's here, on Cranberry Island."

"Who says?"

"You know," said the man. "They. The ones who always say."

Jason fidgeted.

"Maybe you should go for a walk," said the man. "Work off some of that energy."

Jason stopped moving.

"I'm not offended," said the man. He ate the last piece of his fruit. The gulls had been leaving one by one and now were all gone. "In fact, I'm going back to my house. Too much sun's no good for me."

The man began gathering his belongings. Jason helped.

"Good luck," the man said as he stood. "Hope you find it." His voice lowered. "I did. Once."

"What do you mean?" Jason asked.

"The day this happened." The man pointed to his eyes. His expression changed, as if he were trying to see something far away.

"The beach at that place was a low granite shelf, covered with rocks of all kinds, a geologist's dream. I saw the stone by the edge of the water, mixed in with the rest but different. Very different.

"It resembled a human heart, a living, beating heart, dark red, the water glistening on it like drops of blood. I stood there staring at it, watching the waves splash over it. I could have sworn the water turned red when it washed off the stone. I leaned closer, reached for it, but I didn't touch it. My hand shook and I couldn't."

He paused. A few gulls fluttered in close, then flew off.

"Then a wave came, a big one. Smashed me into the rocks, knocked me unconscious. When I came to, I was blind."

"Blind?!"

The man nodded. "Doctors haven't been able to figure out why." He chuckled. "But I know. Fear. Fear blinded me. Kept me from picking up the stone and blinded me."

"Fear of what?"

The man shrugged. "Power. Limitless power."

"I think I'd like that."

"Yes, you think so now. But when you can have it, it's different. Awesome. Unimaginable."

"What happened to the stone?"

"Washed out, I guess. So if you see it, boy, don't let your fear do what mine did to me. Reach for the miracle."

Jason watched as the man walked off, then continued on his way north, looking at every stone, wondering if there was really something to look for after all.

Alone at the house, Lee examined herself in the long bathroom mirror. Her breasts were still taut, still had the firm lift they had when she was in her twenties. Her belly was smooth, her hips full but not fat, her thighs and legs curvy but not heavy, with no cellulite pockets to spoil their smoothness. Not having had the baby hadn't been all bad. Her body looked great.

Lee picked up the bottle of coconut tanning lotion and poured some into the palm of one hand. The creamy white lotion reminded her of cum, but with a pleasant tropical fragrance. She dipped the fingers of her other hand into the lotion and drew her hands apart, smiling as sticky strands formed in the air between her fingers.

She worked the lotion into her skin with loving care, moving her fingers in slow circles around her stomach, dipping again for more lotion, touching her breasts and smoothing the lotion on, feeling the soft weight of her flesh, the tautness of her nipples. She massaged each nipple in turn, then pinched them playfully. Lee gasped with the pleasure of it, sucking in her breath and smiling at herself in the mirror, watching the nipples stiffen.

She rubbed herself all over with the coconut cream, working the lotion into her feet, ankles, legs, thighs, and buttocks, doing her arms, shoulders, neck, and face, and as much of her back as she could reach. She was preparing for her daily walk toward the Colony and might stop at the Nude Beach to take the sun. All of her had to be protected.

When she was done, Lee cleaned the excess cream from her hands and sat on the toilet. She touched a finger to her clit. Her other hand went to a nipple. A soft breeze pushed through the open louvers on the outside bathroom door, cooling her.

She thought of Ralph. The few times he wasn't drunk he had been a wonderful lover. She thought of his hands touching her, his lips on hers, his strong back, his magnificent cock driving home again and again until she would cry out with pleasure, then cry tears after she came, tears full of the happy love she had for him in the beginning.

Lee bit her lip as she caressed her flesh. She teased herself until she had to be rougher, then rubbed hard, harder, breathed faster, squeezed the clit between two fingers, pinched the nipple, rocked and moaned and came and came and came with new tears in her eyes.

She sat for a while afterwards, then peed, enjoying the feel of her bladder emptying. She wiped herself then stood and put on her bathing suit. Her breasts filled out the black bikini top nicely and her hips weren't too wide for the bottom. The suit was old, she needed a new one. Maybe later in the week she'd get over to the Mart.

Lee finished in the bathroom and gathered her beach things. Towel, Dean Koontz novel, lotion, bottle of Evian, and tee-shirt all went into a mesh bag. She put on her beach hat, a big floppy straw hat with a red fabric rose sewn on it, and her sunglasses. She was conflicted about going for a walk without her sister, but Anna liked staying around the house or sitting on the beach near the house. Lee couldn't sit around. She had to take her walk, had to use the energy that burned inside her.

Lee reached the sand and stood for a moment watching the eternal volleyball players bat the white ball back and forth, screaming and yelling at each other to do this or do that or do something else *allie grant so crazy to get killed that way fighting over a volleyball game that no good father never gave a rats ass for the boy now his poor mother is alone*

Most of the boys had fine bodies. She licked her lips and walked on, her gaze next finding the lifeguards *now id like to get to know them what would they say lees fucking a lifeguard sucking his hard dick oh god why do i think about this all the time jesus well it could be worse after all i dont rape them and i dont even go after really young ones usually look at the pecs on that one oh god lets get over to nude beach see whats up like that fat guy who looked like a whale what did i call him a blister waiting to be burst poor fucker burnt to a crisp hope he didnt lose his dick out there in the sun not much to lose not like jason bet hes got something down there all right god what am i thinking my own nephew jesus*

She strutted past the lifeguards, a blank expression on her face, enjoying the idea that she was stirring them up, stiffening their sturdy cocks, making them swell in their Speedos with her succulent breasts, her luscious ass, her delectable legs *too bad i dont have on heels theyd be creaming off right now glad i keep in shape its the walking does it best thing for you walking in the sand every day keeps those calves tight*

Enjoying herself, Lee went to the edge of the water and bent over to examine nothing, really, but to put on a show for the lifeguards and anybody else who wanted to look *i must be sick to do this fuck it makes me hot wonder if annas right a sex fiend had good training all right ed you fuck*

She stood and walked on, watching the joggers, the tireless Kadema players, the sunbathers, the babies wrapped to keep from burning, the kids, the couples, the oldsters, and listening to the scraps of conversation that filled the air. She walked faster, taking long strides on the yielding sand, feeling it try to hold her, keep her back. She breathed deep.

Lee passed the final row of houses and was soon alone on the beach, with no one as far as she could see in either direction. In the distance stood the Colony's tower.

Lee's side hurt. It felt like a stitch and surprised her. Maybe she had walked faster than she should have, fast enough to strain a muscle. Maybe she was just getting old. She took her towel out of the beach bag and threw it down. She sat. The ocean lapped at the shore. Here and there a gull flew. When one cried out, it sounded like *a baby oh my god why do those damn birds always sound like babies to me more than ever these days menopause threatening maybe thats why all that could have been poor little fucker jamie it would have been so nice then you had to die inside oh god im not thinking about it anna is so lucky to have jason i hope she knows how lucky she is a son of her own a wonderful bright boy to call her own nobody to ever remember me ever remember*

Lee got to her feet, picked up her towel and bag, and resumed walking. After some time saw her first nude sunbather. A slim brunette in her late teens, attractive *never did it with a woman wonder what its like not me dont think id care for it like sausages too much*

Lee put down her towel and set the bag next to it. She saw the brunette look her way. Lee smiled. The girl smiled back. Lee sat and gazed at the ocean *maybe it would be fun get a dildo to stick inside like those movies with ralph that ramrod put a little oil on it use it together suck those titties of hers what am i thinking*

When Lee glanced over the next time, a young man had joined the brunette. He was mid-twenties, well built, short cropped sandy hair and a Speedo that bulged with his equipment. The Speedo came off fast and Lee appraised his thick member and heavy testicles. He sat down next to the girl and they talked. She didn't look over at Lee anymore *fucking marines have landed look at that guy fuck i guess just as well dont want to start up as a lez at my age old bull sucking after the young cunts juicy like to suck him though nothing wrong with that hose could take it all in nicely thank you suck it till it squirts love that stuff better not undress jason might wander by give him an eyeful he wouldnt forget for a while what about that what about*

Her nipples hardened as she thought of sex. Lee looked at the sky, a bright clear blue sky with only a small white cloud here and there for decoration. Not a day to fall asleep on the beach. She stood, then wrapped the towel around her waist. She decided to walk a little further towards the Colony to see who else was around. After a few hundred feet she found out.

A cluster of nudist families had gathered like a herd of walrus Lee once saw in a Nature Channel documentary. Mothers, fathers, kids, babies, even a few oldsters, had swarmed onto this part of the beach and made it their own.

Lee sized up the men who, for the most part, looked woebegone, with no more starch left in their dicks than in cooked spaghetti. The wives were baggy and many of them were fat, which surprised Lee. Most nudists she had seen liked to keep trim. Maybe they were just starting out. A baby cried *perfectly healthy they said then the next week we dont know what happened your son*

The infant was a boy too long in the sun. His skin bright pink. Mother and father argued. Lee kept walking.

"...left him just sitting there..."

"...under the umbrella..."

"...not enough lotion..."

"...had plenty..."

"...burned..."

"...he'll live..."

Lee walked faster *hell live what a laugh they were wrong took it from her after it was dead slipped out so small wouldnt let me hold the little corpse carl not even there fuck that fuck oh god he blamed me wasnt my fault poor little thing little jamie then doctor roberts there wouldnt be anymore no more babies for you no more no son like jason want one like him want*

The waves at this section of the beach were rough. They beat against the shore, slapped whitecaps and foam against the sand, shoved the shells and stones in, then dragged them out. Lee put down her things and walked into the water. She wanted to swim.

Swim for a long time.

When Jason got back to the house, he called Phil's cell phone to tell him about the blind man on the beach but there was no answer. He left a message. Phil's parents made him use a cell phone for his calls because he was always tying up their regular line with his computer. Frustrated, Jason took the Ross out, heading south on Midway.

As he sped up to pass a girl on a tricycle, the bike's gear chain fell off. It had always been trouble, always dropping off at the worst times, usually when Jason was trying to impress somebody with the his speed or whizzing by a pack of jerky little kids. Fortunately, he never lost control when it happened and always managed to come to a slow stop before dismounting and inspecting the damage. Sometimes he could wiggle and nudge and coax the chain back into place. This time he couldn't.

It meant a trip to Vern's Bike Shop, over on Navy, just off Midway. Vern was probably the oldest man on the island, Jason thought. Vern the Bike Man.

Jason walked the Ross to Vern's, sweating in the hot still August day. The trees seemed to sag and the sound of the ocean in the distance seemed more like the lapping of a quiet river against its bank than the pounding of the Atlantic against its shore. The wooden boardwalk that was Midway felt splintery and hard against Jason's bare feet, for he never wore shoes while biking on Cranberry Island. Never.

As he neared Vern's, he could hear the old man shouting.

"Damn shirts aren't even clean. What's the matter, washer broken again?"

"No, Vern." A woman's voice.

"Well, do 'em again. Do 'em till they come out or..."

The sound of an electric saw from a neighboring house drowned out the end of his sentence. For a small place, Cranberry Island supported hordes of building contractors.

"What?" The woman.

"White! Do 'em till they come out white!"

The electric saw again. The end of the woman's sentence.

"...do it."

"What?"

Jason reached the walkway that led to the Bike Shop. It occupied the lower level of Vern's house, an old weather-beaten structure on stilts. The shouting had come from above.

"Got a bike needs fixing," Jason called.

Sudden quiet from Vern and the woman. Then Vern.

"Who's there?"

"I got a bike, it's cha-in fell off."

Vern appeared at the top of the flight of stairs that led down to the shop. "What's wrong?"

"The chain," said Jason. The electric saw made him pause. "Fell off," he said during a silence.

Vern disappeared inside. Jason stood in the sun looking at his bike and all the other bicycles that perched on their kick stands, leaned against walls, or lay on their sides in the Bike Shop. Hanging on hooks or scattered on wooden shelves and work tables were wrenches of different sizes, screwdrivers, hammers, tires, cans of WD-40, inner tubes, chains, bells, seats, screws, wires, gears, nuts and bolts, lights, reflectors, wheels, mud guards, brake cables, and pedals, all layered in grease and speckled with grime.

Vern reappeared and came down the stairs. He was a big man with only a few thin strands of grey hair dangling wherever they fell over his craggy face. Vern's deep tanned, barrel-shaped chest, on the other hand, was covered with a mat of tangled growth. His skin was like old leather, worked by the sun and the rain into a tough protective coat. A ratty piece of rope tied around his waist held up a pair of baggy tan pants and he wore the oldest, dirtiest sneakers Jason had ever seen. Vern's clear blue eyes fixed first on Jason and then on the bike.

"Got a Ross there," Vern said.

"Yeah," said Jason.

"Nice," Vern said. It was his highest compliment.

"Thanks."

"Know much about 'em?" Vern asked, running his hand along the frame.

"Bikes?" said Jason.

"People been riding 'em since 1840. Scotsman named Macmillan built the first real bike. Then there was the ordinary, you probably seen pictures of it, with that great big front wheel sometimes five feet high."

"Yeah," said Jason. "I've seen them."

"Know why they built 'em that way?"

Jason shrugged.

"Get over the potholes. Yeah, they had 'em back then."

He kneeled down to take a closer look at the chain. "Tough to ride, those big wheel bikes. Tough to mount."

A voice from above interrupted his work.

"Vern, you coming back?"

Jason couldn't believe his eyes. At the top of the stairs he saw a young Asian woman in her early twenties, dressed in the short black dress and starched apron of a formal maid. On her trim legs she wore sheer black nylons. Shiny black high heel shoes adorned her feet.

"In a minute," Vern replied.

"You pay four hours, that's all you get," she said, going back into the house.

Vern winked at Jason. "Now her," he said, "she's easy to mount." Vern leaned the Ross against a wall, then inspected the front wheel, moving it back and forth with his hand.

"Gotta little wobble here. You know how many bike accidents are caused by mechanical failure?"

"No," said Jason.

"Fifteen percent. Gotta keep your machine clean, fastened tight, no wobble in the wheels. Okay?"

"Okay."

Vern scratched his head. "You can pick it up tomorrow."

"Tomorrow?" said Jason. He would lose the whole day.

"I gotta use the girl while…"

The electric saw cut through his words. Vern leaned the Ross against a wall. "Come by first thing."

He turned and climbed the stairs. Jason listened to the whine of the electric saw and started away. He heard Vern and the girl resume their conversation.

"What happened to my shorts?"

Electric saw.

"What?"

"My shorts. They turned pink."

"Pink?"

Electric saw.

"…god damn it."

"Vern, watch your mouth. Why'd you put a red towel…"

Electric saw.

"What?"

"Red towel in there."

"Didn't…"

Electric saw.

"…'em over. Use bleach."

"That's gonna take more time."

Electric saw.

"…gotta get 'em clean, god damn it, can't wear 'em like this, lookit that."

Laughter.

Electric saw.

Jason walked to the beach.

When he got there, he started in the direction of the Colony but after about half a mile lost interest in walking. Jason got on his knees and dug in the sand.

He remembered his trips with his mother to Aunt Lee's place on the Jersey shore when he was small. He remembered how he loved digging in the sand and how his mother and aunt used to amuse him by making sand castles, burying his feet, and digging holes and trenches for the water to fill.

The sand, rough and smooth at the same time, ran through his fingers to accumulate into small hills. He flattened them as he had as a child, like a giant monster gleefully destroying cities, a Godzilla on the rampage, King Kong, Mothra, Gorgo, Rodan.

Jason scanned the empty beach and decided to take off his shirt. He knew ultra-violet light was good for zits, and liked to give them a good burn whenever he had the chance. He slipped off the shirt and angled his back to the sun. Then he dug some more.

He remembered filling his bucket with sand, then turning it upside down to make small mounds he would work together to form castles, castles he decorated with shells, stones, twigs, dried starfish, seaweed, and whatever other treasures the sea might have left on the shore. Castles that he could look at and dream about for hours. Castles that were the homes of great Kings and Queens, Princes and Princesses, Knights and Nobles. Castles on Earth and on planets no human had ever seen.

Today he didn't have the patience for castles. Today he just wanted to dig, to pull the sand out in handfuls and make a space where there had been none. He made a hole deep enough to climb into and climb into it he did, up to his chest. He sat looking over the Atlantic like a soldier in a trench watching for the enemy. The sun beat down. He wished he weren't so afraid of the water. Then he would jump right into the waves and splash all day, like everybody else.

He imagined the ocean devoid of water, as were the arid seabeds of Mars. He tried to picture the great abyss that would now lie before him, barren of all but the hardiest plant life. He wondered how deep it would be, what the sand and rocks would look like, and how it would feel to walk on the bottom, an explorer on a small, dry planet millions of miles away.

As Jason daydreamed, he saw a young girl walking in his direction with a small unleashed dog running well ahead of her. She was eleven or twelve, dressed in a white one-piece suit and a green baseball cap. She was pretty flat up top but her face was cute and long blond hair flowed out from under the cap. Hair that reminded him of Carol's.

Jason weighed the embarrassment of the girl seeing his exposed zits against the benefit they were getting from the sun and decided to cover up until she had passed. If only he had Healit-All to use on them. That would take care of his problem. Jason draped his tee-shirt over his back and went back to contemplating the Martian landscape.

The dog moved out of Jason's view but he soon heard it come up behind him to sniff and dig in the sand. When the dog quieted, Jason became uneasy. The next thing he knew, a warm liquid was soaking into his shirt and trickling down his back. The girl came running, yelling "Stop it, Max!"

Jason burst from his hole, his wet shirt falling from him, and turned to see the dog, a terrier, staring up at him, its leg still in the air.

"Bad dog, bad dog." The girl came over to put a leash on her pet.

"He peed on me," Jason said, more to himself than to the girl, shocked that he had been mistaken for a fire plug.

"Sorry," she said. "He's never done that before. Must have been the way you were sitting. Sorry."

"He peed on me," Jason repeated, retrieving his shirt from the sand, not believing.

"Maybe you should go in the ocean," she suggested.

"I don't have a towel," Jason said.

She thrust her towel at him. "Take mine. Please. It's the least I can do."

"Thanks," said Jason, thinking fast. "The sand is better. I'll just roll around in the sand."

She shrugged. Jason wanted to ask her name but couldn't get the words out.

"Come on, Max," she finally said, pulling at the dog.

"Good-bye," said Jason, his voice cracking. The girl waved and walked off. When she was far away, Jason lay back in the sand and rolled from side to side to clean himself, like a dog. Then he rinsed his shirt in the ocean and put it back on, shivering from its cold wetness. He walked home.

"We lost our faith and went around wondering what life was for."
Jason put down the *Martian Chronicles* when he heard a commotion of dogs outside the house, sounds of barking, growling, snorting, snuffling,

and the click-click-click of dog claws on wood. He saw his aunt with a man. Both were wrestling with two mean looking Rotweilers.

"Leave 'em outside," Jason heard his aunt say.

"They don't like to be tied up," the man replied.

"My sister's here. She's not crazy about dog hairs all over."

Jason saw the man bend down to leash the dogs to the railing. They whined and whimpered.

"It's okay, okay. Gonna be all right."

Aunt Lee opened the door and walked in with the man. He was beefy, hairy, shorter than her, with a greasy black moustache that looked like something you would avoid stepping on.

"Hi, Jason," his aunt bubbled. "This is Greg. Greg, Jason."

Greg mumbled something unintelligible and Jason said "Hi."

"Greg has a house on Sailor. Sit down, sit down," Aunt Lee directed Greg, opening her hands to indicate anywhere. "I'll get you a beer."

Greg crossed the room and flopped onto the couch. Jason could have sworn he heard Greg's lumpy body, wet and sandy from the beach, squish as it worked its way into the creaking sofa like the blob from the old Steve McQueen movie.

Aunt Lee opened the refrigerator and took out two beers. She opened them and gave one to Greg who took it without a thank you and drank greedily, a man at last at the oasis. Beer spilled onto his chest. Outside, the dogs clawed at the door.

Lee sipped her beer in a more civilized fashion, wiping the foam from her lips with the back of her hand.

"Where's your mom?" she asked Jason, pushing her hair back.

"At the beach. Didn't you see her?"

"Guess not," Lee answered. "But it's a beautiful day, isn't it Greg?"

Greg drank, burped. Jason said nothing.

"Well young man, I suggest you get yourself out there," his aunt continued. "There's places to go, sights to see, people to meet. If you want to read, you can do that just as well on the beach as in here and get the fresh air and sun, too."

Jason looked at his aunt and then at Greg, who was playing with the his long belly hairs, twirling them around his fingers. Then Jason figured it out. They wanted to fuck.

He smiled at his insight and made believe his smile was because of his aunt's suggestion.

"Good idea," he said. "Maybe I'll take a shower first." Jason's smile broadened as he stalled to make them wait. In fact, Jason had showered as soon as he had returned from the beach, to wash off the dog's baptism and the sand clinging to it.

"That's silly," said Lee. "You'll just get all sandy and have to take another one."

"Yeah," said Jason. He thought of continuing to delay them, then had a better idea. He stood up.

"Maybe I will go."

"That's my boy," said Lee.

"Watch those dogs," said Greg. "They're excitable today." He finished his beer and crumpled the can.

"I'll use the back way," said Jason. He waited for Greg to burp but there was only silence. In the silence, Aunt Lee went to the fridge and got her catch another beer.

Jason went to his room and retrieved his towel, then went out the bathroom door and around to the shed get a beach chair. When he came back in for his book, Lee and Greg were giggling on the couch. Jason saw a swelling in the crotch of Greg's bathing suit.

"Have fun," said Aunt Lee. "See you later."

"Okay," said Jason. He went out the front, avoiding the Rotweilers who had settled down to chew on the deck furniture. Jason carried all his things to the beach and set them up near his mother, who had dozed off. When ten minutes had passed, he returned to the house as Blue Shirt on a mission. To find Phil and Bunny.

He approached the safe house from the back, stealthily climbing onto the deck, fully alert, ready to flash away like lightning should he be discovered by Homer's men. He crept along the deck until he reached Bunny's room, where he crouched under the open window, listening.

"...oh, give me..."

"..open wide..."

"Uhnnn...uhnnn..ohhh..."

Giggling.

"...deep..."

"...this on..."

It became quiet. Jason strained his ears but could hear nothing. Then came soft moaning and the rhythmic thumping of bed against wall. He cast a quick glance around to see if anyone from another house was watching. The coast was clear and he slowly raised his head to spying height.

There they were! Through the worn lace curtain Jason could see Phil and Bunny naked, Phil on top ramming home his meat, Bunny's legs spread, arms wrapped around him, eyes closed to receive his love in darkness. No wonder Homer was jealous.

Phil's back had even more hair than his front, Jason saw, and thought he resembled a warthog as he quivered and lurched in and out of Bunny's cunt. Jason heard what sounded like a fart and his nose wrinkled as thought of the gas filling the room. They didn't talk about that in *Wide Open Legs*.

Bunny opened her eyes and looked right at him.

Jason jerked away from the window as if hit by a laser. He ducked down and took a step back, falling over his own feet and landing on the deck with a loud thump. Around in front, the dogs came to life, barking to wake the world.

Jason rolled off the deck and dropped onto the sand, then scrambled under the house. Blue Shirt caught by surprise but not taken prisoner. From above he could hear fragments of conversation.

"...that noise..."

"…from another house…"

"…someone outside…"

"…dogs…"

"…forget about it…"

"…take a look…"

"…come here…"

His aunt was pretending nothing had happened. Jason wondered if she had seen him, wondered if she knew he had seen her. He waited until the rhythmic moving of the bed started again, then crab-walked out from under the house and headed to the beach. He wanted to splash ocean water on his hot, sweaty face.

At dinner, Jason sat with his mother on his right, Aunt Lee across from him, and Greg to his left. Annabelle served the meatless lasagna while Lee poured Chianti for the adults and a soda for Jason.

"I'm so glad you could join us," Aunt Lee cooed. "Anna makes great Italian food." Greg had dressed for dinner in a torn bathing suit and a tee-shirt reading "Save The Dolphins—Eat Pussy Not Tuna." The letters were done in a hard-to-read gothic font that saved everyone from complete embarrassment.

"Don't get his hopes up," said Annabelle. "Lee, you gave me too much wine. I'll fall asleep at the table."

"Don't be silly, it's just a drop. And don't put yourself down. The lasagna's good. Isn't it, Greg?"

Greg nodded, digging into the food like a starving man, piling so much on his plate that Jason thought there might not be enough for everyone. But Aunt Lee had foreseen this possibility and had told Annabelle to prepare lots of the pasta. As they ate, Jason tried to read his aunt's face, looking for anything that might reveal whether she had seen him at the window. Once or twice when she smiled at him, he was certain that she had. The rest of the time he was just as certain that she hadn't.

"You know Jason, the water was beautiful today," Aunt Lee said after one of her smiles. "What I don't understand is why you two never go in. You've been coming here for years and never go in the water. I just don't get it."

"The water's rough out here," said his mother. "That's all."

"Nonsense," said Aunt Lee. "Tell her, Greg."

Greg ate without responding.

"Greg. Tell her." Aunt Lee insisted.

"What?" Greg said, after a forkful of lasagna and a big slurp of wine.

"About the tides here."

Greg rested his elbow on the table and held his fork in the air like an antenna, then glanced up and to the left. He half-closed his eyes.

"Tides in the Atlantic along Cranberry Island are among the gentlest of the waters near any of the east coast barrier reefs. Oceanographers attribute this phenomenon to natural underwater formations off the coast of Maryland that extend twenty miles out to sea.

"These formations provide protection against strong tides and, while ineffective in holding back the ocean during severe storms or hurricanes, retard the erosion that would normally be expected to occur on a barrier reef. Rip tides and other currents dangerous to swimmers are for the most part unknown in this area."

Everyone had stopped eating. When Greg finished his impromptu lecture, he was the first to start again, plowing the fork into the food on his plate.

"Is all that true?" Annabelle asked in amazement.

"He's got a photographic memory," Aunt Lee said, as if boasting a son's accomplishment. "Read the Encyclopedia Britannica by the time he was eighteen and remembers it all."

"That's not possible," said Jason.

Greg burped. "I did. I do."

"Go ahead," said Lee. "Ask him something. Something you know about."

Jason frowned. Greg seemed about as intelligent as a turd. Jason hated that this lump was fucking his aunt.

"Didn't you just finish a science project?" Annabelle prompted. Jason remembered his astronomy research for Mr. Hall's class.

"All right," he said. "Octans."

"The constellation?" Greg asked. Jason nodded, already impressed that Greg even knew what it was. Greg took another gulp of wine and glanced up and to his left again, then half-closed his eyes.

"Octans is a dim constellation visible only in the southern hemisphere. It is interesting chiefly because it contains the point in the sky that lies precisely above the earth's south pole. This is called the south celestial pole. The closest star to the south celestial pole is Sigma Octantis. It is a giant white star of magnitude five point four."

Jason's mouth fell open. His mother frowned, not believing that anyone could be as smart as or, God forbid, smarter than her son. Aunt Lee smiled at her man's trick. Greg cleared his throat and continued.

"Octans received its name in the seventeen-fifties from the French astronomer Louis de Lacaille. Originally he called the constellation Octans Hadleianus after the double-reflecting octant invented by John Hadley in 1730. The octant measured angles between celestial objects and the horizon. It was the predecessor of the modern sextant.

"The stars that compose Octans are mostly third- and fourth-magnitude and range from seventy to more than three hundred light years distant. Octans covers an area of two-hundred ninety-one square degrees and contains thirty-five stars brighter than the sixth magnitude."

Greg burped. He went back to his food. Jason could only gape in amazement. Everything Greg had said was right. Everything.

Greg left right after dinner and Jason helped Aunt Lee and his mother clean up, even though his aunt told him not to bother. Jason was still in shock over Greg's performance and felt like doing something, anything, to take his mind off of the meatloaf's giftedness. Besides, being close to his aunt in the kitchen and inhaling her sweet perfume gave him a lot to think about. He imagined himself her husband and constructed an elaborate love making scene that would happen after the dishes were done.

At eleven o'clock, his mother and aunt had gone to bed and Jason abandoned his fantasy. He hooked his laptop to the telephone to call the Crossing Network. Within minutes, he had contacted Phil.

JACKER69:   Goodbuddy. What's happening?
genzero: where were u when i needed u? i tried to call earlier
JACKER69:   I was out. What about?
genzero: i found a guy who's seen the stone
JACKER69:   What stone?
genzero: the resurrection stone

There was a long pause at Phil's end.

genzero: you smoking again?
JACKER69:   Smoking?
genzero: do I have to type everything twice?
JACKER69:   Why not?
genzero: so you smoking or not?
JACKER69:   Whatcha think?
genzero: u r smoking
JACKER69:   A little light stuff.
genzero: it rots your brain
JACKER69:   Egghead on drugs.
genzero: i can hear it sizzle
JACKER69:   Thru the wires?
genzero: i talked to a guy who'd seen the resurrection stone
JACKER69:   What'd he say?
genzero: he was afraid to pick it up and got hit by a wave and hit his
              head and went blind
JACKER69:   He's blind?
genzero: the gulls were eating his food on the beach
JACKER69:   Eating his food on the beach?

genzero: what am i talking to a mirror?

JACKER69:   :-D

genzero: stop laughing and listen. he thinks it's here, on cranberry island.

JACKER69:   Sounds like bullshit.

genzero: i thought you believed in it

JACKER69:   That doesn't mean I believe every joffer's story. What in hell would the Holy Stone be doing on Cranberry Island?

genzero: its gotta be somewhere

JACKER69:   If you don't believe in God, how can you believe in the Stone?

genzero: don't know. this guy said he saw it

JACKER69:   And that makes it true.

genzero: maybe, maybe not

JACKER69:   I mean, if you have one, then you have the other.

genzero: so there's no stone

JACKER69:   You're that sure there's no God?

genzero: how can there be? look at what goes on in the world, war, famine, disease, babies born blind while others are healthy, it's all so stupid and unfair how could there be a god and if there were who the fuck would want anything to do with him? Nobody.

JACKER69:   Not if you put it like that.

genzero: how else is there to put it?

JACKER69:   Reincarnation.

genzero: come on

JACKER69:   Explains it all. There are no innocents here. We all bring our karma, like that blind baby or the healthy one, they're spirits in new bodies continuing on their paths.

genzero: paths to where?

JACKER69:   Enlightenment.

genzero: bullshit

JACKER69:   Listen, we're born feeling separate from God, it's part of the human belief system. We spend our multiple lives dealing with it, trying to fill the emptiness. But we're really connected to God all along. Enlightenment is waking up to that fact.

genzero: so i'm asleep

JACKER69:   Right.

genzero: and when you smoke grass, you wake up?

JACKER69:   No, it just takes away the pain of separation. It's an attempt to medicate myself. I struggle with it. We all struggle and every now and then one of us wakes up to the truth.

genzero: like who?

JACKER69:   Christ, Buddha, Paul, John, George, Ringo. Anybody can do it.

genzero: i'm sure of it

JACKER69:   Sometimes it happens after a lifelong search. Sometimes it just happens, like Saul.

genzero: was he a beatle, too?

JACKER69:   Saul of Tarsus.

genzero: enough of that

JACKER69:   What's wrong?

genzero: saw my aunt fucking today

JACKER69:   Now that's news! Fucking who?

genzero: guy from out here. greg

JACKER69:   Where'd they do it?

genzero: in the house. middle of the day. i watched through the window

JACKER69:   That's my man!

genzero: do people fart when they fuck?

JACKER69:   Who farted?

genzero: he did. then i almost got spotted

JACKER69:   Fart blew your cover?

genzero:	funny
JACKER69:	So you caught 'em doing the deed. Good work. Next time, use your camera.
genzero:	yeah
JACKER69:	It depressed you, seeing your aunt fucking?
genzero:	guess so
JACKER69:	Maybe you're jealous.
genzero:	he's a creep
JACKER69:	Greg?
genzero:	real slob
JACKER69:	Lots going on out there.
genzero:	not for me
JACKER69:	Stop feeling sorry for yourself. Go find the Stone.
genzero:	yeah
JACKER69:	And pick it up! Don't want to go blind. What was that joffer scared of anyway?
genzero:	the power

"Jason? What are you doing?"

Jason nearly jumped out of his chair. It was Aunt Lee, wearing a flimsy tee-shirt and silk panties through which, in spite of the dim light, he could discern a dark, triangular patch of pubic hair.

"Just finish-ing up on the network."

"It's late."

"Yeah."

"It's hot."

She opened the refrigerator. Its cold light illuminated her breasts through the thin fabric and added shadows to her nipples, emphasizing the points at which the shirt draped over them.

Snake stretched.

Aunt Lee tilted her head back and drank water from a bottle in the fridge. Jason ached with wanting as he watched her suck at the bottle, watched her breasts rise and fall with her breathing.

Snake throbbed.

Lee finished and returned the bottle to the fridge. "Good night."

"Night, Aunt Lee."

She walked back to her room. Jason's heart raced as he glued his eyes to her hips and legs. He imagined her in high heels.

Snake burned.

JJACKER69:	Where'd you go? Hello??
JACKER69:	Hello??? Jason?? Where are you???
genzero:	it was my aunt
JACKER69:	Got up to blow you?
genzero:	she had on this thin top and now I can't walk
JACKER69:	Joff in place.
genzero:	right here right now
JACKER69:	Contact LOVESlace.
genzero:	i'll go nuts, rather do it in my room
JACKER69:	Don't go blind.
genzero:	no
JACKER69:	Put it to good use, write some porn.
genzero:	want to live some
JACKER69:	Sure. Say, how's that story coming?
genzero:	story?
JACKER69:	You sent me part of it. About that detective in the future.
genzero:	Blue Shirt
JACKER69:	Yeah. You finish it?
genzero:	i suppose so
JACKER69:	Enthusiastic, aren't you. What happened to your hero?
genzero:	he survived sort of

JACKER69:   Can you send me the rest of it?

genzero: what do you have so far

JACKER69:   He was talking to this woman about what happened to her husband. The guy who got headaches.

genzero: i'll email the rest

JACKER69:   Thanks. Why do you write that stuff?

genzero: dont know what else to do sometimes, sit around the house under guard by my mother

JACKER69:   I wonder if that's what inspired Shakespeare?

genzero: his mother?

JACKER69:   Time on his hands.

genzero: maybe

JACKER69:   You said something interesting in the stuff I read.

genzero: glad i impressed you

JACKER69:   You always impress me, kid. It was about evil, where you said you couldn't understand how they could do the evil they did.

genzero: right

JACKER69:   People commit evil because they feel completely separate from God.

genzero: so the nazis were just people who felt separate from god?

JACKER69:   Exactly. And the greater the belief in separation, the greater the fear, the greater the need for self-preservation, the greater the capacity for evil. Their name tells their story.

genzero: ???

JACKER69:   Nazis. Not-sees. They could not-see the truth, that we all are one, that there's no real separation, that what I do to anyone, I do to myself. It's all on that website I told you about

genzero: deep

JACKER69:   I can see you're very interested. Get anywhere with those anagrams?

genzero: haven't worked them

JACKER69:	You have to be profoundly disturbed not to do anagrams.
genzero:	sometimes i feel like I've got no insides
JACKER69:	Cold and dark in your gut?
genzero:	cold dark empty
JACKER69:	I know it well.
genzero:	what you do for it?
JACKER69:	Smoke. Joff.
genzero:	i thought you were enlightened
JACKER69:	They're part of my religion.
genzero:	all seems pointless
JACKER69:	Sounds like OMR Syndrome.
genzero:	omr???
JACKER69:	Old Man River. Tired o' living, scared o' dying.
genzero:	WHAT DOES IT ALL MEAN?
JACKER69:	O sad ruins. O disaster.
genzero:	WHAT?
JACKER69:	Dinosaurs, o sad ruins. Asteroids, o disaster.
genzero:	cute. but what about those ohs
JACKER69:	Exclamations. They're oh-kay.
genzero:	what does it all mean?
JACKER69:	We were the dinosaurs.
genzero:	i thought we came from apes
JACKER69:	No. We never "descended from the apes." The truth is that our souls, at low levels of consciousness, manifested as dinosaurs, apes. all the animals.
genzero:	you've turned it upside down!
JACKER69:	Right side up. Our physical form doesn't give rise to consciousness. Consciousness gives rise to physical form. As we wake to our divinity, our consciousness takes on more advanced forms.
genzero:	evolution is metaphysical

JACKER69:	Precisely. Evolution is part of the process of awakening to God. It's part of the plan. God's plan is LOVE. EVOLution.
genzero:	so that's it???
JACKER69:	Yep. Here's one more anagram: mINe
genzero:	i dont get it
JACKER69:	Want a clue?
genzero:	no i've had it…how does this shit help you live anyway?
JACKER69:	That's up to you.
JACKER69:	OK. See u tomorrow.
genzero:	boot up jack in take off
JACKER69:	Part of the net.
genzero:	part of the nineties

Before signing off the network, Jason e-mailed the last chapters of Blue Shirt to Phil. When they were sent, he logged off and unplugged his computer. Jason got up and went to the front door. He opened it and stepped out.

A thick fog had gathered in the chill night air and settled over the houses like grey cotton candy. Porch lights glowed like eyes peering into the dark through moist lenses.

Jason breathed in the enveloping mist, enjoying its damp, cold, clean feeling. He held onto the deck railing and did a stretching exercise, all the while listening to the night. From the beach came the sound of the Atlantic beating against the shore. A lonely sound to Jason. Hypnotic, romantic, dark.

Crickets racketed away, their intense chattering an insistent song of a life that Jason would never understand, never comprehend. That amazed him. That something so palpably in his consciousness, so much a part of his environment, should remain a mystery. Even if he studied the bugs, even if he spent a lifetime researching, examining, investigating, and writing papers about them, he would never truly know what it was like to be a cricket making cricket sounds, moving in cricket ways.

The fog came in waves now, imitating the ocean. It rolled in from the beach, filling the island's crevices and crannies with its shadowy bulk. Jason finished his stretching and slapped at a mosquito perched on his arm. A smudge of blood replaced the insect.

Jason walked the deck around the house, being careful not to take heavy steps that might wake anyone. Overhead were clouds and not a star in sight.

Jason wondered if it all meant anything. After a while, he decided it probably didn't.

Blue Shirt Files—2009.9.BG3

The safe house was an apartment on what used to be called Central Park West. Since the park had been bulldozed and paved over in 2006 to drive away the homeless squatters, the avenue was now known as Westpave. The fancy residences had gone to seed but there were still a few nice ones left.

As my cab rattled up the avenue, I reflected on what had become of New York. The city was largely deserted, with less than two million people left in the entire tri-state metropolitan area. Subways still ran on some lines and there were a few bus routes and taxis, with limos for the remaining rich. There was little of what could be called industry, mostly a few stock/bond firms, lotto parlors, the sex markets, and the food/entertainment/health services. Everywhere was decay and collapse, which was true all over the country, all over the world.

President Cranston, an independent who ran on a platform of America first (keep out the immigrants) continually promised to revitalize the economy but everyone knew it was just talk. That's all there was left. Talk.

A block away from Phil's place, I told the driver to stop. I got out and walked the remaining distance.

I got nervous when there was no answer at the door, so I let myself in with my passkey. The apartment was dark and quiet. I knew something bad had happened and I was right.

I found Phil in the bathroom, on his back in the tub, his throat cut ear to ear. Bunny was gone. I figured one call to Lt. Harper that night was all I could make before he started wondering what I was mixed up in, so I said goodbye to Phil, wiped my prints off everything and left, leaving the door ajar so somebody else would find him and report the murder. I rubbed my eyes and looked at my watch. Nearly midnight. I knew what I had to do next. See Dr. Blinker for some more eye drops.

The unrelenting heat had changed all kinds of habits, routines, and ways of doing business. No one could work during the day, when temperatures sometimes reached 110 degrees with humidities of 80 to 90 percent. There wasn't enough electricity to power ACs under those conditions and working without an AC was impossible. So most people worked at night, between 8 PM and 6 AM. We were like a city of vampires, moving about at night and hiding from the sun during the day.

I couldn't find another cab, so I had to walk to Blinker's office on East 53rd street. He wasn't expecting me and I certainly wasn't expecting what I found when I got there.

Blinkers was dead, face down on his desk with one sleeve rolled up and a hypodermic in his hand. All the look of a suicide but I knew better. Blinker was most of the well-adjusted men I knew, a family man with good health, a fine career, even some money stashed away. This was no suicide, even though the note someone had left talked about depression. Somebody had forced him to write the note, then shoved a poison needle into his arm.

I looked at the pictures of his wife and kids on the desk. Now they had no one. I hoped to God, even though I didn't believe in

God, that he had good insurance. Something to see them through. I'd hate for them to be on the street.

The work had the look of Rattler and his boys and when I found a small brown bag surrounded by scattered crumbs I knew they'd been here. Blinker either knew something or they thought he knew something that cost him his life. But what?

I searched Blinker's office, looking for anything that would tie him into the world of Bunny and Homer Glands. His files had been stolen but I knew where the doc kept his microfiche back-ups and soon had streams of records rolling across the screen. I found my own file and stuck it in my pocket for the next doctor. Then I saw the file of James Unger. The name was infamous.

James Unger had worked as an air traffic controller at Kennedy Airport and had been responsible for an accident in which a Boeing 737 carrying Secretary of Defense Carl Wallace had been flying. Unger's error had brought the plane down in Queens, killing all 90 passengers and dozens of people on the ground.

According to his file, James Unger had come to see Dr. Blinker six months after the accident complaining of headaches and blurred vision. Dr. Blinker had tested him for everything but there was no clear diagnosis. Unger had been to see Blinker four times, with his headaches and vision problems steadily growing worse. He'd died three weeks ago. Eye diseases don't usually kill.

Then I saw a possible connection. One line, a few words buried in one of the reports. "Glands Biochips infused 3/20/04." Bunny had said there was a flaw. Was this it? Did the Biochips damage the brain after a time? Could they cause death? That would certainly put a crimp in the Homer Glands empire. Did Homer have his goons get rid of Blinker to cover something up?

It was time to make a call. I pocketed the Unger file and picked up the phone. When I was connected to Glands' office I asked for the great man and told the receptionist that I had a message from his wife. Homer's face filled the viewscreen, a granite face with large jagged features like those carved on Mt. Rushmore. Under a full mane of flowing white hair, his brow furrowed in concentrated anger.

"Blue Shirt! Where the hell's my wife?"

"She's safe," I lied, wanting to seem in control. "But a couple of other people aren't so lucky. Like Jonas Blinker."

"I don't know any Blinker. What the hell is this all about? Have you kidnapped Bunny?"

"Not a chance. She tells me you want her dead. True?"

He laughed. It sounded like barbed wire scraping across sand. "Why would I want her dead?"

"You tell me."

"Well, I don't. Now where is she?"

I checked my watch. Glands had probably already dispatched his boys to Blinker's office. I had to get out of there.

"Sorry, got to go. I'll call again."

"Wait," he said. "I'll pay you to get her back to me."

"I already have a client," I said. "And she doesn't want to go back."

I hung up, stuffed a few bottles of eye drops in my pocket, and headed for the door. When I opened it, Scone, Rattler, and Pickett were standing there! I guessed my knot tying needed more work.

I slammed the door in their faces and ran for the back stairs. I always cased out every place I went, mentally noting all the exits. I pushed through the door leading to the stairs and took the stops down two at a time. I heard my pursuers cursing and running behind me as I reached the bottom and grabbed the handle of the basement door.

It was locked.

Thursday

After breakfast, Jason settled in on the back deck with his chair, paper, pens, pencils, and his poetry notebook. The cool morning invigorated him, gave him energy to accomplish the goal he had set for himself upon waking, inspired him to achieve his purpose, to carry out his intent, his plan, ambition, dream, aspiration, hope, longing, wish, yearning, desire, aim.

To write a poem for Carol. A love poem.

Not that he ever intended to show it to her. It would be his poem of unrequited love, his paean, his song to her, a song that would never be sung, whose beauty would therefore be all the more intense, all the more luminescent because of being unarticulated, like the rose born to blush unseen.

Jason loved poetry. Writing poetry was far different from constructing his Blue Shirt stories. When he wrote poetry, he didn't have to think about plot or characters or dialogue, just about feelings and ideas and the words that best expressed them. Besides writing poetry, he read other poets, copied their poems, and imitated their styles. He had filled two notebooks with his poems, fragments of poems, and ideas for poems. Unlike his stories, Jason had never shown his poems to anyone.

His style was eclectic. He wrote free verse but sometimes tried a rhyming form for the fun of it. He had wanted a rhyming dictionary but his mother hadn't seen the need for it and with the budget they were on, it had become an unnecessary expense.

He opened his notebook and read a poem he had written the year before, about Cranberry Island.

mystery

around the rows of summer homes
on cranberry island

                              phone lines sag

in cats cradles

                              between oak poles

what whispers tell that sparrow
to perch on the wire

                              that gull

to rest on the oak?

Jason looked at the phone lines overhead, strung parallel to the electric power line. Three small birds rested there, chirping, chattering, heads darting from side to side, finally flying off. He wondered if gulls just naturally avoided anything sagging and went right to the more solid structures or if they tried the lines and fell off before learning not to use them. He'd never seen a bird fall off of anything, so he guessed they somehow knew where to land.

The sun warmed Jason's face. From somewhere came the occasional whine of an electric saw, then the rat-tat-tat of a hammer. A light breeze rustled the tree branches. A baby cried, then was still. A dog barked.

Jason thought about Carol, wondered what it would be like to hold her. He had never held a girl, not even at the Friday night dances in the gym that he sometimes went to when he found the courage but at which he never, ever talked to one and certainly never, ever asked one to dance.

He wrote.

she is pale, she is alabaster

Carol wasn't really pale but it sounded better than tanned. Poetic license.

standing near the ocean
in the summer sunset
                    she is rose

He had never seen her standing in the summer sunset but imagined it might be like that. Rose colored. From the setting sun. Or maybe sunrise. Same color. Sunset sounded better. More romantic. More mysterious. Sunset it would be.

He remembered riding on a bus with his mother one summer evening, the air warm with the smell of the season in the city, the sky streaked with rose, with gold, the buildings a hazy purple in the dwindling light. Jason remembered the feeling of being alone, of being the only person left on the planet, in the solar system, in the galaxy, the universe.

He tapped the pen on his knee, glanced at Carol's house. It was quiet. Jason listened to his heart beat for a few seconds, then wrote.

her heart is a flower
opened only by the moon

A seagull sailed by, wings still, riding a current of air. Jason watched it circle a house, then head for the ocean. He remembered the gulls that had stolen the blind man's food, how aggressively they scavenged. He wondered if the Resurrection Stone was real.

Jason tapped his knee, then continued.

> *her heart is a flower*
> *opened only by the moon*
> *to touch a cooler breeze*
> *then soothes the day*

>   *she surrenders*
> *to the night wind like a gull*
> *in the calm of a glide*
> *not trying to push the air*

When he glanced up, he saw Carol on her deck, wearing a white shirt tucked into blue denim shorts. She was doing laundry and he watched her bend, lift, stuff laundry, bend, lift, stuff laundry, until the machine was loaded. She put in the detergent, closed the machine, and started it. She glanced in his direction and smiled. Jason smiled back. She walked along the deck and turned the corner of her house, disappearing from view. Jason heard a door open and close.

He wrote.

> *i am caught in a tidal sweep*
> *unable to change my course*

Jason wondered about his course. What he would do with his life. His mother wanted him to be a scientist because he showed promise in chemistry, physics, math. But he was good in English, too, and liked it more than anything except maybe math with its sets, infinities, number relationships, prime numbers, imaginary numbers, topology, perfect numbers. Six. Twenty-eight.

Chemistry was fun, too. Mixing things, figuring out what they would do together. Like people, you put them together and strange things sometimes came out. But with chemistry you could predict the strangeness most of the time. With people you never could. He had learned that much.

He wrote.

a ship at sea and lost
follows the dipped folds of gull's wings
into phantom ocean currents pounding.

Done. He knew it was finished. He read it over again, not changing anything. Sometimes they came out perfect the first time. He made a neat copy of the poem in his notebook.

Jason wiped the sweat from his forehead as he worked. The day had warmed so gradually that he hadn't noticed, reminding him of the story of the frog you put in cool water that you slowly heated. The temperature changed imperceptibly and the frog never hopped out, remaining in the water until it was cooked.

When he finished copying the poem, Jason decided to take a shower. As he soaped himself under the hot water he imagined his aunt coming into the bathroom, wearing only her bra and white silk panties. Snake stiffened as he fantasized. Jason soaped it well.

She would pull back the shower curtain and her mouth would drop open in awe at the magnificent size and power of Snake. She would fall to her knees in supplication before it and Jason would move to her. Lee would cup his bulging scrotum in her hands and draw his enormous organ to her lips. She would kiss and suck it while her supple fingers worked into his balls until they burned like red hot stones, the heat of which filled Jason's belly with a blazing need for release. He soaped harder, using his fingers to imitate his aunt's imagined massaging.

Jason tried to control himself, to prolong the pleasure, but he soon reached the point of no return. He stroked harder as he imagined Lee sucking harder, wanting his hot semen to fill her mouth, wanting to taste its fatty slipperiness, wanting to swallow it again and again to quench her desperate thirst.

There was a knock at the bathroom door.

"Jason?"

His mother.

The first shot of his semen splattered against the tiled shower wall as he tried to answer. All he could get out was a muffled grunt.

"Umnh."

"Jason? You in there?"

A second shot of semen slammed into the tiles. He cursed as he squeezed off a third shot.

"I'm coming in." Jason heard the doorknob turn.

He'd forgotten to lock the door! Startled, he turned to face the shower curtain as if that would keep his mother out.

"Nomai'mallright," he croaked before the fourth shot hit the curtain. The door opened.

"You all right?"

"Ma, I'm fine, just trying to take a shower, okay?" He pushed his spurting penis between his legs. Sperm squirted onto his thighs.

"You're taking a shower this early?"

Jesus!

"Yeah, ma. Is there a law?"

"You don't have to be rude. I need to use the bathroom."

"I'm in the shower."

"Can you finish up? I need to go."

He cursed under his breath again.

"Give me a minute, okay?"

His mother shut the door and Jason washed away the evidence of his pleasure. He had to get out of the house.

the beach another planet sun red ocean light green sky yellow a space traveler there was the crab monster laser blasting it to shreds five legged starfish an ally   together clean up this place me and the starfish blasting crabs and then there are the jelly fish blobs of protoplasm resting in the sun gathering strength from sunlight lorgos legions   the most vicious creatures invisible in the water till they grabbed you and sucked your life out cute ass up ahead in a bikini black with jagged red stripes a blond must be 23 24 25 with her surfer friends laughing standing with their boards wet suits all rubber do they fuck in their rubber suits i wonder safe sex all right a little stone take that jelly fish bounces off the protective rubbery surface blast it with the laser the world made free what a life all i need is a girl carol when it gets dark i will be watching a stranger is watching ha ha ha in the dead of night watching every move pretty girl waiting to make my move watching and waiting waiting waiting patiently until the time is right a heavy stone to drop a clam shell shatter it   nice cracking sound break another one the same way and another   a good dropping stone heavy black lined grey stone listen to that crunch crack sand feels good sky bright bleached out of color by the sun blazing a desert a dessert the second ess you always want more dessert but not more desert miss cronin said that need more shells to crack drop crunch   look at those girls going into the water laughing at the waves looks pretty rough going right in not for me looks rough they made it past the waves standing splashing at each other pony tails waving wonder if they were horses in past life like phil would say crunch fire laser they are everywhere blast blast blast a close one lots of stones broken shells on this part of the beach catalogue and classify   sea glass bright in the water there a red stone lookit that red one like a heart   lying near the water looks alive so real red glistening water slick in the sun veins looks like the blind guy said only a stone what a stone go blind from fear pick it up the heart stone has to be goddamn phil this is crazy where did he get that story could this be it looks like it has ventricles what a strange rock maybe it is magic granting wishes chambers of the heart   would it twist in the hand like the monkeys paw something horrible would happen what to wish for theres a sexy redhead lying face down on her towel bikini top strap off throw water on her have her jump up with no top on see her breasts they look like pillows shes lying on all alone make my move say hello ask the stone what to do   move on better fish to fry what fish aunt lee now there was a fish bet she knew how to do it greg in

there theres a wish a blowjob from lee could wish for anything or maybe for the redhead to lose her bikini top or fuck me right there on her towel in the sand
        a good wish why not what about smashing the face of an enemy like that joffer allie somebody did that already   just a stupid stone anyway heavy that guy said he went blind probably from joffing getting dry loses its look a bit wet in the ocean blood red glistening again nows the time wish for a blowjob from aunt lee why not to get laid but a blowjob would be easy fast in her room she would invite me in pull off my pants suck me dry
what if theres only one wish would it be to get laid or money fame live forever the stone did it twitch was it beating like a real heart only one wish i could wish for other things no focus the power into one wish
did it twitch   was it the stone or imagination

When Jason got back to the house, he called Phil. His friend answered, sleepy.

"Hello?"

"Phil. It's me. You awake?"

"Yeah, yeah. What's up?"

"I found something."

"Your manhood?"

"The Resurrection Stone. You can't believe what this thing looks like. I've got it right here in front of me, wet, glistening."

"Maybe you should zip up."

"I'm serious. It's deep red, veined, looks just like a heart. A human heart."

"What makes you think it's the Holy Stone?"

"I don't know. A feeling."

"A hope?"

"Maybe."

"Weren't you afraid to pick it up?"

"I didn't think about it."

Phil said nothing.

"Phil?" Silence. "Phil, you there?"

"Yeah, just got distracted. What you going to do with it?"

"I don't know. What can I do? Make a wish?"

"If it's real, it's not a genii like Barbara Eden. It's the power of God."

"So what do I do? Create a world? Let there be light? Besides, it's been floating around for two thousand years. Maybe it lost its power."

"Not the power of God."

"You don't believe any of this, do you?

"I'm not sure what I believe. I heard about it, your blind guy said he saw it. Whether it's real and whether you've got it, I don't know."

Silence. Sunlight filtered through the curtained windows. Children laughed outside. A radio blared for a moment somewhere. The stone pulsed.

"It's beat-ing." Jason's voice cracked.

"What?"

"It looks like it's beating. Like a heart."

"Jason, take two aspirin. Put a cold compress on your head. Call me in the morning."

"I'm telling you..."

"Jason, listen to me. It's a stone. It's not alive. It can't beat. It's not a real heart."

Silence. Jason touched the stone. It felt warm.

"It's the Heart Stone, Phil. I know it."

"What you going to do?"

"I think I'll wish for a blowjob from my aunt."

"That's great. The power of God and you wish for a blowjob."

"It'd be a test."

"Some test. Must be nice out there in the sun, thinking about blowjobs all day. When's this happening?"

"I didn't say when."

"When you leaving?"

"Monday."

"Labor Day?"

"Yeah."

"Hear about the storm?"

"What storm?"

"Hurricane Eric. Off Carolina."

"That's all we need, get flooded out."

"Better get your blowjob fast."

Jason thought of his aunt blowing him. Maybe if he put his cock on the stone and wished. Maybe he shouldn't.

"Jason, you there?"

"Yeah, but I'm getting off. I just wanted to tell you about the stone."

"Where you going?"

"I had an idea. Gonna go look for that blind man."

"You know where he lives?"

"Somewhere on Marine."

"Good luck. And no playing with yourself. Save it for your aunt."

"Right."

"Be on the Net tonight?"

"Guess so."

"Talk to Loveslace."

"Maybe."

"See you."

"Okay."

Jason picked up the Ross from Vern and went to look for the blind man. He started his search by turning left from Midway onto Marine toward the ocean, looking at each house as if he would somehow intuitively know which was the house he sought. But he didn't see the blind man or anything that gave him a clue as to the man's whereabouts.

When he reached the end of Marine on the ocean side, Jason turned and pedaled slow all the way to the bay side, again scanning the houses that lined the walkway. Nothing. Not many people were around.

Jason reached the bay and had an inspiration. He would ride over to the Island Mart and ask about the blind man. The store was the communications hub of Cranberry Island, gossip central for the community. And it was there that Jason found his answer.

George Wensel remembered the blind man coming into his store early Wednesday morning to buy a melon and cheese. The man had said little beyond asking directions to the beach and wasn't seen again until he boarded a ferry back to the mainland later that same morning. As for the story the blind man had told Jason about living on Marine Walk with his sister, Wensel mentally inventoried the population along Marine and found no one with a blind relative and, as he expanded his mental search like a computer program accessing more and more data on its hard drive, found no blind man in the community or on the entire island, not now nor in his considerable memory except for the one who had visited for a few hours the morning of the day before.

Jason rode home, wondering.

When he walked into the house, only his mother was there. In the bathroom.

"Who is it?" she called when she heard the front door.

"Just me."

"I'm in the bathroom."

"I know."

"I'm having cramps." Jason never understood why she had to describe her symptoms to him as if he had to be updated continually on the condition of her bowels the way listeners were updated with the headlines every few minutes over the radio. He sometimes wondered how she managed to work at a job when she seemed to be in the bathroom all the time. He shrugged it off as another mystery of life.

Jason went to his room and sat on the bed to look at the stone. It was about the size of his clenched fist, streaked with what could easily be mistaken for veins. As he studied it, the room became dark and Jason thought that a cloud had passed over the sun, although the sky had been clear all day. Jason blinked, finding it hard to focus in the increasing gloom. He took a deep breath but no air flowed into his lungs. He gasped and thought about something he had once read, the idea that the atoms of oxygen could, at random, all move out of a room, leaving anyone inside to suffocate. Jason choked and jumped off the bed.

"Jason! Jason!"

His mother's voice came from afar, sounding more like a distant echo than someone a few feet away. Jason stumbled out of his room, clutching his throat, almost crashing into the bathroom door.

"Jason? Is that you? I need toilet paper."

Toilet paper! Jason coughed, trying to catch his breath.

"Jason?"

He inhaled deeply and found air. "Okay, mom," he called. "I'm coming."

Jason took a roll of toilet paper from the closet at the end of the hall and left it outside the bathroom.

"It's on the floor," he said.

"Thank you," his mother replied. Jason returned to his room, shaking from his brush with death. The sun was back, the stone appeared normal, and Jason could breathe. All the oxygen atoms had returned, once again distributed evenly throughout the room, bumping into each other with orderly quantum randomness.

Jason decided to do his yoga exercises to calm himself. He had started working from a book six months earlier and, although he could not do the more complicated exercises, found the simple ones relaxing. Jason took a beach towel and went out to the back deck.

He began as usual by sitting on the towel with his legs crossed in a half-lotus position and reading a short passage from the book.

"Life in the so-called real world, the world of material striving, with its inevitable changes in fortune and with the uncertainty that attends the outcome of every action, can never provide a lasting happiness. Social standing, personal wealth, honors, the adoration of millions or of just one, are things that are gained or lost as the winds shift, as the tides turn. The individual who associates happiness with any of these things will find that happiness transitory, elusive, not permanent. The one who commits suicide because of the loss of a worldly attachment, be it a loved one or money or the respect of others, is the most extreme example of how dependency on the material world can have devastating consequences."

Jason put the book down and did a shoulder stand, leaning back on his shoulders and lifting his trunk, hips, and legs straight above him. It brought the blood to his head and, he hoped, would nourish his brain for the rest of his exercises.

After a few minutes, Jason resumed a sitting position and did a few simple twists to the right and to the left, then toe-touching that he incorporated from a more western form of exercise. He resumed his half-lotus and did alternate nostril breathing in which he used one finger to block first his right nostril, then his left nostril, hoping to stimulate his brain as the book promised.

When he finished, he closed his eyes and contemplated what he had just read *phil would agree material life a trap i dont know what else is there life of the spirit life of the mind the brain is material itself and the brain holds the mind which is how we think doesnt that just put an end to the argument*

i mean if the brain is material than how can we be anything but material phil says about the spirit driving who knows i like these exercises but dont know about this philosophy so what is that meditation i saw i am not the body not the blood not the energy not the mind not the thoughts not the ego not the astral self i am immortal soul that illuminates these things remaining unchangeable in spite of their changes bullshit feel more like shit than immortal soul most of the time attached to the material wanting to get laid be a lifeguard is fear an attachment i am afraid of the water some kind of negative attachment maybe it is   i dont know what else am i attached to my mother no she is attached to me more than i am to her i want to get away she holds on tight cant wait for college at least in stuyvesant ill be away hang out in the chess club or something spend less time at home   this is bullshit what did it say the adoration of millions position wealth honors my

*name is ozymandias king of kings look on my works ye mighty and despair
hows that for futility suicide to follow   star meditation inhale i am a star
expand breath out contract expand contract a giant blue star*

expand   contract

*   expand   contract*

*   expand*

   *i would like to have some worldly success maybe even get laid i guess thats
an attachment well to live in the world you have to do something cant go to a
mountain and sit there*

*   contract   i guess the idea is do things without
being attached not easy i am attached to the snake what does that mean the
wealth of millions would like to have it i wouldnt get too attached no not me
not ever me no no no*

Jason opened his eyes to see Carol staring right at him.

"That's yoga, isn't it?" she asked.

He nodded. "Looks relaxing," she said. "I'm off to the store for my mom. See you later."

She walked around to the front of her house, out of sight. Jason sat for a few moments, no longer able to concentrate. Then he got up and went inside.

After lunch, Aunt Lee and Annabelle went to the beach while Jason stayed in the house. He felt like playing Pod Attack. Just as he was about to start, he heard a racket of dogs outside, then Greg's voice.

"Easy, easy, we'll get you some water."

Jason rolled his eyes. Exactly what he didn't want.

"Anybody home?" Greg called. "Anybody here?"

Jason dragged himself to the door and opened it a crack, looking down at the dogs. They were foaming at the mouth.

"Thirsty," Greg explained, responding to Jason's worried expression. "They just need water. Can you get some?"

Jason shut the door to keep the hounds from charging inside and found an old bowl that he didn't think his aunt would mind being used to service thirsty dogs. Especially Greg's thirsty dogs. Jason brought the water to the door and opened it, handing the bowl to Greg.

"Thanks, kid. Thanks a lot." He put the bowl down and the dogs slopped their tongues into it as if they had just crossed the Sahara. "They thank you, too." He tied their leashes to the railing.

"My aunt's not here," said Jason.

"Can I take a leak?" Greg asked.

Jason nodded. How could he refuse?

Greg entered and went straight to the bathroom. Outside, the dogs made loud slurping noises as they drank. When Greg came out of the bathroom, he saw the Omega Game System.

"You got Pod Attack?"

"Yes," Jason replied.

"How far you get?"

"Level Six," Jason said.

"Not bad," said Greg. "Ever do two-player?"

"No."

"Wanna try it?"

Jason shrugged. He didn't, but at the same time didn't want to be rude. "Okay."

"Great." Greg went to the door.

"Be a minute," he said to the dogs outside. "Gotta whip Lorgo."

Jason attached the second player's controls and turned them over to Greg, then settled down with him in front of the TV. For the first time, he pressed the button for two players. Lorgo spoke.

"SO, FOUL WORMS, TWO OF YOU DARE MY WRATH? THEN KNOW THAT LORGO SHOWS NO MERCY. PREPARE TO MEET THY DEATH!"

Jason and Greg each worked a set of weapon and flight controls as Lorgo attacked, fighting together against the swarms of pods that swept over the screen toward their fleets. Jason kept Greg covered as Greg blasted away at the pods, then Greg covered Jason as he fought. They moved quickly through the first three levels, acquiring lives and ships at the expense of Lorgo's pods. The evil one cursed them as they attained Level Four.

"DESPICABLE VERMIN, YOU WILL KNOW MY FURY AS YOUR SHIPS FALL TO MY POD SWARMS."

"All right!" Greg shouted. "We got him worried now."

Indeed, Jason had never made it this far with so many ships in his fleet. They had done well in disposing of pods and each had 23 ships available to them. Jason prepared for the onslaught of Level Four pods but instead cried out in surprise as a diffuse cloud formed within the space controlled by his fleet.

"Wait, wait," he called to Greg as fire tunnels moved toward his ships. "This isn't supposed to happen until Level Five!"

Greg laughed. "It changes on you!" he said. "If you have more than a certain number of lives when you enter a level, it'll change the level, make it harder. We're still in four but fighting the pods of five."

Two of Jason's ships vanished before he was able to respond to the attack. Energy could be transferred between the two fleets and Greg helped support Jason's shields until they had the pod clouds under control. They advanced to Level Five with 19 ships in Jason's fleet and 24 in Greg's.

Lorgo spoke.

"YOU HAVE SEALED YOUR DEATH WARRANTS, SCUM! THERE IS NO ESCAPE FROM MY WORMHOLES!"

The TV vibrated as a vast wormhole opened on the screen, immediately sucking in one of Jason's ships and two of Greg's. The wormhole grew and drew in two more ships, threatening to devour both fleets in a matter of minutes.

"This is it, kid," Greg yelled. "He means business!"

"What do we do? How do we fight it?"

"Like this," Greg said, lining up his ships and driving them into the center of the hole. "Go right in! Go right in!"

Jason watched what seemed to be the certain suicidal destruction of Greg's fleet, but the ships survived. "Go in, go in," Greg encouraged.

Jason lined up his ships as Greg had done and drove them into the center of the wormhole. As the mass of the combined fleets overwhelmed the cohesiveness of Lorgo's wormhole it collapsed. They reached Level Six.

And Lorgo spoke.

"SWINE, YOU FIGHT WELL, BUT NEVER WILL YOU SURVIVE MY ELITE HOME GUARD. YOU WILL NOT LEAVE MY SYSTEM ALIVE!"

The Home Guard consisted of huge mother ships capable of launching numberless small pods that flickered in and out of view, disappearing here, reappearing there, like fireflies flashing in space, deadly fireflies that sprayed out flaming globes of energy that ate through ship's hulls.

"Use torpedoes!" Greg cried. "Low energy, wide dispersal, it fucks up their cloaking devices, then use your lasers."

Jason did as he was told, dodging fireballs and firing torpedoes everywhere. He started to lose ships, one, then two, then three, but wasn't making any headway against the pods. Greg was having more luck and had even managed to destroy a mother ship.

"Hang on," said Greg. He moved a half dozen of his ships close to Jason's and fired off a wave of torpedoes that momentarily stunned the attackers and froze them in space.

"Now!"

Jason and Greg used their lasers at full intensity to pick off scores of the defenseless pods, then focused on the nearest mother ship. It blew apart and Jason and Greg advanced their fleets, blasting pods and destroying mother ships at will. As they progressed they scored points and their fleets increased. When they reached Level Seven they each had 50 ships.

Lorgo raged.

**"UNSPEAKABLE FILTH, WHO DARE
INVADE OUR HOME, MEET AT LAST
YOUR END. I GIVE NO QUARTER!!"**

In Level Seven they landed on Lorgo's planet and their ships transformed into robot fighters that were attacked by hordes of pods launched from ground bases. The pods fought hard and Jason and Greg were soon down to less than a dozen fighters each. But they had penetrated to Lorgo's Palace and Level Eight.

**"YOU FIGHT LIKE DEMONS!
CAN NOTHING STOP YOU? MY
PALACE FORCES WILL SERVE
YOUR ROTTING FLESH TO THE
HUNTING ANIMALS!"**

But the Palace Forces could not stop them. Inspired by Greg, Jason advanced his fighters in the face of great odds, taking huge chances and being wildly successful.

"Way to go!" Greg called. "We got him, we got him!"

With the remnants of Lorgo's troops at their feet, Greg and Jason took their fighters to Level Nine, the Throne Room. Jason jumped back as the television exploded with light and sound. Lorgo swept off his hood, revealing a massive face twisted in fury.

"YOU HAVE MET YOUR MATCH HUMAN GARBAGE, AND NOW YOU DIE, WE ALL DIE! HA, HA HA, HA, HA, HA, HA, HA!!!"

Lorgo's maniacal laughter filled the room as he pressed a button marked self-destruct. A timer sequence began an ominous countdown.

"We've got a minute to defuse it," said Greg. "It's in one of the palace chambers. Follow me!"

Jason and Greg moved their fighters through a maze of corridors and passageways that led out from the Throne Room. In the background they could hear Lorgo's laughter and the chilling voice of the self-destruct counter.

"49, 48, 47, 46, 45..."

When a fighter entered the wrong chamber, the chamber would collapse in on the fighter, destroying it. Each lost fighter increased Lorgo's glee.

"Keep looking," said Greg. "We'll get it."

Jason had half a dozen fighters left with at least twenty chambers to search. Greg was in the same shape.

"Where? Where do we look?" Jason asked as another of his fighters died and the self-destruct count got to nineteen.

"There's no map," said Greg. "Use your intuition."

Jason studied the screen, not moving any of his fighters. A red haze backgrounded the picture and flashed as each number was called out.

"16, 15, 14, 13, 12, 11..."

Jason studied the rooms while Greg swept through them, losing one fighter after another. When the count reached five, all of Greg's fighters were gone and Lorgo laughed like a madman.

Jason had a hunch. More than a hunch. He knew which was the right chamber. In a flash he moved one of his fighters into it and pushed a console button just as the count reached 1. The self-destruct sequence aborted.

The screen shimmered and they heard Lorgo's wail of defeat and his final challenge.

**"SO, FIENDS, YOU HAVE BEATEN ME.
ENJOY YOUR TRIUMPH WHILE YOU
MAY AND KNOW THAT I AM HERE
ALWAYS, WAITING FOR YOU TO TRY
AGAIN! HA, HA, HA, HA, HA, HA, HA!"**

Lorgo's image disappeared and the game shut itself off. Greg and Jason, drenched in sweat, smiled at each other. They laughed and slapped each other's hands in a high five.

After a dinner to which, at Annabelle's request, Greg had not been invited, Jason booted up the laptop to browse CrossNet. Earlier in the evening, when Jason had been in his room, he had heard his mother and aunt arguing in whispers about Greg.

"He's a slob. A disgusting slob. With those Hounds of Baskerville."

"He's very bright."

"Because he's got a camera for a memory. I don't think that makes him bright. I don't want him coming to dinner."

"Annabelle, it's my house."

"And I'm your sister. And I can't stand him. I can't eat when he's here."

"Isn't that a little extreme?"

"No. He makes me sick."

"Anna."

"Really, Lee. Please. After Jason and I are gone, then do what you want."

"Is it really that bad?"

"Yes."

"Well, all right then."

"He's no good for you anyway."

"What do you know about what's good for me?"

"I may not know what's good but I sure know what's not good."

That had been the end of the discussion and the end of Greg as long as Annabelle guarded the door. Jason searched for LOVESlace in the conversation rooms, but couldn't find her. As he moved from screen to screen, he was amazed again at the vast range of human interests, strivings, ambitions, desires, and at the intense need people had to listen and be heard. He wondered if that was how to fill the emptiness Phil talked about.

Then Jason found his friend.

JACKER69:   Good numbers to you, goodbuddy. What's happening?
genzero: beat lorgo
JACKER69:   Pod Attack?
genzero: two player game
JACKER69:   Who'd you play with?
genzero: greg
JACKER69:   The creep?
genzero: he's not so bad
JACKER69:   How'd he take it?
genzero: greg?
JACKER69:   Lorgo.
genzero: pissed off. you play it much?
JACKER69:   Too old. Burned out.
genzero: at 18?
JACKER69:   Who says I'm 18?
genzero: your profile
JACKER69:   That could say anything. I bet loveslace is 56 years old with baggy skin and warts and lives in a trailer in the Ozarks. That's the beauty of the Net. You can be who you want, create yourself.
genzero: but it's not real if you lie
JACKER69:   What's a lie? We lie all the time. When a woman puts on makeup, she's lying. When a joffer puts on a toupee, he's lying.

genzero:	that's not the same
JACKER69:	No? What about when you talk yourself up to get into a volleyball game?
genzero:	those are lies about one or two things, not about everything. you can build a profile that's got nothing to do with who you really are
JACKER69:	Sure it does. It's who you are in your mind.
genzero:	it's not real
JACKER69:	The mind is the only real thing. Think about phone sex. Ever do it?
genzero:	my mother would destroy me if she saw bills from those numbers
JACKER69:	It's all in the mind but it's real sex.
genzero:	It's fantasy
JACKER69:	Sex is fantasy. Lingerie, perfume, lipstick, soft lights, words that mask the reality. It's a game.
genzero:	people are getting conned over the net
JACKER69:	People are getting conned everywhere. You always have to keep alert.
genZero:	what about making real connections with real people?
JACKER69:	I'm not real?
GenZero:	sure, but I mean face to face real contact
JACKER69:	Trouble with seeing people face to face is you might not like the face and then you can't hear what's being said. What if I were all ugly and twisted? Would you have been my friend?
genzero:	don't know
JACKER69:	So what's the better way to make contact? I bet there are some blacks and whites who've gotten close on the net who might have never talked face to face.
genzero:	maybe
JACKER69:	What's better?

genzero: there's a distance here. emotional distance
JACKER69:   And that can't happen face to face?
genzero: i guess so…then what's really real? what's really true?
JACKER69:   God.
genzero: why did I know you'd say that?
JACKER69:   You're getting smart.
genzero: i self-destruct one minute after I hear that word
JACKER69:   Your problem is, you confuse God with religion.
genzero: what do you mean?
JACKER69:   Religion distorts the truth because religious beliefs are influenced by the ego.
genzero: whats that mean?
JACKER69:   The ego believes in separation and people try to overcome the feeling of separation by belonging to things.
genzero: is that bad?
JACKER69:   The intention's good, but the problem is that ego relationships include some and exclude others.
genzero: us and them
JACKER69:   Ego ties its survival to the survival of its group. Once we believe our survival depends on group survival, we'll do anything to keep our group alive.
genzero: like destroy competing groups
JACKER69:   And competing beliefs. Holy War. The Crusades. Inquisitions, Witch hunts. Pogroms. The most zealous are the most afraid.
genzero: so the desire for God brings evil
JACKER69:   Only because ego believes it's doing something necessary to preserve itself. Evil is the extreme actions the ego takes to survive.
genzero: i still don't believe in God
JACKER69:   What you going to do with the Stone?
genzero: don't know. it makes me nervous

JACKER69:	How?
genzero:	looks too much like a heart
JACKER69:	It makes you nervous because you're afraid you can't control it.
genzero:	what?
JACKER69:	When you control things, you feel powerful, strong. People use control to cover up fear.
genzero:	you're getting back to God
JACKER69:	That's all there is.
genzero:	theres blade runner
JACKER69:	True.
genzero:	i'm reading a book by him
JACKER69:	Who?
genzero:	asimov…you remember, they had his name on an apartment building next to the Bradbury where Sebastian lived.
JACKER69:	Right.
genzero:	yeah, right/okay, gotta go
JACKER69:	Just when it's getting good.
genzero:	boot up
JACKER69:	Jack in.
genzero:	take off

Jason left Phil, his heart racing as he thought about his friend's last response. Anybody who had seen *Blade Runner* knew that Asimov's name wasn't on any building. Phil would have to be blind not to know that.

Stone blind.

He wished he were tired, wished he could get into bed and sleep, but he was wide awake with questions about Phil and with a terrible yearning for something he couldn't identify.

Jason decided to go for a late night walk and left the house, strolling down Gilbert toward Midway where he headed north.

The full moon's light gave the foliage a metallic lustre. A sea breeze agitated the trees, making them wave and flap like children dressed in silver leaves doing an excited dance with more energy than form. In the distance, Jason heard fragments of music through party noise.

wouldn't it be nice

Jason kept walking. A house on Marshall blazed with light.

say goodnight and sleep

Paper lanterns strung around the deck shone red, green, orange, yellow, blue, white, like a necklace of stars. The Beach Boys yearned.

hold each other

People drank, danced, talked, laughed. Revelers spilled out onto the boardwalk. The girls were beautiful. Jason stopped. He saw Carol.

happy times

Her hair glowed. She moved like a dream in her airy summer dress, an angel of the night, a mermaid enchantress from a fabulous undersea kingdom. She danced with a guy Jason had never before seen. The breeze picked up and a chill touched Jason's heart.

might come true

Jason moved through the mob surrounding the house, his eyes locked on Carol, hoping he had seen wrong, hoping that it wasn't her, there, dancing with someone else.

But it was her. Jason kept walking until he reached the end of Midway. He jumped down into the sand, knowing that it would change to a soft, marshy wetland in less than a hundred steps. He walked, listening to the music fade behind him.

The night air hummed with mosquitoes, crickets, moths, flies, and frogs all out to eat or be eaten. Jason didn't want to be at the bottom of that particular food chain any longer. He squashed a mosquito that was feeding on his arm and turned to start the walk home. This time he went quickly past the party, paying no attention to the late summer madness.

wouldn't it be nice

Blue Shirt Files—2009.9.BG4

Like the Boy Scout I had never been, I was always prepared. I pulled my gun and with my other hand took a flash pellet from a compartment in my belt buckle. Just like Batman.

Rattler appeared at the top of the stairs and I knew that Scone and Pickett would be right behind him. I threw the pellet over his head at the wall and closed my eyes. I heard the soft whoosh of the flash pellet exploding and the startled cries from the thugs as a blinding white light filled the stairwell. The pellet would glow for five seconds and leave them blinded for several minutes, plenty of time for me to get away.

I counted the time and, after I got to five, opened my eyes. Rattler had drawn his gun and was aiming it in my general direction. I fired off a round, the roar of the gun in the confined space slamming into my ears like a freight train smashing into a mountain side. Rattler dove for cover and I raced up the stairs.

Scone and Pickett weren't so enthusiastic about using their weapons. They were more worried about their eyes than anything else, with Scone rubbing his and Pickett whimpering that he was blind. I ran by them to the first floor and found the door. It was open.

I put my gun away and walked out into the night, looking for a cab. I needed to get to my office fast and regroup. Halfway down the block I heard the soft whirr of hard plastic wheels on concrete. I turned in the direction of the sound and saw what I expected to see.

Rollerpunks!

Across the street, three of them were moving in on the target, a middle-aged man carrying a briefcase and a shopping bag. Trudging home after a hard night's work and an easy mark for the young thugs heading his way.

Rollerpunks were muggers on rollerblades, usually operating in gangs of three or four. The mostly deserted urban streets made a perfect hunting ground for these scavengers whose chief weapons were speed and surprise.

The slammer would be the first to hit the target, knocking him or her down with a blow to the ribs or with a short club thrust into the back of the knees as the rollerpunk raced past. About fifteen feet behind the slammer came the grabber, who picked up whatever the target had dropped as a result of being knocked down. And fifteen feet after the grabber came one or two cleanups who knocked the target down again if he or she was getting up, or picked up anything the grabber had missed.

The law was clear on rollerpunks. Shoot on sight.

Shoot To Kill.

I pulled the Smith and Wesson and went into my shooter's stance. There was no way to get the slammer, who was too close to the target for me to try a shot. I waited for the hit and saw the man go down, his bag and case flying from him. The grabber crouched as he darted in for the pickup.

I fired at him, two quick shots that I knew had no hope of connecting at this distance and with my bad eyes, but that I hoped would scare the punk off.

The loud reports of my gun startled him and he kept going, ignoring the target's possessions. I fired again, this time at the cleanup punk and, to my surprise, saw him fly into the side of a building. I'd gotten him!

The target was on his knees, gathering his things. He looked at me and I waved to him, trying to reassure him that I was on his side. He ran off.

I put away my gun and hailed a cab, leaving the downed roller-punk to the charity of the streets. It was all he deserved.

"Graybar building," I told the cabbie as I got in. He inspected me in the mirror.

"I can pay," I said, flashing a few notes of Bunny's Americash. He took off without any argument.

As I sat in the cab, I checked my clothes for a microtransmitter. It was the only way that Rattler and his goons could have tracked me so fast. Sure enough, I found one glued to the bottom of my shoe, in the little space where the heel meets the sole. They'd bugged me during our first meeting, before I regained consciousness. I ripped the bug off and threw it out the window, then checked the rest of me. I was clean.

As we moved through the deserted streets, I thought about what I knew.

Bunny Glands was afraid Homer would kill her for her affairs and was safe only as long as she had the scoop on the Biochip. Homer had hired three of the meanest characters in the city to do his dirty work. And two men were dead: Phil Crane and Jonas Blinker. Men I liked and counted on. On top of everything, Bunny had disappeared. The question was, did Homer already have her or had she gone underground on her own?

I suspected that if Homer had Bunny, then Rattler, Scone, and Pickett wouldn't still be after me, unless it was pure revenge. I didn't think they operated that way. As bad as they were, they were professionals and didn't kill anybody unless they got paid for it. And in Americash.

So Bunny was probably on her own, holed up somewhere or maybe gone from the city. Maybe to Canada. That's where I'd like to be, up North where there was still an environment left to enjoy.

"...twenty-seven fifty, buddy." It was the cabbie.

"What?" I said. I'd been deep in thought.

"I said, that's twenty-seven fifty." I looked out the window and saw the Graybar. We'd arrived. I paid and got out into the steamy night. A few derelicts lay in the doorway and I stepped over them. I hoped my AC was still working.

When I opened my door I smelled something familiar. Strawberries. I looked around and, saw Bunny Glands sleeping on the couch, still wearing that skin tight dress. As I shut the door behind me, the sound of its soft click woke her.

"Well, hello. Fancy meeting you here," she said in a sleepy voice.

"Where else should I be?" I asked, crossing over to her. She moved her legs and I sat down on the edge of the couch. "What happened at the safe house?"

"Somebody found us," she said. "Your friend Phil held them off while I got out the back. Is he all right?"

"He's dead. Who were the men?"

"I didn't see them. But there was more than one."

It couldn't have been Pickett, Rattler, and Scone. They had been busy with me. Homer had a big payroll.

"You've got to kill him," she said.

"Kill who?"

"Homer. He'll kill me if you don't get him first."

"I'm not a hired gun," I said. "I do investigations."

"But you do kill people," she persisted.

"Only when I have to," I said. "And right now I don't have to kill Homer."

"You want to bring him to justice."

"Yes," I said. "If that's what it comes to."

"Homer owns every judge left in the city," she said. "There's only one way to bring him to justice."

"It's not my way," I said, tiring of the direction the conversation had taken. "If that's what you want, you can have your money back."

She gazed into my eyes. "No," she said. "I need you." She reached out, touched my cheek.

"I'm sorry about your friend," she said.

"Me, too," I said. "He was a good one."

She looked at me with eyes that invited me into her soul.

"If there's anything I can do," she said, her voice smooth as satin. "Anything at all."

The next thing I knew she was in my arms and we were pulling each other's clothes off. She liked her sex and knew how to get all the possible pleasure she could out of it. We did it the first time on the couch, then on the floor. After the third time, on the couch again, I fell asleep beside her.

When I woke up, she was gone. The dull light of morning seeped through my shuttered windows and I could feel the start of the day's heat, like an oven just turned on. I lay nude on the couch, on top of my sweat-soaked clothes, remembering the night's passion with Bunny. It was hard to believe Homer would want to kill her. It was hard to believe any man would want to kill her. I guessed that jealousy could drive a man to extremes.

I had a splitting headache and got up to get aspirin when I saw something that made me stop in my tracks. A puncture mark on my left arm, in my vein.

I examined the mark closely. It was from a hyponeedle.
Bunny's lovemaking hadn't been all pleasure for her. She used
my time asleep to inject me with something.

But what? And why?

Friday

The clock read 6:41 AM and Jason didn't want to be awake. He had just been about to dream fuck Cindy, had just watched her slip off her bikini bottom and bend over the counter at the Island Mart, had just started to move toward her, Snake ready, hard and dripping with love, when he'd come out of his sleep and into the new day.

Snake was still ready, projecting from between Jason's legs stiff and throbbing. Jason had to joff, he knew that, Snake gave him no choice. He also had to take a vicious piss and rolled out of bed to put on his bathing suit. He pressed Snake down and slowly opened his door to check for any other early risers. His mother and aunt were still asleep, the doors to their rooms closed. Jason tiptoed the few steps to the bathroom and shut the door behind him, not making a sound.

As he pissed, Jason saw a pair of his aunt's white silk panties hanging over the towel rack. He contemplated their shiny smoothness and his eyes traced their delicate fringed borders, coming to rest on the little tag at the waistband that displayed the brand name *Parisian* in lacy script. He shook the final drops from his penis and, surprising himself, leaned toward the rack and took the panties.

They had a faint musty fragrance, nothing too noticeable, nothing unpleasant, mostly neutral. But the feel of the silk and the knowledge that they were intimately familiar with his aunt's most private parts made Snake twitch. Jason thought only for a moment. His heart racing with the thrill of the theft and the fear of being discovered, Jason grabbed the panties and returned to his room.

After closing the door, he took out *Wide Open Legs* and leafed through the worn pages, looking for someone appropriate to the morning hour. The sex ads near the back of the magazine caught his eye and he scanned their florid text.

"Make Your *Cream Dreams* Cum True"

"Connect For Real Women!"

"Oral Fantasies"

"Feel   The   Heat   Live   1-On-1 Uncensored"   *"Kinky Sex Acts"*   "Oral"   "Lesbian"   "The Wet Line"

"I'll Make It Hard For You"

"No 900 Billing Charges"   "TABOO"

"Wet Hot Pussy Live" "Dirtiest   Stuff Ever!"

"Call For Real Girls"

"Oral Orgies"

"Anal Parties!"   "Back Door Fantasies"

"Hot Shaved Lips"   "I Command You To Call!!!"

"69 Forbidden Sex Videos"   *"Sex Starved Housewives"*

"Real Women Who Need Dicks"

"XXX Phone Talk"   "Join Us In The Gutter"

"Sluts And Tramps"

"Hot Talk 24 Hours—It's New It's Different It's Better"

"Lesbian Talk"

"What Would You Do With 3 More Inches?"

"Gay Interludes"   "Black And Asian Dolls"

"We Service Special Interests"   "Hard Core Action"   "Fat Fucks"   *"Big Assed Babes 1-900-111-7593"*

"Two Girls Hot & Horny"

"2.99 Per Minute"

"Lonely For Your Cock"

"Strange Sex Fantasies"   "Hot, Wet, Eager

To   Please"   "Wanted: Stiff Dicks"

"I Can Make U Cum 011-392-392-9087"

"Let's Get Off"

"Anal Fetishes"   "Leather Dreams"   "My   Lips   Are
Burning For You"   "Amateur Videos"

"All Tastes Welcome"   "Bizarre Rituals"

"Incest"   "Leg Men"   "Foot Fetishists"
"Surprising Photos"   "1-800-555-5551 They Do It All"
"Silk Stockings"   *"SLEAZE"*

"Fashion Models Free Video"   "Sex Toys"

"Spanish Fly Formula"   *"Women
Who Take It All!"*   "Hear Us Do Dildos"   "Open
Cheeks"

"Listen To Us Shave Each Other"

"Help Me Get Off"   "Greek Party Line"

"Talk Is Cheap And So Are We"

"The Dirtiest Ever"   "Munch My Muffin"

"100%   SATISFACTION"   "Call Now"   "Bigger Penis In
One Week"   *"Fuck My Ass"*

"Erotic Dancers, Naughty Nurses, Hot Stewardesses, More"

"Our Lines Are Open And So Are Our Legs"

"Young Men, Older Women"

"I Want to Suck!"

"KISS MY TITS!!"

He passed the ads and found Sue, one of his favorites because she wore
a white bra and panties like Aunt Lee's. The brazen pictures displayed Sue
posing on a bed, peeling off the flimsy garments and exposing her cunt for
the men of the world to examine.

Jason rubbed the underside of his penis with the panties, all the time staring at Sue. He imagined her lipsticked mouth around his cock, sucking him. She thrust out her breasts and he stroked, she bent over to reveal her ass and he stroked, she looked into his eyes and opened her cunt with her fingers and he stroked and stroked and stroked until he came, spurting his cum into a wad of tissues.

When he finished, Jason wondered at the depth of his depravity. Snake would stop at nothing. He shook his head in amazement and was about to sneak back to the bathroom to return the panties when he noticed it.

A spot of his semen.

Jason's hands trembled as he scrutinized it. A small drop of his seed rested on the waistband, mute testimony to his madness. When he recovered from the initial shock, Jason dabbed the spot with a tissue, leaving a stain smaller than the nail of his little finger, but which, however, appeared larger to him than the stains on Lady Macbeth's hands.

He wet the tissue with his saliva and rubbed the spot as clean as he could then blew on it to dry it off, almost completely erasing the evidence of his lust. Jason hoped that Lee wouldn't use the panties that morning. When he had calmed down, Jason returned the panties. He flushed the tissues down the toilet and went back to his room.

Instead of quelling his desire, using the panties had fired him to greater lust. He wanted more than pictures in a magazine. He decided to do what he had thought about and ask the stone for a blowjob from his aunt. How bad could the karma be for a blowjob? Besides, the chances of anything happening were remote. Very remote.

He decided there would have to be a ceremony. Jason took the Resurrection Stone into the bathroom and locked the door. He put down the toilet seat lid and rested the stone on top of it, then retrieved the panties one more time. He draped them over the stone, leaned close, and spoke in a whisper.

"I want Aunt Lee to blow me."

The door knob turned. Jason's heart stopped.

"Jason? Lee?"

Jason's mouth fell open in disbelief. His mother.

"I'm using the toilet," he said. "Can you wait?"

Silence. Then, "I need to go."

"All right, ma. Give me a minute, okay?"

"Okay."

Jason waited for his mother's footsteps, but none sounded. She was standing at the door, a silent sentinel at her eternal post.

Jason's anger flared. He couldn't even make his request three times as he had wanted, lest his mother overhear. In defiance, he bent close to the stone and kissed the panties, then replaced them and flushed the toilet. He wrapped the stone in his towel and opened the door. His mother smiled in relief. Jason sighed. He had done all he could do.

At breakfast, Jason spread butter over his English muffin, making sure to fill every crevice with creamy yellowness. Next would be jam, red raspberry with seeds. Delicious. He took a mouthful of juice to jolt his taste buds to life.

"Too much butter will give you zits," said Aunt Lee, sounding a little like his mother.

"I'm immune," said Jason. "I'm from another planet. There are no zits there."

"That would be nice," his mother said.

"It's true," said Jason. "No zits, no tooth decay, no smelly armpits, and nobody gets sick from all the good things to eat like chocolate and sugar and butter and cheese and red meat and ice cream."

"Sounds pretty good to me," said Aunt Lee. "What about dandruff?"

"Doesn't exist," Jason answered, turning to his mother who was dabbing margarine on her muffin. "And no bowel problems."

Annabelle smiled weakly. "Wonderful."

"So if that place is so great," said his aunt, digging into her grapefruit, "what are you doing here?"

Jason watched as Aunt Lee slid a grapefruit segment into her mouth.

"Exploration," he said. "Finding new civilizations."

"Where no one has gone before," said Aunt Lee.

"Right. And colonization."

His mother took a sip of her tea. "So you're planning to stay."

Jason looked out the window at the beautiful day. "As long as the weather holds," he said. "Looks pretty good so far."

"We may be in for something over the weekend," said Aunt Lee. "That hurricane's prowling around out there. The one with your name."

"Do you think it'll hit?" Annabelle asked.

"Don't worry, ma," said Jason. "I'll set up a Weather Inversion and Negation Device to break up the storm and bring out the sun."

"Excellent," said Aunt Lee. "That'll do it."

"When are you going back to Baltimore anyway?" Annabelle asked.

"The fifteenth. School starts on the twentieth."

"Wow," said Jason. "How come so late?"

Aunt Lee shrugged. "That's how they do it. Lucky for me. I guess it doesn't work that way on your planet."

"Afraid not," said Jason. "We still have a few barbaric and primitive customs."

"Like starting school right after Labor Day," his aunt said. Jason nodded. He finished the remnants of his muffin and took his dishes to the sink.

"Where are you exploring today?" his aunt asked.

"Around," Jason replied. "I'll be getting orders telling me exactly where to go."

"Good luck," she said.

"Don't get too much sun," his mother said. Jason laughed.

"Do I look burned?" he asked, showing off his still pale skin. "I hardly look like I've been here."

"Don't put so much lotion on your face," said Aunt Lee. "Get a little brown."

Jason saluted. "Excellent idea, Commander. To blend in with the native population."

His aunt laughed. "Precisely. Oh, by the way, Jason, you left your poetry notebook on the back deck yesterday. I put it in your room."

His poetry notebook! Jason's brow furrowed. How could he have left it lying around? "Tha-nks," he said.

Lee smiled. "I hope you don't mind, but I read a couple of your poems. They're nice."

"Jason never lets me see his writing," Annabelle said.

Jason felt the warm rush of blood to his face. He hadn't wanted anyone to read his poems.

"That's okay," Jason lied. He went to his room and hid the notebook in the bottom of his suitcase. Then he decided to go for a ride on the Ross and forget about everything.

"Be careful," his mother called after him she always did. Jason said nothing in reply, instead remembering Bobby, his best friend from kindergarten to third grade, and how they used to watch cartoons together *especially Road Runner played hide and seek ran races bobby always won barked at dogs to hear them bark back laughed laughed laughed but then hit by a car splashed on the street like a bug left to die by someone speeding they never found who did it left to die in the street roadkill going for ice cream on a bright fall afternoon close to halloween we were planning what to wear for trick or treat my mother was going to take us bobby liked to dress up as batman i was the joker didnt know till that night doing chores with ma a haircut the dentist check for cavities loose teeth bobby just had one come out got a dollar from tooth fairy his dad saturday afternoon things i was in the dentists chair when he got hit found out later funny thing was we were so close but when it happened not knowing anything was wrong almost expected some kind of telepathic link with bobby that close getting a tooth filled thinking about having to finish arithmetic homework and a book for school wanted to be out of there thats when it happened bobby crossing the street to the deli when the car came fast around the corner out of nowhere lightning on a clear day smashing down my friend the closest friend i ever had his parents only child massive brain injuries doa in the er roadkill we always laughed at those cartoons didnt find out until i got home always together doing everything sesame street chocolate ice cream with chocolate sprinkles and fudge topping and trading cards and spit and poker with danny who was nine fresh baked cookies playing at aunt lees one summer when bobby came to visit we were six learning geography in miss perrys class he loved geography had a big globe at home he could look anything up and know where everything was his fierce laughter when he asked a stupid riddle how is a cat different from a football you get four points when you kick a field goal with a cat when we got home i called bobby a friend of the family answered serious and quiet its jason could i speak to bobby the friend quiet hello could i speak to bobby theres been an accident what happened hows bobby must have broken an arm or something what a story hed have to tell hes dead what do you mean hit by a car killed instantly the friend said are you all right i hung up knew there was no god or anything bobby wouldnt come over again or talk on the phone eat ice cream laugh or cry or run or jump or play cold inside empty sat shivering there ma saying what happened are you all right bobbys dead looking mouth open shut open what do you mean thinking a joke we always joked around but it was no joke hes dead ma bobbys dead and I was at the dentist and never even knew it happened at the dentist when he died alone roadkill left there slippery red she really worried about me after that*

Jason came out of his reverie and, on a whim, turned onto Sailor, a walk he ordinarily didn't take for two reasons. First, it ran only from Midway to the ocean, the only walk not to go all the way to the bay. Second, it was a narrow boardwalk with broken planks and uninteresting, run down houses. Most of them were small, looking like shacks compared to the homes found elsewhere.

As he rode, he heard music and ahead of him saw Greg and his dogs sitting on the deck of a dilapidated house. Greg spotted him and waved. The music boomed.

there'll be love

"What brings you over?" Greg called.

"Just out for a ride," Jason answered, remembering his aunt saying that Greg lived on Sailor.

"Well, come on in," Greg said. "Let's talk."

Jason wasn't sure he wanted to talk but just as he was about to make an excuse, his bike's front wheel dropped into a gap in the boardwalk where two planks were missing and he flew off into the bushes, the Ross landing on top of him.

"You okay?" Greg asked as Jason got to his feet and brushed himself off. He'd received no injuries and the Ross was undamaged.

"I think so," Jason answered.

"Good for you, kid. Now let's talk."

Jason sighed in defeat and joined Greg on the deck. The house was very shabby, with dirty windows, paint peeling from the sea green walls, and a sagging deck. The deck chairs were rusted and broken, the grill lay on its side with used charcoal scattered next to it, and garbage overflowed the trash cans with bottles, newspapers, and kitchen waste mixed together without regard for the Cranberry Island recycling program that assigned wet trash to black bags, cans and glass bottles to white bags, plastic bottles and containers to blue bags. Newspapers and magazines and other paper trash had to be bundled separately and not bagged.

At Greg's, it was all one big pile.

Greg gestured toward the dogs. "You haven't really met 'em, have you? Castor and Pollux."

no more war

"From Greek myth," said Jason.

"Yeah," said Greg, scratching Castor behind the ears. "Gemini. Nice dogs, eh?"

The slobbering Rotweilers were anything but nice. They were big and vicious looking, with tight snarly faces that had no trace of playfulness in them. Pollux was the larger of the two, built like a battleship, a sleek black battleship that Jason could imagine tearing into a grizzly bear and ripping it limb from limb.

this world you see

Castor was no runt, either. The dog had a long scar across one flank, no doubt from a past battle, and one ear had been half chewed off.

"What happened to him?" Jason asked, pointing at Castor's scars.

"He's a she," said Greg. "Take a look."

Jason realized his mistake.

"I like to keep a bitch around. She's a fighter, though."

Greg took a pull on his beer and laughed. "Little dispute with a Pit Bull in the park a few years ago. Damn owner egged his dog on, let her bark and growl till she built up her courage then loosed her, made believe she got away. Bull took a piece of Castor's ear then they really went at it. Clawed her nice across the flank when they were rolling."

Greg pulled a Big Jim beef stick from his pocket and fed it to Castor.

what a life
> *what a life*
>> *what a life*

"How'd it end?" asked Jason.

"Tore her throat out. Got her down and tore her throat out. Should have seen the owner freak, saw his dog piss itself and die. Right there in the park. Everybody watching. Tore that Pit Bull's throat out, didn't ya?"

Castor wagged her tail, hoping for another treat. Greg patted her head.

"Wanna take 'em for a walk?" Greg asked.

"Not much good at walking dogs," Jason said.

"Who says?" said Greg. "Bet you're great. Did great at Pod Attack."

"Naw, it's okay," said Jason.

Greg took another swallow of beer and snarled, his face contorting, twisting, transforming, Jason thought, into a doglike shape.

"You scared?"

Jason's heart fluttered. Yes, by God, he was scared. Scared of taking those monsters anywhere. Scared of even being around them. His throat went dry. Maybe that's why Greg always had a beer, he thought. To wet his throat. Maybe he's scared.

"No," said Jason.

"Then take 'em. Make you a man, walk dogs like these. You wanna be a man, don't you?"

Yes, Jason thought, but not this way. Never this way. Jason felt a rope constricting his neck, a noose drawing tight from which there was no escape.

oh oh oh oh

oh oh oh oh

"Where'll I take 'em?"

"The beach. Just keep 'em on a short leash and if you see other dogs, keep 'em apart."

"What if the other dogs aren't leashed?"

Greg laughed. "Fuck 'em then, they die." He handed the leashes to Jason. "Go on. And cover their shit with sand. Don't pick it up or nothing. They don't like it."

And we better not do anything they don't like, thought Jason. Not anything.

i promise

The dogs leapt to their feet and almost pulled Jason off the deck, so eager they were to get going.

"Don't let 'em drag ya," he said as Jason ran to keep up. "Give a pull now and then to slow 'em down."

Jason gave a tug and to his amazement the dogs did slow down. But not for long. Soon their exuberance overcame their discipline and they were moving as fast as they could without actually running. Jason had a bad feeling as the music subsided behind him.

what a life

        what a life

                what a life

The dogs pulled and Jason followed, down the short flight of wooden steps that led to the sand, the fine beige sand that Jason loved. Hot from the sun. Hot against his feet. Hot for the dogs, who started panting even harder, panting and slobbering like the Hounds of Hell.

The beach, much to Jason's horror, was packed. And even though the sign clearly said NO UNLEASHED DOGS along with NO DISROBING NO PICNICKING NO LOUD RADIOS NO SWIMMING EXCEPT IN MARKED AREAS NO SURFING AFTER DARK NO NUDITY NO DRUNKENNESS and NO FIRES, Jason saw several unleashed dogs running free, chasing frisbees or sticks or just running alongside their jogging owners.

Jason looked back at the house, where Greg sat on the deck, beaming. That fucker fucked me, thought Jason. Do you want to be a man? Fuck you. Double fuck you even though we beat Lorgo. Dumb hairy bastard. But who was dumb now? Jason had the dogs. Jason was the dumb one.

Jason steered them through the beachgoers, avoiding blankets and babies, trying to catch a look here and there at tits or ass but trying at the same time not to be distracted to the extent that Castor or Pollux might leap off in an unexpected and dangerous direction. As he moved through the mob, Jason noticed something.

People gave him a berth. A wide berth. If they were standing as the dogs approached, they moved back. If they were sitting or lying down, they shrank away. Jason began to give the dogs some leash, letting them awe the masses as he followed along, master of the twin stars that flew before him, Apollo crossing the sky.

The wind blew through his hair, the ocean roared, the sun beat down, the clouds drifted by, and Jason ran with the dogs. Ran free. Jason laughed. He was having fun.

Then it happened. Jason saw it coming but knew he could do nothing, knew he was powerless over what must be, what had been written to happen long before he had ever reached this earthly place, this spot on the beach on Cranberry Island.

A Pekingese, small and arrogant, free of its owner's grasp, blocked their path, yipping in what Jason took to be dog for "Fuck you." Jason saw a middle-aged woman several yards away waving a leash and looking fearfully at the Rotweilers.

"Fifi!" she screamed. "Fifi!!"

Jason couldn't believe anyone still named a dog Fifi. Castor and Pollux, now there were names. He dug in his heels and pulled on the leashes but the dogs had been challenged and, being the dogs they were, had to respond. They charged poor Fifi, dragging Jason behind them.

The little dog, at last sensing the stupidity of its provocation, turned to run but it was too late. Pollux reached the lap dog first and snapped at its hindquarters. Fifi yelped as the Rotweiler's jaws closed on its flesh and yelped a second and last time as Castor's teeth sank into its neck, breaking it with a sickening crunch.

Pollux released Fifi and Castor swung the Pekingese into the air and let it go, as if throwing away a small rubber toy. The middle-aged woman who had raised Fifi from puppyhood shrieked in horror as the dog landed providentially at her feet and Jason knew he was in trouble. Major trouble.

"You killed my dog!" she screamed at Jason. "You killed my Fifi! Call the police, call the police! He killed my dog!"

Jason couldn't speak. Around him stood a mob, looking down at the dead animal and at the vicious hounds that had snuffed out its life. A life dedicated to the happiness of a middle-aged woman.

The onlookers muttered, murmured, whispered. "Vicious…killers… shouldn't be allowed…muzzle…have 'em shot…kid should have known…can't believe it…snapped its head off…threw it…ugly…on the beach…poor thing…poor lady…poor dog…."

Jason pulled tight on the leashes, not knowing what to expect. He'd seen movies about lynch mobs and could feel the pressure building around him. Would they string him up? Take the leashes and make a rope and hang him from the lifeguard tower?

A firm hand took the leashes from him.

"Your dog was off its leash." Greg had arrived.

"I saw it all, lady," he went on. "Your damn angry dog was off its leash, running loose, barking at everyone and jumped right in front of my dogs. It's all your fault."

Greg pulled at the leashes and started to walk off. He put his other hand on Jason's shoulder and indicated it was time to leave the beach. Jason did not object.

The lady screamed on, but the point had been made. NO UNLEASHED DOGS. Unleash at your own risk. Castor and Pollux were the victims. Fifi was the criminal. Just desserts.

The crowd parted to let Greg, Jason, and the two dogs through. When they were clear of the people, Greg turned to Jason.

"How d'ya feel?"

"Sick," said Jason.

"Right," said Greg. "Your first kill. Now you're a man."

When Jason returned to the house, Aunt Lee and his mother were sunbathing on the deck. He glanced at his aunt without trying to be too obvious about it. She had on just her bra and panties. Jason wondered if they were the ones he had used earlier.

"What's up, Jason?" she asked. His mother glanced disapproval at her sister.

"Greg's dogs killed a Pekingese on the beach."

They both sat up in surprise.

"Killed a Pekingese?" said Aunt Lee. "What are you talking about?"

Jason told the story, watching their reactions. His mother was shocked, disgusted. Aunt Lee seemed amused.

"I don't want you talking to him again," Annabelle said when Jason had finished. "He's crazy."

"He's not crazy, Anna," said Lee. "You're the crazy one, afraid of every-one, nervous about everything."

Annabelle looked from her sister to Jason. "Go inside," she said to her son.

Jason went in, glad that his aunt knew about his mother's neurosis. It made him feel less alone to know someone else reacted to her the same way as he did. He stood in the hallway leading to his room, listening to the fragments of conversation from outside.

"…no clothes on…"

"…didn't think he'd be back…"

"…bathing suit…"

Jason pictured his aunt in his mind's eye, resting in the lounge chair, white bra, white silk panties, long tanned legs, tits like honeydew.

"…around him…"

"…for God's sake…"

"…lunatic…dogs…"

"…an accident…"

"…waiting to happen…"

"…lighten up…"

"…get dressed…"

Jason heard a lounge chair scrape against the wooden deck. His horni-ness emboldened him and he sat on the nearest couch to get a quick look at his aunt as she came in. She opened the door and the blazing sunlight illuminated her like God's thought glorifies an angel. Her body shone as pure gold and her hair flamed as a dazzling crown. The vision obliterated in an instant Jason's plan for a casual glance. Lee smiled.

Jason gaped.

After she passed him and closed the door to her room, Jason took a deep breath to recover, then went outside to ponder life.

Later, Annabelle came in to use the bathroom. When she finished, she found Lee in the living room in her bathing suit, skimming a magazine.

"You okay?" Lee asked.

"Pretty much. Look, I'll go down to the store and replace all the TP I've used."

"Don't be ridiculous." Lee tossed the magazine on the couch and stood. "Can I go in?"

"If you don't mind the smell."

"Jesus, do you have to be so graphic?"

"Sorry," Anna said.

"You know, you can use a match for that."

"For what?"

"For the smell. One of my kids told me. Light a match, it burns up the gas. Better than room spray. And cheaper."

"By your students you'll be taught."

"I guess so."

Annabelle got herself a soda while her sister used the bathroom. She sat at the table and took a small sip of the sparkling cold drink, enjoying the taste but afraid the bubbles would give her gas. Lee finished and joined her.

"Outside of your problems, you having a good time here?" Lee asked.

"Always do," said Anna. "And Jason loves it."

"Does he? He doesn't seem to have any friends. No one comes around or calls. Except for that computer friend. Seems strange just talking on the computer."

"At least he doesn't kill dogs."

"We're back to Greg?"

"You just use him for sex, like a toy. You use all men for sex."

"Better than you're doing."

"It's hard with Jason around."

"Don't you have a life of your own?"

"Of course. But dating isn't easy these days."

"Tell me about it."

From outside came the sound of gulls shrieking. The ocean drummed at the shore. Anna took another sip of her soda. "You seeing a shrink these days?" she asked her sister.

"No," said Lee. "Should I?"

"That's up to you. Just curious."

"Why?"

"Wondered if that stuff with Ed still bothered you."

"Good old Uncle Ed."

"The bastard."

"You got him good."

"Spatula in the pants."

"In the balls."

They laughed. "It's okay," said Lee. "That was a long time ago. I survived."

"What do you see in him?" Anna asked.

"Who?"

"Greg. I mean, he looks completely burnt out."

"Had lots of promise once."

"So did we all."

"He couldn't stand the noise."

"Noise?"

"All the memories," Lee explained. "Everything he read, heard, experienced, always right there, always available, instantly, unavoidably there, jostling around in his brain like jumping beans on speed. It made him crazy. By the time he was twelve he was on drugs to blot it all out. To quiet his mind. Later, he started drinking. Wrote a book or something, it never came to much. Says he's working on another one."

"You feel sorry for him."

"I guess so. Sentimental jerk, that's me. But he has an amazing mind."

"We have to call mother," said Anna.

"What made you suddenly think of her?" Lee asked.

"An amazing mind. Hers is gone."

"We'll call later." Lee stood. "Now I'm going to the beach. Want to come?"

"You're not mad, are you?"

"About what?"

"What I think of Greg."

"No."

"I'm just not comfortable with him."

"It's all right."

"Don't be mad."

"I'm not."

"Sure?"

"Sure."

"Okay. Let me lotion up."

It squirmed in the grass, slippery brown and yellow stripes moving like shadow and light, shimmering across the grass, disappearing, reappearing, a mirage, an illusion, a rope of ancient fear slithering from where Jason saw it to where he couldn't see it.

It had the Resurrection Stone. Jason had been playing with it and dropped it from the back deck. The red stone lay in the grass, the snake guarding it, moving around and around it, watching over its prize.

Jason had to get it back. He had to go into the grass and pick it up. He watched the snake but it refused to move, instead stayed near the stone.

Jason did not have the patience of the snake. He feared that some other kids might come along and see the stone and, not worrying about the snake, would carry it off. Jason had to act. He glared at the snake with grim determination and spoke in his deepest possible voice.

"I'll be back."

He would need a weapon and went to the storage shed to arm himself. The shed held a veritable arsenal of snake-fighting implements: a shovel, hoe, hammers, a saw, screwdrivers, wrenches, awls, rasps, drills, even a box cutter for slicing the head off an intrusive reptile. Not that Jason had ever cut anything off of anything living. But now he had to kill a snake. Or scare it away. But he knew it wouldn't scare. He knew he would have to terminate it. Terminate with Prejudice. That's how they said it in the CIA. Terminate with Extreme Prejudice. He was the Terminator. Invulnerable. Unstoppable. Merciless.

He selected the hoe for long range attack and the hammer and box cutter for infighting. He brought his weapons out to the deck and took another look into the grass. The snake lay there, coiled around the stone, waiting for him.

He went to his room and put on a long-sleeved shirt and jeans over his bathing suit, then donned socks and sneakers and went back out onto the deck. He stuffed the box cutter into a pocket and slid the hammer through his belt. He carried the hoe, a spear for snake fishing, as ready as he would ever be. He could delay no longer. It was now or never. Take the action. Make his move. Do or die. Kill or be killed. Fish or get off the pot. Shit or cut bait.

He jumped the few feet off the deck into the grass. The snake ignored him. The hot sun made Jason, in his armor, sweat profusely and his eyes burned from the perspiration. He rubbed his face, tried to clear his eyes. They burned even more and he used his shirt sleeve to dry himself. When he could see again, the snake had vanished.

Jason's heart stopped. He had to force himself to breathe as he searched in the grass for his invisible enemy.

He moved in on the stone, cautious, remembering what they said about snakes in the grass. Snakes are sneaks. Even the words were the same, anagrams of each other. Sneak. Snake. Phil would love it. Mine. In me. What's mine is in me.

At last he stood right over the stone, his opponent seeming to have left the field. Jason searched the area again, hoe at the ready. Nothing. Not even a shadow to fight.

Jason reached down and picked up the stone. It shone in his hand, bright red in the brilliant sunlight. Triumph.

Then he felt something slip up his pant leg. Something smooth and quick. Something long and slender. Something with a purpose.

Jason yelped and dropped the stone and the hoe, grabbing for the intruder with both hands. It squirmed beneath his fingers and Jason shuddered as it moved inside his clothes. He fell into the grass, thrashing and flailing as if wrestling with a ghost. From the corner of his eye, Jason saw Carol staring at him from her deck. On the boardwalk a trio of young girls stopped to look at him.

The snake slid further up his leg and Jason screamed, the sound rushing out of him like wind from the center of a storm. The snake was going for Snake.

Jason kept one hand on the snake and with the other fumbled at his belt. He would get his pants off, he thought, even with the girls watching, get his pants off and get rid of the serpent.

The belt did not yield to his frantic grabbing. He needed both hands which meant letting go altogether of his relentless foe. Jason had hold of its tail and the snake, itself acting out of fear and the instinct to survive, waggled frantically in its dark trap knowing only to go forward, forward, forward, ever forward.

Jason took a deep breath and let go, tearing at his belt to open it, then pulling his pants down without even unbuttoning or unzipping. Jason heard the girls laugh as they saw the snake fall out onto the grass.

Without thinking Jason grabbed the snake with one hand and reached for the Heart Stone with the other. He slapped the snake against a rock and lifted the stone high in the air, then brought it crashing down. The snake darted to one side and Jason smashed at it again and again, getting closer each time until he scored a hit, a direct hit on the grinning head of the evil thing. He heard the tiny skull crack and knew he had wounded it mortally, but kept on clubbing it, over and over with blood and little bits of snake flying everywhere then the Heart Stone cracked and one piece flew off but Jason kept smashing at the snake with the remaining piece until all that was left was a limp brown and yellow rope topped off with a bloody mass of unrecognizable protoplasmic pulp.

The girls on the boardwalk cheered as Jason kneeled over his dead adversary. His stomach turned as he viewed the remains of the snake and saw the blood on his hands and shirt and on the piece of the Heart Stone he was holding. He gagged and dropped it. He stood, forgetting that his pants had fallen to his knees, and took a step, tripping over himself and landing on his face.

The girls laughed.

Jason got to his feet and pulled his pants up, then ran into the house without looking back. He went straight to the bathroom where he threw up in the toilet, kneeling over the bowl like a religious supplicant. When he recovered enough to stand, he washed off the snake's blood and went to his room to recover.

Jason did little for the rest of the day. Afternoon grew into evening and, as twilight colors decorated the sky, weekenders arrived for the last holiday of the summer. Aunt Lee decided to grill steaks instead of having the spaghetti Annabelle had been planning. But the rough smell of cooking meat that usually made Jason hungry had no effect and he ate little.

After dinner Jason read while his mother and aunt watched television. He was putting off the time when he would have to tell Phil about the broken Resurrection Stone and ask him about *Blade Runner* and about not wanting to talk about Stuyvesant. About his true identity. He finally put down his book and got out the laptop.

"Oh, wait," his mother said as she saw him hooking up to the telephone. "Lee, we've got to call mother. We won't be long, Jason."

Jason handed the phone to his mother and flipped channels, coming to rest on a movie about a blond woman about to steal a baby from a hospital maternity ward. Annabelle dialed the number of her mother's nursing home. Lee came to sit next to her sister on the couch.

"1608, Meredith Henderson, please," Anna said into the phone. She nodded at Lee and waited for their mother to answer.

"Hello, mother? Hi, it's me, Annabelle."

There was a pause.

"Your daughter, Annabelle."

Pause.

"No, I'm at Lee's."

Pause. The blond woman picked out the baby she wanted.

Louder. "Lee's. Lee's."

Pause.

"I'm here with Jason. We're all here. Cranberry Island."

Pause. She put the baby in a shopping bag and covered it with newspapers.

"Mother, this is Annabelle."

Lee shook her head.

"How are you?"

Pause.

"Are they feeding you well?"

Pause. The blond woman walked out of the maternity ward.

"The food. How's the food?"

Pause.

"Have they been taking you out?"

Pause.

"You're not going anywhere? Aren't they taking you out?"

Pause. The real mother discovered her baby missing. She screamed.

"Jason, turn that down." Jason pressed MUTE on the remote control.

"You're supposed to get out twice a week. I'll talk to David."

Pause. Doctors and nurses ran around, looking for the baby.

"David Piper. You know David. He runs the place."

Pause.

"I'll tell him you need to get out more. Do you want to talk to Lee?"

Pause.

Louder. "Lee. Your other daughter."

Anna handed the phone to Lee, who took it with reluctance.

"Hello, mother?" Lee shouted. "It's Lee."

Pause. A man sat in a car in the hospital parking lot.

"How're you doing?"

Pause.

"The doctor says what?"

Puzzlement.

"An operation? For what?"

"She didn't say anything about that to me" Anna said.

Pause. The blond woman with the shopping bag came out of the hospital.

"Let me talk to your nurse."

Pause.

Louder. "Your nurse. I want to talk to your nurse."

Pause. From her window, the real mother saw the blond woman get into the car, not knowing that her baby was in the shopping bag.

"Tell her it's your daughter."

Pause.

"Hello, is this the nurse? I'm Mrs. Henderson's daughter. She said something about needing an operation. Is that right?"

Pause. The real mother was given a sedative.

"Thank you. All right, put her back on so we can say goodbye." To Anna, "Her roommate's the one who needs the operation."

Pause. In the car, the blond woman hugged her new baby.

"Mother? This is Lee. I have to go."

Pause.

"No, I meant get off the phone. Bye for now. Say goodbye to Anna." She passed the phone to Annabelle.

"Mother?"

Pause. The car drove off.

"Mother?" To Lee, "I think she hung up." Anna put the phone down.

Lee shook her head and sighed. "Go ahead," she said to Jason. "It's all yours. Do you think she'll get away with it?"

"Who?" asked Jason.

Lee motioned toward the television.

"Her."

Jason shrugged. "I don't know." A commercial for pop-tarts came on. He hooked up the laptop.

CROSSNET: !!! Welcome to the Love Connection !!!

Men4men	22
NYCM4M	20
Tired BusMen	17
PM Delight	22
SWMSWF	21
NiceLadies	25
DofLesbos	19
Bare It All	25
Marr/Looking	18

Jason found LOVESlace in Bare It All. The screen blinked.

CROSSNET:	!!! You are in Bare It All !!!
TheTruck:	Talk is cheap, know what I mean???
LOVESlace:	Anyway you want.
NYBigGuy:	Hi, I'm new here. What's up?
LeoPard123:	Lace, you like it with gals too?
Android:	Outside of Austin.
genzero:	Lace, could we get together?
LOVESlace:	Welcome, BigGuy. Yeah, gals too.
GentleBob:	Hi everybody!
Paulman:	Used to be a nudist camp there.
LOVESlace:	zero, I need to roam tonite.
James007:	Stuff you run into is crazy.
Android:	There's good ones down there.
genzero:	where you roamin'???
NYBigGuy:	:-) This is a right friendly room!
LeoPard123:	Hey, genzero, wanna go with me?
Paulman:	The crowds are smaller these days, people are afraid because of the ozone.
GennyLee:	What's going on here?
LOVESlace:	Roamin' the net, where else?
genzero:	my heart's only for lace
Android:	The way I figure, something's gonna git ya.
genzero:	LL, my snake has its eye on you
GennyLee:	Is this what you usually talk about?
Paulman:	Yeah, well I don't want my skin to rot off.
TheTruck:	Shut it off genzero, nobody wants to hear.
LOVESlace:	Oooh, that makes me shiver....is it lonnng???
GennyLee:	:-(Take it private you guys, okay?
Crazy4U:	TOS says no porn talk, check it out.
genzero:	a foot, at least
GennyLee:	I'm outta here >:-<!

Android:	I use a new formula sun block, 64 strength. It works great.
LOVESlace:	Why is a snake like a road?
Crazy4U:	You guys are being stupid.
TheTruck	Take it private!!!!!
genzero:	why oh why???
NYBigGuy:	Leo, want to meet in another room?
Sally8888:	Hi, Paulman, how you doing?
LOVESlace:	Slippery when wet!
Paulman:	Hi, Sally8s. What's cookin?
genzero:	i want to get wet. tell me you love me
Crazy4U:	There should be rules against some people.
LeoPard123:	Sure, let's go private in MYPLACE
LOVESlace:	I do, but I have to go.
Sally8888:	Nothing, just checking out the scene.
genzero:	don't go!!! :-(
TheTruck:	Go, please. Both of you.
Android:	Sally, good to hear from you. Been awhile.
NYBigGuy:	C U there

Jason listed the people in the room and saw that LOVESlace had signed off. It was probably just as well, what with his mother and aunt in the room with him. If either of them saw the screen during one of his conversations with LOVESlace, he would be in unthinkable trouble.

Jason watched the chatter for a few more minutes then lost interest and left. He jumped the net, checking out a number of rooms and services, then brought up the NetWorld Map. This was a Mercator projection of the earth on which you could access news and weather information for countries or geographic areas. Jason selected the Eastern United States and asked for the WeatherCast. There was a report on the hurricane.

CROSSNET: !!! WeatherCast Update !!!

Hurricane Eric continues to confound forecasters, lying 300 miles off the coast of South Carolina with winds of up to 80 miles per hour but otherwise stationary. The storm has not moved more than a few miles since its formation earlier in the week and no good estimate can now be made as to its intentions. The weather over the Carolinas continues to be fair, sunny and mild.

Jason jumped for a few more minutes until hooking up with Phil in their private room. He had put it off as long as he could.

JACKER69:	Whaddayu say?
genzero:	something horrible happened
JACKER69:	Tell me.
genzero:	the stone broke
JACKER69:	The Resurrection Stone? How?
genzero:	i killed a snake with it, smashed it on another rock, it broke in half
JACKER69:	You still have it?
genzero:	left it in the yard. not much of a holy relic if it breaks on a snake
JACKER69:	The serpent has long been an enemy of the good. You should get the pieces.
genzero:	of the snake?
JACKER69:	The Stone.
genzero:	fuck 'em
JACKER69:	You're pissed, you wanted that blowjob.
genzero:	fuck you
JACKER69:	You try jumping the net, get your mind off things?
genzero:	yeah
JACKER69:	I was in CyberMarket.
genzero:	pick up anything?
JACKER69:	Found LL.

genzero:	i saw her in bare it all
JACKER69:	Spent a little time.
genzero:	wonder who she really is, where she lives
JACKER69:	You'd go see her?
genzero:	probably too old for me
JACKER69:	Like your aunt.
genzero:	they're all too old for me
JACKER69:	Stop feeling sorry for yourself.
genzero:	what else you do?
JACKER69:	Listened in on the dog lovers, WWF fans, lesbians, even an AA meeting.
genzero:	my old man could have used that
JACKER69:	What?
genzero:	aa —he's wet brain in a va hospital
JACKER69:	You told me he was dead.
genzero:	i lied
JACKER69:	Why?
genzero:	i hate having to explain it all
JACKER69:	So you redefined yourself. Changed your identity.
genzero:	is that why you lied, not wanting to explain things?
JACKER69:	What do you mean?
genzero:	you're an old blind man. you were the blind man I talked to on the beach
JACKER69:	You crazy?
genzero:	i know i'm right
JACKER69:	How?
genzero:	things you didn't want to talk about, school and stuff made me wonder, then i found out the blind man lied to me about having a sister and when i called you after i met him you weren't home, it was morning you're usually home and then i got suspicious and laid a trap
JACKER69:	Trap?

genzero:	in blade runner, asimov's name isn't on any building. you'd know that if you could see.
JACKER69;	You're a good detective.
genzero:	why'd you lie?
JACKER69:	i wanted to pretend I was a kid again. To be young.
genzero;	you hang out with a lot of young guys?
JACKER69:	A few.
genzero;	you some kind of perv?
JACKER69:	No.
genzero:	i cant believe you came here and told me that bullshit story on the beach, whatever even made you think we'd run into each other?
JACKER69:	First of all, it's not a bullshit story. That's what happened to me. As for you finding me, I guess I just knew it would happen.
genzero;	you knew
JACKER69:	I hoped.
genzero:	why? why did you want to tell me that story?
JACKER69:	So you'd know what you were dealing with.
genzero:	a shitty piece of rock that cracked in two
JACKER69:	Don't be so quick to dismiss it.
genzero:	yeah, right
JACKER69:	Look, I'm sorry.
genzero:	yeah
JACKER69:	I think you should get the pieces.
genzero:	pieces?
JACKER69:	The Stone.
genzero:	what for?
JACKER69:	Got to have faith.
genzero:	sure
JACKER69:	I finished Blue Shirt.
genzero:	yeah

JACKER69:	Depressing ending.
genzero:	he survives
JACKER69:	Guess I wanted something more uplifting.
genzero:	what's more uplifting than survival?
JACKER69:	Truth.
genzero:	you're talking about truth?
JACKER69:	Yes.
genzero:	i'm gone
JACKER69:	Wait. How come he doesn't have a real name?
genzero:	he doesn't know who he is
JACKER69:	Who does?

After leaving Phil, Jason roamed the Net, aimless. He felt let down, betrayed, sold out, kicked in the stomach, stabbed in the back. And what was worse was that now he had no one to talk to. No one at all.

Jason stopped his browsing when he came across a category called Electronic Books. He selected a book called *Frightful Tales* and picked out a short story called *Bugs*. He read it quickly.

Jason shuddered when he finished the story and wondered about life on other planets. Had life evolved elsewhere? If there were a God, would It have created life anywhere besides earth? What would be the point? To glorify Itself? Sounded selfish. On the other hand, why was there life any-where? Why was there anything? Why was he even alive?

Jason shook his head at the impossibility of answering the questions he had posed, especially when he couldn't even figure out why Phil had deceived him. He read another story called *The Makinaw*, about a lunatic, then logged off the network and turned off the laptop. He hoped he would never wind up locked away somewhere like the man in the story.

After reassuring his mother that he wouldn't get lost or drown, Jason went for a walk to the beach. He stood on the shore watching the stars, the rising moon, the distant lights of the fishing boats, the ocean washing against the sand.

Jason returned to the house and went to his room. Carol's light was on. He took out his binoculars and knelt on his bed, watching her brush out her blond hair, hair that flowed like a river of golden stars around her shoulders. He focused in as she applied face cream, watched as she organized the things on the top of her bureau, putting a hair clip over here, a tube of something over there, taking a tissue, adjusting the position of the tissue box.

She turned out her lights. Jason put down the binoculars and sat staring into the darkness, wishing he could be with her, wishing he could put his arms around her and stay with her all night.

Blue Shirt
Files—2009.9.BG5

I dressed quickly, had a fast cup of Allsoy, put in my eye drops, and scanned James Unger's records. He had lived with his wife in Queens and I decided to pay her a visit. Unannounced. There was less chance of anyone finding out my plans if I didn't use the phone to call ahead.

I got on the elevator and rode down to the subway level. Most of the commuter trains had stopped running in 2007, when the shaky global economy collapsed and the fast-spreading Kerner's disease killed two billion people world wide by bursting the air sacs in their lungs. People suffocated to death even when they were given pure oxygen. Most of the deaths were in the densely-populated urban areas where the incurable disease had spread like wildfire. The cities were decimated, mere shells of what they had once been. But the F train to Queens still ran and I decided to take it out to Mrs. Unger's place. I got on the subway and looked around at the old graffiti-patterned car, grateful that the air-conditioner still managed to sputter out a hint of coolness.

The world had changed a lot in the last several years. Global warming had heated up everything. The rich had cold water and cool air while everybody else sweated. American industry had come to be dominated by a few large corporations. Europe and the Middle East had dissolved in atomic war, likewise the old Soviet Republics. China and Japan had been largely destroyed by earthquakes and floods, and Africa and South American ruined by disease. Mexico was in revolt. Only Australia prospered, an island unto itself. And then there was Canada.

Canada had become a refuge for millions of Americans because it still had cool weather, clean water, and arable land. America itself had been in decline for years, with most people living in poverty and nothing to export because all the U.S. made anymore was fast food, movies, magazines, CDs, and television shows. When companies saw they could get workers in the Far East to build cars and computers for ten dollars a week, that was the end of American manufacturing.

Me? I'd been thrown off the police force after 18 years for drinking. I made about 40,000 GEC a year doing investigations, barely subsistence. I'd divorced twice and had no kids. My parents moved to Canada in '03. We didn't write or call much. My sister lived in what was left of Dallas after the flood of '04. She was still single.

I got off the train in Forest Hills and soon found Mrs. Unger's place, a run down single-family house with a small vegetable garden in front. Most people out here grew their own food. I knocked and Mrs. Unger opened her door a crack. I showed her my ID and explained it was about her husband, told her I might be able to help out with a little Americash if she answered a few questions. That did it. She let me in.

Mrs. Unger was in her forties and attractive, with long dark hair and a full sensuous face. But a deep sadness came from her. Her house reflected her depression, with old ratty furniture and a dank, moldy smell. There was no life in the place, no pets or indoor plants and hardly any pictures on the walls. She offered me tea but I declined.

"Your husband's condition," I began. "When did it start?"

"Last year," she said. "He started having these headaches and trouble with his eyes."

"What kind of trouble?"

"Bright flashes of light, stabbing pain. He was miserable."

"And that was after the accident at Kennedy?" I was confirming Blinker's records.

She hesitated. The accident had probably been the most horrible thing in their lives.

"Mrs. Unger?"

"Yes," she said.

"Why did he install the Glands Biochips?" I asked. "Was it required by his employers?"

Her face registered surprise. "How do you know about the biochips?"

"That's my business," I said, trying not to sound smug.

She nodded. "They didn't make him do it, not exactly. But he knew if he didn't, his days at Kennedy were numbered. More and more they needed their people to have an instant, constant link with the computers. He used to tell me how strange it was, having the computer right there inside his brain and just thinking a command and having it carried out. I saw him use it on our home PC. It was amazing."

Something puzzled me. "So how did the accident happen? If he had that constant link, how did an error occur? I don't think they ever explained that."

"They didn't," she said. "No one could figure it out. James thought he was giving the right commands. He never worked again."

"So first he had the chips implanted. Then there was the accident. Then he started having the headaches and eye troubles."

She gave me a quizzical look. "Are you saying all this is connected?"

"I don't know," I said. "Could you tell me how it was before he died?"

She shivered, even though the temperature inside the apartment must have been near one hundred.

"The headaches got worse. He couldn't eat, couldn't sleep, couldn't do anything. His doctor had him on pain killers but they didn't help much. When he did fall asleep, he cried."

She stopped. I touched her arm lightly. "Please go on."

"One Friday morning, he didn't wake up. He just lay there, eyes closed, as if he were sleeping the way he used to, like a baby, peaceful and calm."

She started crying. I gave her a tissue.

"I had a terrible thought back then," she said. "A terrible thought."

"What?"

"I've never told anyone."

"It's safe with me."

"I was glad it was over. Glad he didn't have to suffer anymore."

"That's natural," I said. "You loved him and couldn't bear to see him in pain. Don't feel guilty about it."

"I was glad he was dead."

"No," I said. "You were glad he was at peace, that's all. You didn't do anything wrong."

She looked at me, uncertain.

"I didn't?"

"No," I repeated. "You didn't."

I stood. "Thank you for your time and patience," I said. "This has been a great help to me."

My beeper rang. I pulled it out and checked the number. The call was from my own office!

"Could I use your phone?" I asked. Mrs. Unger gestured toward her phone and left the room to give me privacy. I called my office. Bunny Glands answered.

"What happened to you?" I asked. "And what did you inject me with?"

"Biochips, honey. You see, they have a lot of uses. For example, Chip Command Set, Alpha One. Lock to my voice."

A surge of energy rushed through my brain. I felt my jaw go slack, my body become rigid. I knew I should put the phone down but I couldn't. I couldn't move. My breathing became shallow.

"It's something not everyone knows about," I heard Bunny say, her voice distant as if coming through a long tunnel. "They're programmable. Chip Command Set, Action Mode."

The power surge in my mind grew stronger. My adrenaline kicked in. What the hell was she doing to me?

"I have a task for you," she said. "Chip Command Set, kill Homer Glands. End Commands."

I put down the phone. Or rather, I felt and saw myself put down the phone as if I were watching a character in a movie. I was numb, detached, somewhere else, my will submerged under Bunny's commands to the Biochips that had taken over my brain. I was powerless to keep from doing what she wanted. And she wanted me to kill her husband!

"Are you all right?" It was Mrs. Unger. I turned to look at her. God knows (not that there was a God) what I must have looked like, standing like a statue in the middle of her room. I wanted to speak but I couldn't. I started to walk out.

"Wait," she said. "What about my money? You promised there'd be money."

I took out my wallet and gave her a few hundred of Bunny's Americash. She was grateful.

"Thank you. This'll be a great help."

She moved closer, smiling.

"If there's anything else you want, anything I can do for you...."

She'd put on perfume while I was on the telephone and the fragrance suddenly seemed everywhere. A scent like flowers, fresh flowers in a lush garden. I wanted to stay but my programmed brain said no.

"I have to go," I said, or rather, I heard myself say.

Her smile vanished.

"It's business," I said.

She brightened. "Then you'll come back?"

"I have to go," I said. My range of responses was definitely limited in this mode.

I left the apartment and hunted for a cab. Of course, there would be none out here. I headed for the subway. Thoughts ran through my head at cyberspeed.

I was making a plan to kill Homer Glands.

Saturday

Jason woke at 8:49 AM to the wail of a siren. He knew the siren blew only at noon and for fires or other emergencies. Jason lay on his back, watching Snake stand like a tent pole under his sheet.

The siren blew.

Jason got out of bed.

He had to push Snake down between his legs to get his bathing suit on. When he was ready, he went to the bathroom. The door was locked. Through the living room windows he could see his aunt exercising on the deck.

"Ma, I need to go," he called through the bathroom door.

"Give me a minute," she answered.

Jason sighed and said okay. He checked Snake and found it presentable, resting where he had put it. Jason went out on the deck where the sound of the siren was deafening. His aunt lay on a beach towel doing stretches and bends, this time wearing her black bikini and a tee-shirt that read 'Cranberry Island' and showed the sun behind a row of beach houses. Her leg lifts gave Jason a generous view of her crotch, still intriguing even though well covered.

"Why is the sir-en going?" he asked in a loud voice, hardly able to hear it crack over the warbling blasts of sound.

"Maybe a fire. I don't know," his aunt replied.

The siren stopped, its racket replaced by the thumpa-thumpa-thumpa of an approaching helicopter. Above them they saw the hornet-shaped blue and white body with USN stenciled on it approach from the west, circle, then descend to the beach. Annabelle appeared at the door.

"What's all the noise?" she asked.

"Looks like they're airlifting somebody," Aunt Lee said.

Jason followed the chopper with his eyes then had to go to the bathroom. When he finished, he ran out. "I'm going to see what's happening," he called to his aunt and mother as he hurried down the ramp toward the beach.

"Be careful," Annabelle called after him.

The helicopter lowered itself to the sand over by Navy and Jason ran toward it. People had gathered and a couple of the local cops were keeping order. When Jason reached the scene the chopper's blades were slowing and two medical technicians jumped out carrying a stretcher.

"What's happening?" Jason asked a man next to him.

"Vern," said the man. "Heart attack."

"Vern?" He'd seemed in good enough health to Jason just a few days ago. Now he'd had a heart attack? Out of the blue, like Allie Grant, like Jason's grandfather. Like Bobby. Fine one day, dead the next. Jason remembered seeing his grandfather laid out at the wake, dry like a mummy, the face not like in life, instead shriveled like a weather-beaten scarecrow. With Bobby, they never opened the casket.

"…the Navy."

Jason hadn't heard what the man said and asked him to repeat himself.

"Vern. Used to command a destroyer in the Pacific."

Jason had wanted to touch his grandfather and waited until there was a time when he was alone in the room. Then he got close, real close, and put his hand near the corpse. He remembered shaking as he tried to touch the dead flesh. Tried and failed. He had been seven years old.

The medics brought Vern out on the stretcher, an oxygen mask over his face. He wasn't moving. Next to him walked the Asian woman, dressed this time in a shirt and jeans, worried.

"Who's that?" Jason asked.

"Marta."

Jason watched as Vern was loaded into the helicopter. Marta got in with him and the doors shut. The police moved everybody back as the helicopter lifted off, raising a small sandstorm. Jason closed his eyes and turned away as the whirling sand bit into him. The chopper droned off, heading for the mainland. The crowd thinned, people talked in low voices, returning to their lives, wondering how bad Vern was, wondering if he would make it to the hospital in time, wondering if he would live or die, wondering when it might be their turn in the helicopter.

Jason looked at the ocean, the tide rolling in and out, the whitecaps, a distant fishing boat, the flight of a few gulls near the boat, the horizon bleeding into the clear summer sky, the sun shining as if nothing out of the ordinary had happened on the little planet that circled it. Nothing at all.

When Jason returned to the house, his mother and aunt were getting ready to go to the beach. He told them about Vern.

"Poor Vern," said Lee. "He's like an institution around here."

"What's going on this week?" said Annabelle. "First that boy getting killed, now this."

"Shit happens," said Lee. Annabelle went into the house and his aunt took off her shirt and asked Jason to put lotion on her back. She sat while Jason rubbed in the coconut-smelling balm. Aunt Lee arched her back as he moved his hand over her smooth tanned skin, touching her where he had never even touched a girl, reaching all the way down to the top of her bikini bottom, scant inches from her ass. Jason flushed as he felt Snake stiffen. He finished with the lotion and sat down to conceal his embarrassment.

Aunt Lee thanked him and stood. She wore a large, floppy sun hat that made her look sexy and mysterious. Jason could see her nipples pushing against the bikini top.

"You coming to the dance tonight?" she asked.

"Dan-ce?" said Jason.

"The Labor Day weekend dance and cookout at the firehouse. They have it every year. Remember?"

Jason remembered never being particularly comfortable standing around watching people eat, drink, and be merry at the dance in previous years.

"I guess so," he said. "What else is there to do?"

"Sometimes not much for you, is that right?"

"Sometimes."

"I'm sorry."

Jason's mother came out of the house and she and Aunt Lee went to the beach. Snake had subsided and Jason got up and went to his room. The events of the day before, breaking the Resurrection Stone, finding out about Phil, had left Jason feeling disjointed, out of sorts, not himself. As fragmented as the stone he had broken in two. He thought about retrieving it but decided not to. He went back to bed.

Greg finished bathing and brushing Castor. The work had made him hot and he wondered how it was in the city, on the burning sidewalks, in the subways that were always too hot for him. Even in the winter. Hot and noisy.

He remembered Sister Grace, that's what he'd called her, what a ride that had been, August 23rd, 1991, the number Five to Bowling Green stuffed with business people, mothers and kids, the homeless asking for money, teenagers, blacks, whites, asians, latinos, he never forgot anything never forgot   his mind burned as the scene replayed *it takes a hell of a lot to surprise new yorkers feel the graffiti the ads*

PASSION OF LEATHER
GET THE DEGREE THAT GETS THE JOB!
               the nun young and
pretty beautiful clear skin an older stern one with glasses pinching her nose like crab claws FIFTY PERCENT OFF ALL LENSES WITH PURCHASE OF

FRAME her face red boiled lobster eyes small and suspicious a squid in an undersea cave staring out
GET RID OF THAT TATTOO SPACE AGE TREATMENT FOR GENITAL WARTS SAVE \$\$\$
DO NOT HOLD DOORS
FRENO DE EMERGENCIA VALVULA

next to the young one her eyes downcast scrubbed face pale flushed pink lips full pouting deep inside he gave me more than a kiss Herpes Council in spite of no make up looked like a good lay sexy **WITHOUT**
SURGERY *what a waste*
dressed in starched black and white like those penguin jokes don't be lonely—adopt a pet—life's too

short

SILENCE=DEATH

the passion of
leather crowded rush hour coming to a stop "please keep hands off the doors"

(air brakesssss)
jammed train jerked jolted guy bumped into me sorry about that you fuck i wanted to say in your pale blue summer suit carrying a slim brown briefcase if youre so much better than me how come youre riding the subway instead just nodded tight grin fuck you i should have said takes a hell of a lot dr. zitzmore pressed next to jostled her poetry in motion

Dancing a blind jig
on a bright tuesday morning
while everyone goes to work
a man with torn pants lurches
down the block with a bottle
and an angry song
for anyone who will listen.

felt the cheek of her ass my crotch the passion felt her even through the starch
pressed against her train lurched To Activate The Emergency Brake Cord
         valvula listo para comprar
((((DESIGNER BRACES))))
affordable customized for children and adults mother with a two year old in a
stroller nobody ever tell her how dangerous it is bring that stroller onto a sub-
way   packed in no room for it get those wheels caught stupid no
other way to go subway has the advantage of being cheap
                         cock firm tooth colored lingual "do not hold please
keep hands off" her face red free test for depression LOTTERY RESULTLINE
instant updates got my hand wedged against her ass   safety first dont ride
between cars   INTERNET AT A DISCOUNT! too much noise
yielding softness through the starch arm   or pressed into she smiled heart
beat
                 feel

       no pain fast thought of being with her sticking it in deep swelling
moving in her mouth her lips cock ready to burst you have the vote, you have
the power the power and the glory 1-800-FORTUNE CALL TODAY

     WHY FEEL PAIN?

               GAS PROBLEMS?
               BLOATING?
               INDIGESTION?
               TRY GAS-EEZE!

               shmuck looking at me from across the car
what the fuck you looking at you talkin to me then who the fuck
you talkin to de niro

FREE X-RAYS!   *slammed to a stop more people more crowded mother superior hanging on with tentacles the train started nun got her hand down there touched my cock wouldnt look at me like to squeeze her tits*
push push in the bush torn earlobe touched squeezed rubbed   squeezed back tried to go lower to her crack **DR. BENJAMIN DOVER PROCTO-LOGICAL SERVICES**   *saw the mother staring —————> who the fuck you lookin at*
          suddenly knew mother knew something was up   why   walk   around in pain voicemail is the answer CONVENIENT LOCATIONS *the hand squeezed got a finger in her crack probed wanted to be inside fucking her from behind fucking doggie style*
the mother started pulling her away no one could move **PLEASE KEEP HANDS** *she squeezed again around the head knew what to do what was she before a nun squeezed   the mother smelled of tuna she breathed anger   the train bum-pped* ***NEED A PHYSICIAN? 1-   800-DOCTORS***

                    she squeezed hard i came in my pants knew she could feel it twitch the moist load pump out
out   out   out   saw her smile the train doors o p e n i ng people shoving mother pu l l i n g her away squeezed one last time
          she was gone   into the crowd and off whether it was her stop or not
                                             With The New York Post
Reading Books Earns BIG MONEY $$$
          what a ride   wonder what her story was
because theres only one new york   west wind when wilt thou blow the
small rain down can rain   christ if my love were in my arms
and I in my   bed again
                    anonymous

    Jason got up at eleven and rode the Ross over to the Pizza Palace. The pizza, he had to admit, was pretty good even if it wasn't New York pizza. They had different specials every day. The sausage and pepper was the best he'd ever had.

The Pizza Palace was a hole in the wall, a little storefront counter at which no more than two people at a time could place orders. Inside were the ones Jason called the pizza slaves. These were the kids who made and sold the pies: a short, plump girl in charge of kneading the dough and making the basic pizza, a kid younger than Jason who added the specialty items and heated up slices, and a cute girl in her late teens who took the orders and handled the cash register.

They worked in the hot steamy store that had no ventilation except for the front door. Jason ordered and paid for his slice, watching the plump girl's breasts jiggle as she worked the dough. He tried not to see if any of her sweat dripped into it.

Just as Jason got his slice on a paper plate, he heard a commotion from the direction of the liquor store. Shouts, breaking glass, more shouts, curses, a scream. He left the Palace to see what was happening.

A boy in his late teens stood outside the liquor store, bleeding from his head. Attending him were a girl with stringy blond hair and a boy in a bathing suit.

The boy in the bathing suit was trying to stop his friend's bleeding by holding a shirt over the injury. But the injured boy would have none of it. He pushed his friend away and threw down the improvised bandage, letting his blood seep out onto himself and the concrete walk. The girl screamed.

"God, he's hurt, Anthony, oh my god, help him somebody, get the doctor, help him, please!!"

But Anthony didn't want any help. He lurched towards the liquor store, where an angry owner and his assistant stood in the doorway. Anthony challenged them.

"Fuckin' wanna a bottle Johnny Walker, you gotta sell it."

"Not to drunks, we don't have to sell. And who the hell's gonna pay for this window?" said the owner. Jason for the first time noticed that the window of the liquor store was smashed. Bloody shards of glass lay all over the walk. Now Anthony's buddy got tough.

"Fuck would'na happened you sold us a bottle," he slurred, stumbling, his balance no better than Anthony's.

Anthony took encouragement from his friend's righteous indignation and he weaved towards the store. The owner's assistant, a well-muscled boy, moved to meet him.

"Fuck outta my way," Anthony shouted, waving his arm in front of him in a gesture of dismissal. The assistant punched Anthony hard in the stomach, doubling him over, then brought a fist into his face. Jason heard the crunch of breaking cartilage as Anthony flew back and toppled onto the walk, new blood streaming from his nose. The girl threw herself on him, sobbing hysterically.

Anthony's buddy found a bottle in the trash and plucked it out by its neck. He broke the bottle against a wall, sending a gasp through the onlookers. He lifted the jagged bottle, menacing.

"Fuckin' gonna pay for that," he said, as the assistant moved away from him.

Someone ran past Jason, bumping into his arm and knocking the pizza from his hand. Jason looked at the kid who had run by, then at his pizza, lying face down on the concrete, tomato sauce splashed next to it.

The new arrival ran towards the boy with the bottle.

"Timmy," he said, "put it down."

Timmy waved him off with the bottle, its broken edge glistening evil in the sunlight. "Fuckin' gonna pay," he said again. "Gonna pay good."

"Hold it right there." Jason turned toward the voice to see a local cop approaching the scene, billy club in hand. "Put it down. Now!"

Timmy studied the cop, uncertain. His friend spoke.

"He's right, Timmy. Put it down."

Timmy dropped his arm but continued to hold onto the bottle.

"Now!" the cop repeated. Timmy dropped the bottle. It shattered and there were murmurs of relief from the crowd. The cop put Timmy in handcuffs, then spoke into his radio, calling for help. Anthony's girl sobbed, quieter now, still trying to stop her boyfriend's bleeding with the shirt. Anthony sat halfway up, in a daze.

"Wh-at happened?" Jason asked a kid next to him, who, Jason saw, was standing on his pizza.

"Shit-faced drunk," said the kid. "Wanted to buy a bottle. They wouldn't let him. Eddie pushed him outside, they shoved each other, that guy fell against the window."

"Kind of early to be drunk," said Jason.

"Not for them," said another kid. "They're from that party on Marshall."

"On Marshall?" said Jason. "I pas-sed a party there the other night."

"Yeah," said the second kid, "Thursday. That's when it started."

"That's when it started? What do you mean?" Jason asked.

"It's still going on," said the kid. "They're trying to make it to Labor Day."

Jason wondered about Carol. Was she there?

By this time a doctor had arrived and was busy patching up Anthony, cleaning his cuts and applying iodine and butterfly bandages until the wounds could be stitched. A ferry had arrived during the melee and was ready to head back to Ft. Hamilton. The cop spoke to the boat's pilot, who waited for the doctor to finish. When Anthony was ready, the cop, the doctor, Anthony, Timmy, the girl, and a few others walked towards the boat. The liquor store owner and his assistant Eddie began sweeping the broken glass into a cardboard box. That would be the easy part. Clearing the blood from the concrete would be more difficult. The sticky red fluid had by now soaked into the porous walkway and would not be easily removed.

The crowd dispersed, with people ready to get back to their ordinary activities. Jason forgot about pizza and mounted the Ross. He rode toward Marshall.

As he neared the party house, Jason heard none of Thursday night's music. He wondered if the celebrants had already fallen short of their Labor Day goal. But when he got closer, he saw that there were still people on the deck.

Three boys and two girls slept in the sun, lizards warming themselves. None of them moved as Jason parked his bike and went to the door.

When Jason entered the house, he smelled the sweet pungent odor of pot, the same smell that often filled the stairwells and bathrooms at school. The house was dark, the shades drawn to keep out the sun. Jason searched the gloom and saw why there was no music. The CD player lay upside down on the floor, broken open, transistor boards separated from the chassis, components scattered. The tape deck had met a similar fate and rested in the fireplace. Tapes, CDs, paper plates, beer cans, bottles, overflowing ashtrays, food wrappings, plastic cups, crumpled cigarette packs, containers of melted ice cream, littered the room along with pictures torn from the walls, overturned furniture, pizza boxes, and half a dozen vague forms that moved only to take puffs of the joint being passed around or to sip from a common wine bottle. In the middle of the floor, someone had placed a Walkman and turned it up to its highest volume. A song leaked from its earphones, barely audible.

want to know you

One of the kids passed the joint to Jason. Jason said no and the kid passed it around him.

"Is Carol here?" Jason asked.

hare krishna

"Don't know a Carol," said one of the forms. "Wha' she look like?"

"You get the bottle?" said another.

"She's a little taller than me, blond hair, usually wears a pony tail, lives on Gilbert."

"Gilbert?" said the kid. "Who's he?"

"Gilbert Walk," said Jason.

"Anthony? You get the bottle?" Jason heard again.

hara rama

Jason thought of telling them what had happened to Anthony but decided it might not be a good idea. If they all wanted their bottle as much as Anthony, they might vent their displeasure on Jason, the messenger of bad tidings.

"I'm not Anthony," he said. "Just a friend of Carol's. She here?"

"No Carol here."

"Fuck's Anthony?" said another voice.

Jason surveyed the wreckage one more time. He wondered how many times his father had wound up like this, in a drunken stupor in a place he didn't know with people whose only common interest was getting shit-faced.

my sweet lord

Jason went outside and took a deep breath of sea air to purge his lungs of the secondary pot smoke. He got on the Ross and rode off, stopping first at the Island Mart and then heading south on Midway toward Sailor. He had a new mission.

He left the Ross hidden in the trees just off the boardwalk and crept up on Greg's place, quietly moving through the bushes, not using the walkway that led to the house. His mission was find out more about the man called Greg. And he had to beware of the vicious guard dogs.

A few clouds had begun to cover the afternoon sun and Jason felt more comfortable with the somewhat darker conditions, conditions that would hopefully mask his activity. He crept closer to the house and reached the back deck. He peeked over the deck and saw Pollux, resting. Castor was not around.

Jason had planned for the dogs. He took out one of the Big Jim beef sticks he had purchased at Wensel's store and held it ready. When Pollux reared his head, Jason offered the treat. The dog wagged his tail and took it, downing it in a single bite. Jason gave him another and another until the dog reached a point of satiation and just licked the beef without wolfing it down.

Jason climbed up on the deck and started to explore. The house was quiet, with no Greg in sight. Perfect, thought Jason. He could take a good look at things.

Jason crouched and moved with stealth, peering in the dirty windows, trying to make out what was inside. He had his cover story all set. If discovered he would say that he had come over to treat the dogs to Big Jims. When he got there, Jason would say, he found the house deserted except for Pollux and was about to call Greg's name. Just about to call his name.

Then Jason heard something. A soft whimpering. A dog sound. He wondered whether Castor might be hurt somewhere and followed his ears around the house to the source of the sound. He came at last to a window on a side of the house shaded by trees and peeked in.

Jason froze. Inside he saw Greg, naked, holding Castor in front of him on the bed, moving his cock in and out of the bitch's cunt, making quiet grunts to match the dog's whimpers.

Jason couldn't take his eyes away from the grotesque sight. The window was open a crack and Jason again smelled the acrid stink of marijuana.

The dog accepted Greg's thrusts eagerly, her haunches drawn up to enable the man to penetrate. Near them, on the bed, Jason saw a tube of KY-Gel, the universal lubricant that made everyone's way easier. Something sour rose in Jason's throat. He wondered what Aunt Lee would say about this. He wondered what it was like to fuck a dog. He didn't think he really wanted to know.

Jason shrank down low so not to be seen, although he doubted that Greg was seeing anything right now. The man's head was thrown back as his thrusts became more insistent and his grunts and the dog's whimpers became louder. They were coming!

And they did. In spasms of orgasm and with cries of relief, Greg poured his love into Castor. Then Jason realized that once Greg finished, he might notice the spy at his window or hear him fleeing the scene. Better to get out while man and dog were still locked together in passion.

Jason tore himself from the window and crept off the deck then jumped to the grass. He mounted the Ross and took off.

When Jason got back to his aunt's house, he put his Pod Attack game into a black garbage bag and stuffed it in the trash can. Then he remembered it had been an expensive game and that his mother might ask about it someday. He retrieved the bag and put it under his bed. He would just leave it behind, saying he had forgotten it.

On the way to the firehouse for the dance that evening, Jason stopped at the Island Mart to look at Cindy. He smiled at her as he went into the store and she smiled back, right through him to a boy who had come in behind Jason, a lifeguard Jason recognized from the beach. Jason appraised the produce to make it appear he actually had business in the store, then saw a girl with short dark hair and wearing a halter and tight jeans climb the stairs to the non-food section. He followed her.

Jason roamed around the second floor, keeping one eye on the girl and the other on the Mart's wares. But in minutes the girl was joined by what Jason assumed was her boyfriend. They kissed, then giggled over something, then went downstairs, leaving Jason alone. He continued looking around, winding up in a little section of children's books. He smiled as he skimmed through the familiar titles, then picked up one he had never before seen.

The cover showed a seagull flying near a lighthouse. It was a short picture book called *The Clever Seagull*. Jason opened it and read.

Once there stood a fabulous city by the sea. A city of shining white hotels and beaches of golden sand.

In this city lived a clever seagull.

When it came time to eat, all the seagulls except the clever seagull flew to the sea to catch fish. They worked hard diving for their supper.

The clever seagull stayed in the city and caught his supper with a trick. He would fly upside down near some people, roll over in the air, and land with a noisy squawk. The people laughed and applauded and gave the seagull tasty scraps to eat.

Because many visitors came to the city, the clever seagull always had new people to amuse with his trick. He never went hungry. Instead, he grew fat. The fatter he grew, the more he amused people and **the more** *they gave him to eat.*

Then one day a terrible storm swept in from the east. Most of the people fled and the seagulls flew to an island in the south to wait for the storm to pass. But the clever seagull was too fat to fly very far. He took refuge in the city.

The storm lasted two days. When it ended the clever seagull came out to find food. But none of the few people around cared to feed a squawking seagull, no matter what tricks it did.

So he flew to the sea to catch fish. But the clever seagull was slow and clumsy. Every time he dove for a fish it darted away. Time and again the seagull landed in the sea with nothing but a mouthful of salt water for his trouble.

After many failures, the clever seagull struggled to the shore and lay there exhausted and wet, with an empty stomach.

Then he looked up and saw the other seagulls returning from the south. The clever seagull used his last strength to cry out. When his friends saw him helpless on the shore, they brought him food.

The clever seagull thanked them and promised himself never to fish with tricks again. Forevermore he would be a seagull among seagulls, gliding on the bright wind in the clear sky over a fabulous city by the sea.

Jason stared at the final drawing that showed the seagulls flying together. Then he closed the book and put it back on the shelf. He went downstairs.

The firehouse did double duty. Not only did it house the Cranberry Island Volunteer Fire Department but it also hosted a score of community activities: cartoons and movies on Wednesday nights, bake sales to raise money for whatever incidentals the community needed, art shows, kiddie talent shows, pancake breakfasts two Sundays in August, the Fourth of July barbecue, and, to mark the end of summer, the Labor Day Weekend Saturday Night Dance and Chow Down.

As they always were for festivities, the fire trucks had been moved and parked outside of the aging building that had been one of the first structures built on the island. The wide roll-up doors were open and the door frame was festooned with paper garlands, ribbons, and strings of small blinking multi-colored lights. A big poster board sign done in a neat hand announced 70'S DISCO AND FOOD $5 ALL YOU CAN EAT.

A dull red sunset blurred by a thin haze of clouds decorated the western sky as Jason arrived with his mother and aunt. He wasn't hungry. Affairs like this made him nervous. He couldn't dance a step and had nothing to say to anybody. He wasn't even sure why he was there except that he would have felt too alone staying home by himself and joffing. He'd done enough of that for the week.

Jason heard his aunt's name being called and turned to see Greg, beer in hand, coming towards them. Would his aunt believe Greg fucked his dog? Jason would never know because he would never tell. Phil he would tell. Yes, tell the Crossing Net. Or get on a talk show. "Nephews Whose Aunt's Boyfriend Fucks Dogs." Maybe there'll be puppies. Gregweilers.

"Hi, Lee," said Greg. "Get some chow?"

"Sure," said Aunt Lee. "How about you, Jason. Hungry?"

Jason looked inside the firehouse. Only a few couples were dancing. The serving tables were covered with red and white checked tablecloths and laden with platters of chicken, ribs, baked potatoes, corn on the cob, salad, bread, butter, sodas, coffee, and cakes, pies, and cookies. A feast of feasts.

"Not really," said Jason.

"Come on, kid," said Greg. "Celebrate your kill."

"I'll have something later," said Jason.

"I'm going in," said Greg.

"Come with us, Anna," said Lee.

Yes, thought Jason, go with them. Don't hover near me.

"Jason," said his mother. "Mind if I get a bite?"

"No, ma. Go right ahead. I'm fine."

"You'll have something later?"

"Sure, ma. Go ahead."

Jason watched his mother and aunt and the dog fucker walk into the fire house. The music came from a DJ set up just outside the doors, a girl of eighteen or nineteen with long blond hair and a cute face. There were already two guys buzzing around her, bees around the honey. No honey for Jason.

The music played loud disco.

must be the night fever

Jason turned away from the festivities to look out over the bay. Across the water, he could see the lights of the houses on the mainland and, here and there, tracing their way back and forth over the bay, the running lights of ferries and party boats. Jason wondered about Allie's mother. Was she still on the island? Did they have relatives? What was she doing right now? Her son was gone. Dead from a volleyball game. Dead because of Jason. Dead.

turn me on do what you want

"Hi."

Jason came out of his trance. Carol stood next to him.

"Hi." It came out small and weak. He cleared his throat, hoped his voice wouldn't crack, tried again. "Hi."

"Last big weekend," she said. The obvious small talk. What would he say? That he'd spied on her and seen her tits?

"Yeah." She wore a thin white sweater over a red and green plaid skirt. Her hair in a little pony tail. Her perfume the scent of flowers.

"You eat yet?" she asked.

"No."

"Come on. It looks good."

Jason followed her, not believing. The music pulsed, louder now. People were gathering.

i love the night life

They paid and went straight to the food tables. Carol piled her plate high and Jason did the same. He suddenly had an appetite. A great appetite.

get the action going

"Let's sit here," she said, gesturing toward an out of the way table where they would be alone.

"Sure," said Jason. In a dream.

They sat down. Jason tore into the ribs and chicken as if he hadn't eaten in days. Carol smiled.

"Hungry?"

"Guess so," he said. "It's good."

"Always is. You like it here?"

"Yeah. But we only get a week."

"Your aunt's place."

"She's had it for ye-ars." He blushed.

"I know," said Carol. "We rent our place for most of the summer and come out at the end of August."

"You like it here?"

"Love it," Carol said, dabbing at her mouth with a flower-print napkin. "It's so peaceful."

"Not this week," said Jason. "I saw a guy get killed on the beach."

"Allie Grant?"

Jason nodded.

"You were there?"

"Saw the fight and everything."

"Must have been horrible."

"Yeah. Not peaceful. And did you hear about the fight at the liquor store today?"

Carol's eyes widened. "No. What happened?"

"Some kid from the party on Marshall, drunk, wanted to buy a bottle, they wouldn't sell it to him."

"He got into a fight?"

"Fell through the window. Blood all over. Cop arrested him."

how do you like your love

"What was his name?"

"Anthony." Jason paused, then, "Were you at that party?"

"For a while Thursday night. I hear it's still going."

"Wow. You know this Anthony?"

"No. There were a million people there."

Jason took a long drink of soda.

"You had a bit of excitement, too," Carol said.

"What do you mean?"

"That snake."

more more more more

For a moment Jason didn't know what she was talking about. Then he remembered the incident behind his aunt's house.

"Pret-ty embarrassing."

Carol giggled. "I guess so. Kind of funny, though."

Jason grimaced. "Yeah. Funny."

Carol wiped her hands on a napkin. "Wanna dance?"

Jason nearly choked.

"I don't know how."

"Come on," she said, getting up. "It's easy. Just move around."

Jason's heart throbbed in time with the music. Just move around, he thought. Like fucking.

"Okay." Jason stood, legs shaky. She wanted to dance with him? What the fuck was going on?

more than a woman

Carol led Jason to the open space being used as a dance floor. By this time, lots of people were dancing so Jason didn't have to feel totally embarrassed at being seen. He would disappear in the crowd.

She found a spot and started to shake side to side and up and down. "Like this," she said, smiling. Her smile a promise, a beacon for the lost sailor, a star, the light of heaven itself.

here in my arms you'll find happiness

Jason started imitating her the best he could, a puppet on a string, her string. He would do anything she wanted.

more more more more

"Go, kid, go!" It was Greg, yelling encouragement from across the floor. Carol laughed and leaned close. Her perfume filled his brain.

"You're good," she said.

"Thanks," said Jason. Dizzy as they whirled like stars around each other.

The music ended as the DJ took a break. Jason and Carol returned to their table only to find three boys sitting there. Jason recognized them from the beach. The tough kids. Jason Jaybird. Beefy boys with arrogant, disdainful expressions. Rattler. Pickett. Scone.

"Hi, Car," said one, who lounged in what had been Jason's chair. "Who's the date?"

"Not a date. It's my neighbor, Jason." She made the introductions. "This is Jimmy, Billy, Jamie."

Jason nodded at the boys, felt like he was in Macon County. Jimmy. Billy. Jamie. Billy was the lounger.

"Well if it isn't Jason Jaybird," said Billy. Jimmy and Jamie laughed.

"Not funny," said Carol. "Could we sit down. That's our food."

But when Jason and Carol looked at their plates, they saw that the boys had done more than take their chairs. They had eaten the food as well.

"We got hungry," said Billy.

"That's incredibly rude," said Carol. "I can't believe you'd do such a thing."

"Thought you knew me by now," said Billy.

"I guess not," said Carol. "Why don't you take your friends and leave."

"Why don't you get your boyfriend to make us?" Billy challenged.

Jason gulped. He was not a fighter and certainly no match for this bunch of macho pricks. He wished he knew karate. Wished he were Blue Shirt. Then he'd deal with these punks.

"Oh, for God's sake," said Carol. "What's gotten into you, Billy? You on steroids like Allie was?"

Billy uncoiled from the chair like a larger version of the snake Jason had faced the day before.

"How 'bout it, kid? Gonna make us?" Billy swayed and Carol understood.

"You're drunk! You guys are juiced up."

Billy moved close to Jason, who could smell booze on the boy's breath.

"Well?" Billy challenged again.

Jason took a step back and bumped into something that felt like the side of a building. It was Greg.

"Hi, guys," Greg said. "Having fun?"

No one answered him. Greg, his eyes narrow, stepped up to Billy.

"Name's Greg," he said, holding out his hand. Billy extended his.

"Billy."

They shook hands and Greg squeezed. Jason saw Billy's expression change from drunken arrogance to nervous submission in seconds. Greg held on. Billy tried to hide his pain. Jimmy and Jamie exchanged glances, uncertain.

"Nice meeting you," said Greg, squeezing harder. "You look like you wrestle. You wrestle any?"

Billy grimaced. "No."

"Too bad, you got the build for it. Probably be pretty good. Me, I wrestled high school, college, All-State, everything. Great sport. Maybe I'll see you on the beach, give you some pointers. What do you say?"

Billy had turned white. One knee began to buckle. He had the beginnings of tears in his eyes.

"Sure," he squeaked out. The music started up.

don't leave me this way

Greg shook Billy's hand up and down to finish him off, then released it.

"Great. Nice meeting you. Jason, see you later. Have fun. Anything you need help with, let me know."

"Yeah, thanks," said Jason. Billy checked his buddies.

"This sucks," he said. "We're outta here."

They walked away, out of the firehouse, with Greg following a few feet behind them, leaving Jason and Carol standing, staring at each other. Carol was the first to laugh.

"Well, he certainly took care of that. I've seen him around, who is he?"

"Hangs out with my aunt," Jason said. Fucks dogs.

"Nice friend to have," said Carol. She looked at the empty plates and the messy table. "What do you want to do now?"

Jason had no idea. "Dance?"

"Tired of it," said Carol. "How about the dock? Get some air."

"Sure."

They left the firehouse and walked the short distance to the dock. The black water lapped against the wooden piers. Overhead, the stars were mostly obscured by fuzzy patches of clouds. Jason and Carol stood at the edge of the dock, looking into the night.

"A storm is coming," Carol said. "You can feel it. It's so still."

"Eric?"

Carol nodded. "Hurricanes aren't fun out here."

"You've been through them before?" Jason asked.

"Andrew, '92. Terrible."

"We missed it. You have to leave the island?"

"The ferries took us out. Scary."

Jason thought about being on the water during a hurricane. He shivered.

"Cold?" Carol asked.

"Naw."

Carol reached down and picked up a pebble from the dock, tossed it into the water.

"We won't be coming back anymore," she said.

"What do you mean?" asked Jason.

"My parents are selling the house."

"Why?"

"My dad's in the Navy. We're moving to San Diego."

"Vern was in the Navy."

"The bike man?"

"Yeah. He had a heart attack, they flew him out. Your dad command a ship?"

"Teaches computers."

"Neat. So you're moving. Going to miss it?"

"Yes. I love it here."

take the time   do it right

Something deep in Jason stirred, a powerful something he had never known before. He wanted to hold Carol, tell her it would be all right, make it better for her.

"What will you do in the summer?"

"San Diego is summer all year round."

"Is this your last weekend?"

"We've got one more. You?"

"Mom and I head back Monday."

"Where's your dad?"

"Dead."

"I'm sorry. It's tough not having a father."

"Yeah."

you're gonna miss my lovin'

"This is making me sad," she said. "Maybe we should go."

"Yeah," said Jason. "Where?"

"Home," said Carol. "I just want to be in my room. I want to be there a lot before we have to leave."

The music blasted from the firehouse, louder as the hour grew later and the time grew shorter.

more more more more

They walked in silence over the dark boardwalks. Behind them the music faded, giving way to the sound of the waves against the shore. A gentle wind moved through the trees, making the leaves flutter like little wings. The smell of honeysuckle blended with Carol's perfume. Jason stumbled.

"You okay?" Carol asked.

"Tripped on a plank."

She smiled and he thought she was the most beautiful girl he had ever seen.

When they reached her house, the lights were on and the television's blue flame glowed in a comfortable, comforting way. Jason could see Carol's parents in the house, her father puttering in the kitchen, her mother sitting in a chair, reading.

"This is my stop," Carol said. "But you know that."

"Yeah."

"Where's your room?"

Jason pointed to his window.

"Right across from me." Carol paused a moment. "Do you believe in miracles?"

"Miracles?"

"Wonderful things that happen when nobody thinks they can happen."

"Like the Mets winning the World Series."

Carol laughed. "Not exactly like that."

"Then what?" Jason asked.

"I don't know." Carol said. Jason watched as she stood there experiencing the ocean, the sand, the night on Cranberry Island for one of her last times.

"Good night, Jason. It was fun talking."

"It was," said Jason.

Carol moved close and kissed Jason on the lips, a sweet, brief, light kiss as gentle as the brush of a butterfly wing against a rose petal.

She turned and walked to her house. The house she was leaving. The house she would never come back to. The house she loved.

Jason watched her go. When she disappeared inside, he felt his heart go with her. He stood motionless, listening to the ocean, the crickets, the sounds of people partying in neighboring houses, music, laughter, shouts, conversation. Above, stars burned between the clouds in a fiery show of light and color. The damp air chilled his body and he could smell the salt water, the trees, the sand, the breeze, Carol's perfume, the night itself. He could taste the light pink of her lipstick and knew he was in love.

Forever.

Blue Shirt Files—2009.9.BG6

The subway took forever to come. While I waited on the platform, I struggled with the demon that Bunny had planted inside me, a demon of technology that had turned my brain into a computer programmed to murder. I had to use all my will to have any thoughts except those that focused on killing Homer Glands. I made and discarded dozens of plans in seconds as my mind calculated the success probabilities of all the possible strategies I could use to gain access to the great man and finish him.

By the time the subway arrived, I had it figured out. I'd call Homer and pretend to sell out. That would get me an appointment. But before I got to his office I'd wire myself with all the D-5 explosive I had, enough to wipe out a city block. D-5 was illegal, of course, but I had my connections and always found a use for small amounts here and there. Now I would use it all. As soon as I got into his office and saw him in front of me, I would detonate myself. What a blast!

I might have laughed at the lunacy of it if I had been myself. Then again, if I had been myself I wouldn't have been planning to blow up just because somebody told me to. Now that I had a plan, I felt my brain relax and I was able to think a little more clearly. I had to do something.

I decided to get off the train. That, at least, would delay things. But when I tried to go for the door, I couldn't move. My hands held tight to the pole I had grabbed onto when I first got into the subway car and I couldn't move my fingers. I saw drops of sweat fall from my forehead past my eyes and knew I couldn't even wipe them away. I was locked in place until I got to my stop.

This was bad. Very bad.

The subway reached Forty-Second street and I got out, moving mechanically, like a robot, with no will of my own. I walked to the elevator and rode up to my office, unable to change my course or even slow myself down. I was a prisoner in my own body.

I opened my office door and went right for the D-5. I started packing it into a briefcase, with a couple of wires coming out of it that would lead to the detonator. Once I had everything hooked up I would call Homer. Then the fun would start.

My hands didn't even shake as I put the bomb together. Here I was, preparing to kill myself and dozens of other people and my hands were steady as a surgeon's. I wondered at the evil of Bunny, at how she could kill seemingly without remorse to get her way. I wondered at a universe in which such evil was permitted. Thinking about her made me shake inside. Outside, I was a rock.

The phone rang as I was about to make the final connections. My programming knew exactly what to do. It might be Bunny with further orders. I picked up the phone and Archie's pale, pock-marked face lit up the viewscreen.

"Hey, Blue, what you up to?"

Archie the Hacker was one of my best pals and he was wearing the stupid grin he always had when he was up to no good or out hell-raising. I saw his grin change to a look of concern before I hung up.

"Hey, what's…"

I cut him off in mid-sentence, then finished my grim work and checked it. The detonator was a switch I would carry in my pocket and prime just before I entered Homer's office. The moment I saw him, I would press the button. Whoosh. It would all be over.

Whoosh.

I called Homer. His secretary put me right through and his mean face scowled at me, burning a hole in the viewscreen.

"Blue Shirt. What is it?"

"It's Bunny," I heard myself say. "I'll turn her over."

He looked surprised. "Turn her over?"

"To you. For a price."

"I never liked you Blue Shirt, but I thought you had integrity. Guess I was wrong. You're as low as the rest of us."

"I'm coming by your office," I said. "Give me half then and half when I bring her."

"Half of what?"

"One meg Americash."

He laughed. "Nobody's worth that much."

I hung up the phone. That surprised me but It all must have been part of Bunny's program. Less than a minute later, he called back.

"Agreed," he said. "And if you don't bring her…"

I hung up, cutting him off again. I was ready to go, the detonator resting comfortably in my pocket.

I opened the door to leave and stopped in my tracks. Archie was standing there, that shit-eating grin on his face. But I knew what my programming would do and couldn't stop my hand from going for my gun.

Sunday

Jason sat in the living room while outside the August sun filled the afternoon with incessant, broiling heat. He wiped sweat from his forehead and double-clicked on the execute statement in his root directory.

SCREW.EXE.

The screen flickered as a man and woman began copulating in full color computer-controlled video, thrusting in and out, in and out, over and over, a collection of ones and zeros in an endless loop of pornographic recursion, moving against each other without pleasure, digital bodies shimmering, pulsing at 75Mz, soundlessly, endlessly fucking on the laptop's screen.

Jason ogled the naked couple, who resembled himself and Aunt Lee, as they tirelessly pushed at each other. Then their images began to break up, lose their cohesiveness, dissolve into random pixels, and fade into the gray nothingness of a blank screen.

Jason woke from his dream soaked in perspiration and hornier than he had been all week. The clock read 10:12 AM. There was a knock at the door and it opened.

"Ma!"

"Sorry, Jason. It's late. Don't you want to get up?"

"I'm getting up, ma. I'm getting up."

"It's a beautiful day."

"Okay, ma. I'm up."

"Aunt Lee's making pancakes."

"Okay, ma."

The door pulled shut and Jason got out of bed. He looked at Carol's house but there was no sign of her or anyone else.

The day was as hot as it had been in Jason's dream. Hot with a stultifying intensity that drained energy and left everyone to languish. After breakfast, Jason took a spin on the Ross. The heat shortened his trip and by noon he was back in the house.

Only his mother was home. She told him she was taking a water taxi over to the Colony to see a new shop Lee had told her about. Lee didn't feel like a long trip and was doing her own shopping at the Island Mart.

When his mother left, Jason got out his laptop. He remembered his dream and wished he had porn diskettes. He had heard about them but had never seen one. Phil was no help. He was terrified of viruses in downloaded porn. "More scared of them than AIDS," he would say and then stupidly joke, "Can't put a condom on my Pentium."

So Jason settled for the Love Connection. He hooked up to the telephone and signed on. He was just about to enter the Do It Nice room when he heard footsteps on the ramp. The door opened.

"Hi, Jason."

Aunt Lee.

"Whatcha' doing?"

"Noth-ing."

"On a day like this, you'd rather play on the computer than be at the beach?"

"Too hot," he said. Aunt Lee had on shorts and her usual tight halter. She carried a plastic shopping bag.

"Storm's going to hit sometime tonight. That's what they're saying. This'll be the last good day. Your mom leave already?"

"A little while ago."

"I wanted her advice on something. Maybe you could help?"

"With what?"

"Wait."

Aunt Lee went to her room and Jason signed off the Net. He couldn't imagine what his Aunt wanted. Help around the house? He grabbed a towel that had been hanging over his chair, rubbed his face. Hot.

She called from her room. "Jason. Come here."

Jason went. When he reached her door and saw his aunt, he stopped dead. She had on a new bikini, tight and revealing, black with jagged red stripes. She had put on lipstick, a deep red, and he could smell her strawberry perfume. She wore black high heels.

"Like it?"

Jason nodded, unable to speak.

"Come here, come here, come in, come in." She beckoned him.

He entered her room, not able to keep from staring at her breasts pushing against the bikini's taut material, her tanned body, her curved legs.

"Sit down." She nodded toward the edge of the bed.

Jason sat.

"Now, what do you think?" She put her hands on her hips. Posed.

"About wh-at?"

She laughed. "The bathing suit, of course. What do you think?" She turned her back to him, letting her high heels click on the floor, heels that accented her firm calf muscles like the girls in Jason's magazines. She caressed her buttocks with her hands to smooth the material.

"Not too snug? Doesn't show too much?" She bent over to display her ass and patted it. "Here?" Turned to face him. Cupped her breasts in her hands. "Or here?"

Jason's body tingled. His face flushed. He stammered.

"I...I don't kn-ow."

"What do you mean, you don't know? You're a man, Jason. Men know. Want me to show you something?"

Jason shrugged. Aunt Lee reached behind her, undid her bikini top and let it fall to the floor. Her breasts shone like brushed bronze in the quiet room, holding Jason's gaze like the light of God. Jason's throat closed. He stopped breathing.

"What do you think?"

Jason couldn't think. Couldn't answer. He barely heard her through the loud beating of his heart, the blood roaring in his ears, in his brain. Sweat burst from him. Snake strained at his bathing suit, beyond torment. He moved a hand to cover himself. Aunt Lee's eyes fixed on his embarrassment.

"I showed you something, so you have to show me something. Stand up."

Jason was paralyzed.

"Let me help," she said. Aunt Lee reached for Jason's hands and took them in hers. She pulled him to her, helping him to his feet. When he was up, she knelt in front of him.

"I'm going to take off your trunks. Would you like that?"

Jason thought he would pass out. The strawberry perfume rose from his aunt's hot body, filled his nostrils with excitement, promise, passion. He was dreaming, he knew that now. He had to be dreaming. He nodded yes. He would like that. Yes.

Aunt Lee put her fingers into the waistband of Jason's trunks and tugged them down, working them over the engorged Snake that, when finally free, sprang out to bob up and down in front of her. Lee let go the trunks and they fell around Jason's ankles. Her eyes widened as she beheld his equipment.

"You're a man, all right."

Jason burned, unable to move, helpless as he watched his aunt examine his fully erect penis, something no one but he had ever before seen! It jerked, even though he didn't want it to, didn't want his aunt to see his most private stirrings. Then he knew that the powerful Snake, which dominated his body and mind at will, stood helpless against his aunt's desires.

"Do you want to touch me?" she said, her voice low, seductive.

Jason couldn't move.

"Here." Aunt Lee took his hand and brought it to her breast. He felt her warm flesh, the nipple stiff against his palm. "Use both hands," she said, drawing his idle hand to her other breast. "Squeeze."

Jason's hands shook as he pressed his fingers into her softness, pressed and released, pressed again. Aunt Lee clasped her hands behind her head and arched her back, reminding Jason of the time he had rubbed her with suntan lotion. Her breasts jutted out, nipples erect, demanding attention. He squeezed harder and his aunt moaned.

"Play with my nipples," she whispered, feeling a tingle in her belly she hadn't known since Ralph.

Jason hesitated, not wanting to let go of the warm, yielding breasts that filled his hands, wanting nothing but to hold them, to feel them, to revel in their fullness in this glorious dream he knew he must be having.

Aunt Lee blew a puff of air on his hot penis and Jason came to. He rubbed the stiff pink buttons that had so often captivated his eyes. His aunt squirmed and her nipples slipped away from him. "Don't let go," she said, breathing hard, pushing her beasts against his hands, moving slow like a lewd dancer, feeling him enjoy her body, inviting him to do more, begging him, he thought, like Lynne, like Darcy, like Sue, begging him to touch her body as he would touch his own and give her the pleasure he would give himself.

Jason captured the succulent buds between his fingers and lost himself in her flesh, not knowing or seeing or feeling anything except his aunt's breasts and the rubbery thrill of her nipples. He worked on them the way he had seen the girls in *Wide Open Legs* touch themselves, playing with both at the same time, pinching and pulling, then letting go, then taking them, squeezing with his fingers and thumb, kneading them, sometimes hard, sometimes soft, all the while listening to his aunt's gasps of pleasure as she gave herself to him.

She blew on his penis a second time, jolting him to attention.

"Wet your fingers and rub my breasts all over."

Jason responded at once, no longer himself but part of her, part of her body, part of her mind, doing her will and only her will, finding saliva he didn't think he had and lubricating her breasts. His aunt breathed harder. She arched her back even more, surrendering to her nephew's eager touch, bathing in the mounting pleasure, letting it wash over her and take her like an inevitable tide.

Aunt Lee unclasped her hands and brought them around to hold Jason's fingers hard against her. She closed her eyes and shuddered. When she opened her eyes, Jason thought he saw tears. She moved his hands to his side and released them.

"That was nice but I'm all wet," she pouted, a wicked joy flooding her. She dried her breasts with her hands, watching Jason's hard stare, showing herself to him, cupping her breasts in her hands and lifting them, fondling herself to feed her nephew's passion. And her own.

She fixed her eyes on a clear drop of precum that had collected at the end of his penis and she knew she had to be careful lest he spend himself before she wanted him to. His Snake stretched out as full between his legs as the Goodyear blimp.

"You're wet, too," she said, taking the head of his cock between her index finger and thumb, lifting it for Jason to see. She ever so gently squeezed and the drop swelled, threatening to fall. "Look how much there is." She locked her eyes on his. "Do you want me to clean it off?"

Jason made a pitiful, helpless mewling noise.

"That sounds like yes to me," Aunt Lee said, still holding him. "But you have to be perfectly still."

Snake quivered.

"I felt something move," she said. "You have to keep still."

Jason nodded. Snake did not move. It had heard. Still holding the head of his cock between her fingers, Aunt Lee used her other hand to lift a breast and rub its nipple into the moistness at the tip of his penis. Jason gasped, and instead of drying his cock, her work caused another drop to appear.

"I don't think I got it," she said, furrowing her brow and narrowing her eyes to give Jason's organ a full inspection, enjoying her teasing game. She would take her time. "Let me see." She put her hands on his hips and moved him toward her. Jason's entire body stiffened with anticipation as his erection pulsed a breath away from her deep red lips.

"Let's try again," she said. "Maybe I should use my tongue. What do you think?"

Jason couldn't think, but felt his head nodding.

"I agree," said his aunt. She kissed the head of his penis, then dug her tongue into its opening and licked out the sticky fluid. Jason's knees began to buckle. Aunt Lee held him tighter. She drew her mouth away and a thin strand of precum formed between her lips and the head of his cock. Jason moaned as he saw his aunt move her mouth back to his penis without losing the filament. She wiped his cock clean with her tongue and drew back a second time, appraising her work.

"That did it. Look." Jason did and saw his aunt's red lipstick staining the most secret part of his body.

"Lie down."

It didn't sound like Aunt Lee. The voice was low. Throaty. Commanding.

He sat and lay back, supporting himself with his elbows. His aunt knelt at the edge of the bed and slipped his trunks from around his ankles, then put her hands on his knees and spread his legs. The Snake stood at full height, breathing free, throbbing in the summer afternoon air, burning like a rod of foundry iron.

"You're big," she said, tilting her head to view her prize from different angles. "I wonder if I can get all of you in my mouth." Another drop of precum formed and she licked it off. "Let's see how much I can take."

Aunt Lee circled the fingers of one hand around the base of the Snake and held it firm. It jerked. She giggled and talked to it like a little girl playfully scolding a doll. "Are you trying to get away?" She tightened her grip, making Jason feel as if he would burst. "I don't think you're going anywhere but in my mouth. And all of you if I can. What do you think of that?" She licked the underside of his penis, a quick, light lick that made him groan in an agony of delight.

"Did you like that?" she asked. "Say yes and I'll do it again."

Jason, hardly able to breathe much less speak, could only croak out the required answer.

"I can't hear you," his aunt teased.

"Yes," Jason blurted. "Yes."

She giggled again. "I think you'd better say please, just to be sure."

Jason squeaked. "Please."

"Good," said Aunt Lee. She licked him again, longer and slower than before, wanting to prolong the moment, wanting to live this game with her horny young nephew on this blazing Sunday afternoon until the end of time. "You're going to remember this forever," she said. "I promise."

Jason writhed and she knew he wouldn't last much longer. She relaxed her grip then squeezed again, relaxed and squeezed, then wet her lips and kissed his cock from its base to its head, pausing between kisses to tantalize it with the tip of her tongue. When she reached the head, more drops waited. She licked them off, enjoying their sweetness. Jason's mouth fell open but no sound came out.

With her other hand she caressed his testicles, her fingernails like electric probes on Jason's taut pink skin. His balls became hard as billiards. She flicked her tongue back and forth across the sensitive stretched skin of his glans, tasting him, torturing his rigid flesh. She slid her tongue down the length of his silky hardness to his balls, lingering there to explore their tightness, their soft fuzz of hair, cupping them in her fingers as she worked, stiffening her tongue to dig into them, licking them, wetting them generously before gliding her tongue back up the underside of his penis to again slap tenderly at the glans and take him back into her mouth.

Jason heard a guttural, animal noise. He looked but saw no one save his aunt, her eyes half closed, her head moving up and down as her mouth enjoyed his penis, enveloping it, riding in slow motion along its length, taking it all in then letting it slip out but not letting go completely lest it spill its precious contents into the air. His distended cock glistened with trails of her saliva as she held the head tight between her lips, sucking off its oozing drool of precum before drawing him all the way in once more.

While she pleasured him with her mouth, Aunt Lee worked her strong fingers into the balls she had so carefully prepared, massaging the well-lubricated scrotum, moving easily over the slippery fullness, expertly sculpting sensations Jason had never before known, stoking the hot furnace his sacs had become until the liquid seed that boiled within churned toward an inevitable bursting expulsion. His balls spasmed and she sucked out and swallowed the first thick blob of his ejaculate. Savoring its taste, she let his cock slide out of her mouth one last time, wrapping her fingers tight around it to hold back the eruption. Jason's body cried for release and cum seeped out of him like white lava.

She licked up the cum dribbling from his cock and held the fluid in her mouth to help lubricate the blowjob, then released her grip and engulfed all of him, sucking hard, stroking his glans with her tongue again and again and again.

Jason felt the air flow through his throat like wind coming out of a cave and heard the animal sound again.

It came from him.

Jason exploded, eyes closed, head thrown back, grunting again and again as the sperm burst from him, spasm after spasm jolting his young body, Aunt Lee taking him completely, her fingers squeezing and releasing his balls in time with the urgent contractions that propelled his hot semen, her moaning slurping swallowing noises mixing with his own cries, lifting him higher and higher as his thick fluid gushed into her mouth, filling it over and over as she took every drop, over and over until no more came and no more would come.

When he was sucked dry he opened his eyes to see his aunt smiling at him. Drops of his juice clung to her lipstick smeared mouth. She brushed a finger along her lips, gathering the sperm into a single heavy drop that she tasted like the last bit of a forbidden dessert.

A door slammed. "Lee? Jason?"

His mother.

Jason's heart stopped. Aunt Lee jumped to her feet. Whispered.

"Get in the closet."

Jason got off the bed and into the closet as Aunt Lee threw his bathing suit after him.

"Anybody here?" Footsteps approaching.

"I am," Aunt Lee said, cheerful. "Trying on a new suit." She grabbed tissues and cleaned her mouth.

Jason got the door shut just as his mother entered the room. The closet was hot. He held his breath, stood without moving.

"What was that noise?" His mother, uneasy.

"Noise?"

"Like something growling. It sounded like it came from the house."

"I think there were some dogs out back."

"Where's Jason?"

"Not with you? Out somewhere I guess. What do you think of this?"

"Really shows off your breasts."

"I was just putting on the top. So?"

"It still shows off your breasts. Is that what you want?"

"Pays to advertise."

"I didn't know you were selling it."

"Very funny. Okay, let me change. I'll be right out."

"I'm worried about Jason."

"He's fine. Now go on."

Jason heard his mother leave. Aunt Lee opened the closet door and took out a tee-shirt.

Whispered.

"Stay till we're gone."

She shut the closet door and left. Jason was dizzy from his orgasm, from the heat. Outside he could hear their muffled voices. He suddenly needed to piss.

Footsteps. Doors opened, closed. Voices.

"...Colony..."

"...forgot my credit card.."

"...so hot..."

"...left the computer out..."

"...be okay..."

Doors. Footsteps. Toilet flushing. Sweat pouring off him. Bursting to piss. The door to Aunt Lee's room opened.

"...get my bag," he heard his aunt call out. She was telling him they were going. He started to double over.

"...go to the bathroom," he heard his mother say as Aunt Lee closed the door behind her. He couldn't wait.

Jason pushed open the closet door and saw the tissue box on the dresser near him. He grabbed it and relieved himself in the box, letting his pee soak into the tissues, hoping he wouldn't overflow it.

The box held. He finished. Breathed again.

The toilet flushed. Footsteps. A door slammed.

Quiet.

They were gone.

Jason lay the tissue box on the floor and put on his bathing suit. He would count to a hundred and make a run for it. At fifty-six he decided they might come back if he waited too long. He opened Aunt Lee's door. The house was empty.

Jason went to the trash and stuffed the tissue box into the bottom, underneath the breakfast leavings. Then he cautiously went out the back door, not wanting his mother to see him if she were nearby.

There was no one around. Jason tore off his tee-shirt and threw it on the deck. He ran to the beach.

He ran across the sand to the water, weaving through the holiday crowd of sunbathers.

He ran into the water, splashing, laughing.

A wave came and he threw himself into it, letting it wash over him, feeling the cool rush of water on his body, tasting the salt.

He scrabbled around in the ocean, falling over himself as the surf pushed him this way and that. He stumbled to his feet and shook the water from his ears. The sun burned his back.

He jumped into the next wave.

And the next.

And the next.

Annabelle put a tape in the stereo and started to shuck corn for the evening meal. The clear, sweet smell of the corn filled the kitchen as she separated the ears from the corn, brushed off the cornsilk, lay the shucked corn aside. The ocean's rhythm was a steady backdrop to the gentle music, to the sunlight that glazed the hot, sticky afternoon, to the ocean scent that filled the air, to the quiet *cherish the day yes love it is all we have nothing else nothing more just this corn and we all thought it was indigestion couldnt breathe arms in the air lie down call an ambulance hes dead somalia he couldnt survive poor daddy i miss you*

One ear was bad. She'd missed checking it at the market and made a disgusted face. The kernels small and brown, some missing, some rotted. Take it back or throw it out? She put it aside and started on the next ear *that greg fat slob lee will take up with anybody poor girl seems the worse they are the more she wants them good old edward did it to her all right good old uncle ed hit her like a slow bullet should have hit him harder that bastard showing himself to me good thing i had that spatula handy got him out of there fast never told anyone too scared to tell who would believe me then he did it to lee all those years made her suck disgusting bullet proof soul thats what we all need bullet proof souls oh god dear god the way she dresses selling herself eds fault*

The corn done, Annabelle pressed the loosely packed trash down into its container, not wanting to waste any space in the garbage bag. She opened the refrigerator and took out the three packages of chicken drumsticks, six in each, total of eighteen *enough for tomorrow wish jason had someone to invite over no friends out here just here a week each year not much time to get to know people still you can try he doesnt try i dont think he tries at all spends all that time writing that science fiction stuff i never see wonder what its about sex all they think about*

The music stopped and Annabelle went to turn over the tape. When she returned to the chicken she opened the packages and carefully disposed of the wrappings, then put the large wooden cutting board on the counter. She rinsed the chicken parts thoroughly, dried them with paper towel, and put them in the big glass baking dish. Lee liked to line the dish with foil when she cooked to make the clean up easier but Annabelle, being more frugal, preferred to wash an unlined dish than to waste aluminum foil.

She used a marinade prepared from soy sauce, garlic, and hot peppers. Everyone liked it spicy. Annabelle took a measuring spoon from the drawer and dipped it in the marinade, then poured it over the chicken.

The door opened, bringing a flash of light. "Hi, ma." It was Jason, in from the beach or from wherever he had been. He was shirtless and his face and shoulders were red from the sun.

"Jason, what happened? You look burned."

"I'm okay."

He went to his room and shut the door *now that was a conversation i wonder what he does all day by himself wandering around looks so red i hope he didnt get too much sun doesnt find it easy to make friends wonder who he got that from maybe its a gene everythings a gene these days hope he takes care of himself doesnt go swimming have to say that to him so sensitive if i so much as say anything these days he has a fit jason there is so much in the world to be careful of*

Annabelle finished with the marinade and covered the chicken with sheets of paper towel. It was ready for the oven. Or the grill. Lee liked to grill but the fire made Annabelle nervous. She didn't like the way the flames shot up, afraid the eaves would catch fire. Annabelle put the covered chicken in the refrigerator and cleaned the cutting board and utensils she had used, then brought out the lettuce.

Three types for three tastes. Romaine, Leaf, and Boston. She did the Romaine first, tearing off the crisp leaves and rinsing them in the white plastic salad spinner she had put in the sink. Sandy grit ran into the drain. When the leaves were washed she turned the spinner handle to dry them, then tore them and put them into the large salad bowl *good thing he likes lettuce good for the bowels best thing for you what does he eat anyway grabs pizza here a snack there soon be back at work wonder whats happening at the company did jim debug my program wish i knew what was going on there damn thing so many variables cant keep track of them all that damn help file a mess to put together something new to learn i think im getting too old for this stuff all the young kids pick it up in a minute but then they mess it up too so whats the difference besides if i didnt do this what would i do have to make money somehow thank god i have this*

She put the Romaine aside and cleaned the Leaf lettuce. Its soft leaves contrasted with the Romaine. Three types of taste. She creased a leaf between her fingers. It was fresh *have to send money to mamas home next week god it goes so fast how long can i keep her there a nice place but whats the next step down i guess thats the next step for all of us*

Jason came out of his room and passed through the kitchen. He had put on a clean tee-shirt and changed into his shorts.

"What's for dinner?"

"Chicken with spicy sauce, salad, corn."

"Sounds good."

"Would you like to ask somebody over?"

"I don't know anybody, ma."

"Don't you get lonely."

"It's okay."

"What do you do all day."

"Hang out. It's okay, ma."

"I worry about you."

"Ma, it's okay. You listen to too much Sade."

"I like her."

"It's sad."

"Sometimes I like sad."

"I'm going out."

"Where?"

"Around."

"Be careful. Your face is burned, did you put on lotion?"

"Sure, ma. See you later."

The door slammed behind him and she watched as he mounted his bike and rode off *be careful be careful dont let anything happen like bobby*

Annabelle finished the Leaf lettuce and did the Boston. Once all the greens were in place she opened the box of croutons and scattered a few handfuls into the salad bowl. She found a tin of anchovies in one of the cabinets above the sink and put it on one side of the counter for later *nice caesar dressing with this perfect love that fishy taste but no raw egg glad they have this good bottled stuff watch out for salmonella eggs chickens damn things diseased the way they farm chickens its a shame the poor birds cooped up living to be eaten i guess bugs eat us eventually maybe jasons right im too morbid too sad listening to too much sad music i feel like crying sometimes whats the point*

Annabelle made room for the salad bowl in the refrigerator. The music stopped again, leaving the room quiet. Annabelle sighed, as if to fill the void.

She checked the time. 5:47. Clouding up. Annabelle wondered when they would eat and how to time the chicken. It would take at least an hour, that would bring them to nearly seven. She liked to eat early but Lee preferred later dining, sometimes as late as nine or ten. Annabelle turned over the tape. She couldn't help it. She liked sad, quiet music. Always had.

The music played and Annabelle went out on the deck *labor day tomorrow another fall already holidays coming up soon enough what will i get jason what does he want i dont even know this year dont have much money anyway maybe just a game or two for his omega wonder where pod attack is what do you buy a fourteen year old wish his father was here damn gin not easy raising a boy by yourself hard to talk about things hope they taught him about sex at school aids oh my god what a curse wear condoms hope hes heard the message who can i get to talk to him make sure maybe i should no i cant too embarrassing make it all a mess for him maybe i should call his doctor zweifeld ask him to talk to him maybe arrange an appointment a check up before school starts have the doctor look at him say do you know about aids that kind of thing good idea when we get back ill call him cost a bit this is important*

A seagull squawked, startling Annabelle out of her thoughts. The fat bird landed on the roof of the house across the way and stood there, surveying the scene like a king looking down from his castle. The gull cried out a few more times before quieting down.

Annabelle gazed at the beach. The lifeguards had left for the day, leaving their tall white towers lying on the sand, pulled back toward the line of dunes that separated the beach from the houses. People were returning from the beach, looking like pack animals with their chairs and blankets and towels and umbrellas and babies and lotions and books and newspapers and sand toys and frisbees and little rubber footballs and all the rest of everything they needed to survive a day on the shore.

Annabelle felt a twinge in her stomach as she wondered where Jason had gone. She went back inside and returned to her work. A few minutes later Annabelle heard footsteps coming up the ramp, then the sound of a beach chair being propped against the side of the house. Lee opened the door.

"Hi. Doing dinner already?" Lee asked.

"It relaxes me," said Annabelle. "I'm finally starting to feel settled and we have to leave."

"Isn't that always the way," said Lee. "Did you have fun?"

"I don't think I know what that word means."

Lee dropped her beach bag on the deck and came inside.

"You are awfully serious most of the time."

"Being a single mother can make you that way."

"I guess so." Lee picked a crouton out of the box and crunched it between her teeth. She saw the anchovies.

"Caesar salad?"

Annabelle nodded.

"It's still my favorite. Thank you."

"Thanks for having us," said Annabelle.

"You don't have to thank me for that," said Lee. "I'm always happy to see you two."

Annabelle started cleaning up from her dinner preparations. "I hate bringing this up again," she said, "but are you going to visit mother? We could go together."

Lee had another crouton.

"Lee?"

"I find it difficult."

"So do I. But she's our mother."

"She doesn't know that."

"But I do. We do."

"There's no communication."

"How do you know? Something may be getting through to her."

Lee had a final crouton and pushed the box over to Anna.

"Get these away," Lee said.

Anna took the box and closed it. "Will you come?"

"I'll think about it, Anna. I really will."

Jason replayed the blowjob over and over as he rode the Ross from boardwalk to boardwalk. Images of his aunt flooded his mind, of how she had taken the Snake, touched it where only Jason had ever touched it, played with it like a toy, kissed and licked it and sucked and sucked and swallowed its essence to drain it of its strength, to tame it.

When he came out of his reverie, he found himself at Marshall, near the party house.

There was no music but two people were slow dancing on the deck, moving silent in the late summer afternoon like clouds drifting across the sky. They slumped against each other, shuffling their feet in time to an inner tune. Jason wondered if they were both hearing the same song.

Jason rode all the way to the bay on Marshall, then turned left on Bay Walk to Gilbert, then took Gilbert to Midway, where he turned right. When he reached Marine, he turned left to the beach. He thought back on the events of the week. Phil showing up on the beach. Finding the Resurrection Stone. Asking it for a blowjob and getting it. He wondered if the stone had made it happen, then dismissed the idea. It was just an old stone, he thought, of little use and not even good for killing snakes. An old broken stone. There was no God.

When he reached the beach, Jason stopped and checked out the crowd then turned the bike around and headed back to the bay. Once there, he turned left and rode to Navy. When he reached Vern's place he wondered what had happened to the bike man. The shop was closed, the house quiet. There were no neighbors around to ask. Vern had vanished. Commanded a ship in the Pacific. Fought the Japs. Killed the enemy. Won the war. Now lying somewhere, dying or dead. Who wins in life? Nobody.

Jason rode back to the bay and past the stores. Anthony's blood, the color of rust, dyed the concrete walk outside the liquor store. Kids played in the bay under the watchful eyes of their mothers. The Island Mart bustled with activity. Jason stopped for an ice cream, a peach cone with walnut topping, and sat on the dock looking out over the bay.

He wondered if he would ever grow up or if he would die young like Allie Grant. He wondered if he would ever get away from his mother. He wondered if he would ever see Carol again. Most of all, he wondered about his aunt and what she had done. He wanted to tell someone because if he didn't, he would begin to think it never happened, that it had been a dream. Telling would make it real. But he had no one to tell. Certainly not Phil. And Jason couldn't write it down. If anyone found it, there would be trouble. He thought there was probably a law against what his aunt had done. Corrupting a minor. He could use more of such corruption.

Jason finished his cone and got back on the Ross. He rode the concrete walk to Coral, then made a right and drove to the beach past the houses hidden behind the thick tall grass. He heard a warble and saw a cardinal perched on the branch of a tree, its color brilliant. The wind moved slow through the branches and the bird's fiery feathers blazed. Jason stopped.

The bird flew off. Jason waited a few moments, then drove on. He turned onto Midway, passing St. Paul's Church. It was considered something of a miracle building, having survived several hurricanes and a fire since its construction in the fifties. Its lawn sprinkler sprayed the walkway as well as the grass and Jason drove through the cooling shower. He pedaled hard to get up speed for coasting, then rested his feet on the frame to glide like a seagull on a current of air.

Jason all of a sudden felt energetic and pedaled hard, heading north. He had a plan. He would ride back to Marshall along Midway, then go to Bay Walk and take the concrete to Coral, turn and go back to Midway, then do each of the walks again as he had just done them, from the beach to the bay. It was to be his last time here for a year and he wanted to take it all in, every bit of the island he could see from his blue Ross.

He rode like the wind through the last afternoon of summer.

After dinner, while Jason was helping clean up and while his mother was outside taking the air, Aunt Lee whispered to him.

"Come to my room later."

Jason almost dropped the glass he was rinsing.

"One o'clock," she said, then went back to clearing the table. Jason checked the clock on the wall. 10:43. He would go crazy by one. Crazy. His mother came in.

"Lee, my goodness, you gave me so much wine at dinner I think I'll sleep till Christmas."

"It's your last night here," Aunt Lee said. "It called for a celebration."

"Well, I'm going to try to stay up for the news. I want to see where Eric's going. Then I'm off to bed."

At eleven his mother was watching the news and Jason was in the shower, soaping and scrubbing himself more than he'd ever done in his life. He cleaned places he had never thought about cleaning before and had to restrain himself from rubbing the Snake more than he needed to get it clean. He didn't come out until nearly half past eleven. The women were watching the late weather report.

"…may veer eastward by morning but at this point a hurricane watch is in effect for coastal areas. Expect high tides and flooding starting after dawn. Rain will be in excess of six inches and tides will be ten to twelve feet above normal if Eric strikes."

"Are we safe here?" his mother asked.

"The worse that can happen is that we evacuate," said Aunt Lee, glancing up at Jason wrapped in his shower towel.

"Evacuate?" said Jason.

"The ferries will take us out if there's trouble," his aunt said. "Nothing to worry about."

Jason went to the door and peered out. "Seems quiet right now."

"It's on the way," his mother said. "I don't like it."

"Could veer off," said Aunt Lee. "They said that."

"I hope so," said Annabelle. She yawned. "I can't keep my eyes open. I'm going to bed." She said good night to Jason.

"I'm taking a shower," said Aunt Lee.

Jason blushed and hurried to his room. His balls itched and he wanted to pull on Snake until he came but knew that would be stupid, the stupidest thing he might ever do in his life. He decided to look at *Wide Open Legs*.

For the next hour, Jason turned pages, remembering how his aunt had posed for him in her new bathing suit, how she had let him touch her, taken off his trunks, spread his legs, licked his balls, sucked him, drank his cum, and loved it. Snake wanted more.

At twelve-thirty he had to get out of his room. Jason opened the door quietly. Light showed under Aunt Lee's closed door but not under his mother's. Jason went out on the deck.

The day's heat had dissipated but it was still warm. A haze covered the moon and few stars shone. Jason searched for Orion, knowing it was early to see much of his favorite constellation. He thought he made out the red Betelgeuse low on the horizon, but wasn't sure. Rigel would be much too far south to see at this hour. Shines 55,000 times brighter than the sun, 900 light years away. Something Greg undoubtedly knew.

Music played here and there, marking the final parties of summer, Labor Day parties. Jason wondered what Carol was doing but when he checked her house, all was dark.

Frustrated, restless, impatient, Jason went back inside. He took a drink of water and went to his room. He put *Wide Open Legs* back in *PC* magazine and into his drawer. If he saw one more picture he would cum in his shorts.

At one o'clock Jason, heart pounding, legs weak, went to his aunt's room.

The door was open a crack but the room was dark. Jason peered in, wondering if his aunt had forgotten him and fallen asleep, perhaps to dream about Greg. Then he heard a whisper.

"Come in."

Aunt Lee opened the door and took his hand, pulling him inside and shutting the door behind him. Her strawberry perfume filled the air.

She turned on a lamp that lit with a soft pink glow, an incandescence that transformed the pearls of the choker she was wearing into a delicate string of small moons, each reflecting the muted light. She had on her white silk panties and a satiny white bra that barely contained her breasts. She sat him down on the bed, propping him against a pillow, then sat next to him.

"You know what happened this afternoon?"

He nodded. Snake rose. She rubbed his thigh.

"That was playing. This is sex." She brushed her hair back. "I gave your mother so much wine she'll sleep through anything. It's just you and me."

Jason had trouble breathing. Rain pelted on the roof and against the window.

Hard rain.

Blue Shirt Files—2009.9.BG7

Before I could draw the gun, Archie lifted a small tube and aimed a light into my eyes, a strobe that flashed faster than I could think.

"You've been programmed," I heard Archie say. "The goddamn Glands Biochips."

My body sagged and my hand left the gun. I was beginning to take back control of my mind and body. Thank God (not that there was a God) for Archie, the best hacker I'd ever known. I gave him 1000 more points toward Lifetime Master.

"How did you know?" I asked.

He shut off the light and examined my eyes.

"You had the Stare. Can't miss it. You're okay now. Strobe burns it out. They keep it a secret, but a few of us know."

"Come inside," I said. We went in. Archie's eyes widened as I carefully unloaded the bomb and detonator.

"Bunny Glands," I said. "Programmed me to kill her husband."

"Homer Glands? Why?"

"She wanted it all, I guess. His money, his empire. That's usually the way it is. She set both of us up real nice. Had me thinking he wanted her dead, had him thinking I'd kidnapped her. Figured we'd kill each other off and she'd be free of him and whatever I knew wouldn't matter."

"What a woman," Archie said with grudging admiration.

"And there's more," I went on. "She said there's a flaw in the chip."

Archie nodded. "The deaths. Brain burn-out. After four years, the brain goes."

I got scared. "I've got those things inside me."

"I'm sorry." What else could Archie say?

"All right," I said. "Can't do anything about that now. I'm going over to Homer's place the way I said I would. Got to see how this plays out."

"Sounds dangerous."

"Not as dangerous as when I had this," I said, pointing at the now defused D-5. I winked at Archie. His ugly ghost-like face had never looked so good.

"Thanks, guy," I said. "That was a close one. You were nearly dead."

"I didn't think you were reaching for a lollipop back there," he said. "When you get programmed, they don't like you to break free."

I nodded. "You're right about that." I took off my shirt and wrapped my Permavest around me. It would stop anything that came from a gun. The problem was, the heat made it unbearable to wear and I used it only when it seemed absolutely necessary. This was one of those times.

I put on my blue tee-shirt and checked my gun.

"Okay, I'm ready." I said. "Let's go."

We took the elevator down and shook hands before we parted.

I took a cab to Homer's office, Glands International, which occupied what used to be called Lincoln Center. His secretary let me in as soon as I said my name.

Homer was flanked by Pickett, Rattler, and Scone, and part of me wished I still had the bomb. But after Rattler took my gun they kept their distance.

A huge pile of Americash lay on Homer's desk.

"Here's your money," he said. "Now what about my wife?"

"I don't know where she is," I said. "And if I did, I wouldn't sell her out."

"I thought we covered that before," he said. "Where the fuck is she?"

"She injected me with biochips and programmed me to kill you," I said. "That bullshit I gave you over the phone was just to get in here, so I could blow you to kingdom come."

Rattler, Scone, and Pickett looked nervous. Homer just got pissed.

"Bunny wouldn't do anything of the sort. I'm tired of you, Blue Shirt. Rattler, get this garbage out of here. Permanently."

Rattler and his buddies came toward me but I moved first, lashing a kick into Rattler's hand that sent his gun flying across the room. I used my advantage of speed and surprise to smash kicks into Pickett and Scone, knocking them to different corners of Homer's office, then put a fist into Rattler's balls that took him out.

"That's enough."

It was Homer. He had an automatic pointed at me.

"Stay right where you are," he said. "When these three wake up, they'll finish what they were hired to do."

I didn't look forward to that, but there wasn't anything I could do. He had the drop on me and was too far away for my karate. Just then, the door opened.

It was Bunny.

Homer was as surprised as I was. Why would she be here if I was supposed to blow this place to smithereens? Then I got it. Bunny had been monitoring my chips and knew when her programming got fried. This was her backup plan.

"Bunny, where've you been? This lunatic says you're trying to kill me."

"Would I kill the goose that lays the golden eggs?" she cooed. "Besides, I love you. What's going on here?"

"He says you injected him with biochips, programmed him to come here and off me."

"I know about James Unger," I said.

That got to Homer. His sneer of control turned to a look of concern.

"Unger? What the fuck do you know about him?"

"He doesn't know anything, honey," Bunny said. "Finish him."

"And I know about the mole on Bunny's thigh," I said, playing my ace. "Way up on her thigh."

Homer turned red. He glared at Bunny as if he might shoot her. In the corner, Scone moaned. The boys were coming around.

"How the fuck does he know that?" he demanded to know. "How the fuck does he know about that?"

For the first time since I'd met her, Bunny didn't know what to say. So I filled in for her.

"She seduced me," I said. "When I was asleep, she shot me full of chips, then programmed me over the phone. Just the way Unger was programmed to bring down that airplane and kill Secretary Wallace." I had just made the connection and threw it in for shock value. Wallace had been opposed to one of Homer's little projects, implanting biochips into F-117 pilots. Once Wallace was dead, Homer had been able to go ahead with his plan. It had made him millions of government money.

"He knows fucking everything!" Homer exploded. "This is all fucked up! Who has he told, who else knows? Bunny, what the fuck are you up to?"

Bunny started to cry. It took Homer by surprise, her sudden show of vulnerability. She reached into her purse as if going for a tissue, but I knew better. She pulled out a small semi-automatic, lifted it straight out in front of her and shot Homer in the face. Pickett had recovered enough to get his own gun out and fired several rounds into Bunny. I grabbed for Homer's gun as he fell and moved to the side of his desk.

Pickett had used explosive shells that tore Bunny apart, blasting holes in her body from inside. I fired at Pickett's head, killing him instantly.

Scone fired a shot at me, missing. I returned fire and finished him off. That left only Rattler, who by now was on his feet and coming at me, gun blazing.

I took three shots in my Permavest before I could return fire. I got lucky and put one right between his eyes. Rattler went down, finished for good.

In the distance I heard sirens. Homer's secretary must have called the cops when she heard the shooting start. I knew there would be lots of questions to answer. The half-meg of Americash on Homer's desk looked real good and for a moment I thought about picking it up and getting out of there. The money would never be missed. No one would know.

Check that. I would. And it wasn't worth it. I took a deep breath and looked out the window. The butterflies still danced in front of my eyes and now I had biochips in my brain that would kill me in four years unless I could find a cure. And I wasn't the only one.

Thousands of people had the implants. How could they be helped?

The sirens drew closer. I'd tell Lt. Harper the whole story. Then I'd go home. Maybe have some scotch. Maybe watch a flick on TV.

Maybe ride the F train to Queens.

Eric

deep quiet   ocean

                                 time

                                         purpose

roll   sway

                      h   e   a   v   y

s   w   e   l   l

t o s s

                  t o s s

                                    t o s s

    currents pound

sun

air

energy

movement

up

w   i n   d

up

up

warm   up
water v a   p   o   r

stir

stir

gather

energy

turn   time
time

        turn   in time

toss

                              toss

toss

deep near Sargasso

                              gulfweed   meadow

float   float   warm

sun

                              air

e   x   p   a
n   d

                      s

        t

            i

r

c o o l c o n d e ns e
           co ol   c on de nse
      cool   condense

                                        turn

turn
                        spin

                                        spin

gather build turn condense dr op l e t s   dro pl e ts   d rop lets
      droplets

                  crystals
v a p o r   rise condense cool
spin   turn   spin   turn

                                 heavy drops
                    rise
        small
                    rise
raindrops
      thicken clouds   darken cumulonimbus
flash   thunder   FLASH!

      w i nd w   i   n   d

flash w in d thunder flash thunder wi n d
move move move   follow sun   follow sun
turn spin move   flash FLASH flash

move
GROW
                  G R O W

                                        G R O W

fasterfaster   turn   spin
                                       rain move follow sun
whirl whirl   flashfasterfaster thunder
warm water
                             draw up funnel inside clouds grow mass
      gather gather more move west warm water   warm
water drink   huge clouds pour back down drink
warm cold warm cold wet wind rise hard rain down can rain lift high high
spin turn whirl fastfastfaster west west west west
west

          calm eye

push over ocean flash west   follow sun

over sweet warm water thunder whirl faster fasterfasterfaster

more more raindrops heavy heavy lift fall lift fall more slow   drink
more dark
          water become larger heavy stronger want
more more west stronger stronger
          stronger
rain down spin turn spin turn
                                        wait over warm water
wait

move follow sun into night night into dark west
                    to pour down
on that huge place that waits
                                        dry that place ahead that
must find again whirl fury down
on that which waits always waits
until it is no more but a shadow of time
destiny
                    to join
push drive more more west
always always   always   FLASH!
to
                    rain

down

                              HARD   storm   surge
rain
                    rain   rain
                              rain   rain   rain
rain   rain rain rain rainrainrainrainrainrain rainrainrainrainrainrain
rainrainrainrainrainrainrainrainrain**rain**rainrainrainrainrainrainrainrain
RAINRAINRAINRAINRAINRAINRAINRAINRAINRAINRAIN
RAINRAINRAINRAINRAINRAINRAINRAINRAINRAINRAIN

Labor Day

"Jason, get up! We've got to leave the island!"

His mother's shrill voice cut through Jason's sleep like a blade. She hovered over him, wide-eyed, hair uncombed, frantic.

"It's the storm," she said. "It's here."

Outside, trees thrashed and the ocean rumbled as if the entire Atlantic were about to rise out of its bed and fall on them. His window rattled and its panes pressed inward as if straining to burst into the house.

Jason got up and shut the window, his feet immediately wet from puddles the storm had swept onto the floor.

"Get your things. I'll wake Lee," his mother said, rushing out. "They're leaving in half an hour."

Jason checked his clock. 9:54 AM.

"Who's leaving in half an hour?"

"They're evacuating the island," his mother replied. "Last boat's ten-thirty."

"Last boat?"

"Then the storm'll be too bad for boats."

Terrified at imagining his watery death, Jason went to the bathroom and had diarrhea. From the television in the living room he could hear the strident warnings.

"…in effect as Hurricane Eric moves inland. The storm took a surprising turn toward the coast last night and is expected to cause heavy damage…"

As if to confirm the report, a blast of wind blew open the outside bathroom door, slamming it into a plastic laundry hamper. Jason almost jumped off the toilet seat. He peered out into a screaming darkness and his bowels moved again. A tree branch smacked into the side of the house.

He heard his mother. "Jason, are you all right? What was that noise?"

"I'm okay, ma. The door blew open."

"Do you want me to come in?"

"No."

Jason finished on the toilet and closed the door, getting soaked in the process. He dried himself hurriedly, wanting to think about the night with his aunt but afraid to think of anything but survival. He went to his room to get the laptop and brought it to the kitchen to wrap in plastic bags.

"Good idea," his mother said as she watched him work. He put the laptop in a plastic bag that he sealed with tape. Then the computer went into its case and the case went into another bag. It would take a deluge to get through that, and, as the house shook from the storm's violence, a deluge is what they were having.

The television went on about the storm.

"…torrential rains and flood tides. Residents in low-lying coastal areas are directed to head for higher ground and mobile home dwellers have been ordered to gather their belongings and leave as Eric closes in.

"The Governor earlier declared a state of emergency along the coastal areas and urged residents to make emergency preparations. Forecasters said Eric could bring 12 to 15 inches of rain and flood tides eight to ten feet higher than normal. Maximum sustained winds are 85 miles per hour."

"Where's Aunt Lee?" Jason asked.

"Getting ready," his mother said. "I'm packing food. Anything special you want?"

"No," said Jason. The thought of food made him ill.

"I shouldn't have had that wine. It put me out like a light. I woke up and saw the storm, turned on the TV."

Jason left the water-tight laptop in the kitchen and ran to his room. He passed Aunt Lee, dressed snugly in sweater and jeans. Over the sounds of the storm he could hear his mother and aunt talking as he packed.

"You don't seem too worried."

"If I worried about every little storm I'd be worried all the time."

Wind gusted. Garbage cans fell over.

"What happens if we don't make the boat?"

"Everybody makes the boat."

"Hurry," his mother called to him. "We've only got twenty minutes."

Jason ran to the kitchen with his bag.

"Do you have slickers?" his aunt asked.

"No," said Annabelle.

"It's okay. "You'll use garbage bags, the big ones. I'll fix them up for you. We do it all the time."

Jason wished they had slickers. Leaving in a garbage bag didn't appeal to him. He went back to his room to make sure nothing was left behind. Under the bed he found the trash bag with Pod Attack wrapped in it.

He grabbed it and ran to the kitchen, adding it to the pile of luggage. Now he had everything.

Except the Resurrection Stone.

In spite of his fear, in spite of the fact that he had no real belief that the stone had any magic or mystical properties, Jason knew that he had to take it with him. Knew with sudden unshakable certainty that he could not leave it behind.

Aunt Lee had prepared slickers for Jason and Anna by cutting head and arm holes in two 30-gallon black trash bags. Jason put his on and flew out the door. His mother called after him.

"You forgot your things!"

But Jason was already outside, the rain driving into him, the wind tearing at the protective bag. Here and there he saw people leaving, bright in their orange or yellow slickers, hunched down against the storm, dragging their wagons behind them, the luggage encased in plastic sheets or garbage bags, small caravans of alien travelers on the fearsome stormscape of a drowning planet in a dangerous galaxy.

Jason splashed through the sodden grass to the back of the house where conditions were swamp-like. His feet slipped out from under him and he fell, then scrambled to his hands and knees to search for the pieces of the stone, squinting his eyes to keep out the blinding rain. The ground felt alive, sucking at him, as if wanting to draw him under, like the soil of an evil cemetery in a horror story, a cemetery hungry for another victim, hungry for another helpless soul to feed the empty bellies of its gaunt inhabitants.

"Jason! Jason! We have to leave for the ferry!"

His mother sounded distant, hysterical. Then he heard his aunt.

"Jason! For once your mother's right. We've got to go."

Jason cursed, sinking into the mud as he crawled across the grass in his desperate search. The rain poured down, relentless, and furious bursts of wind tried to tear the garbage bag from him but he kept on, a madman on a desperate hunt. He had to find the Resurrection Stone. He had to.

"Jason!! Jason!!!"

He grabbed at something red and his fingers closed on it, only to discover it was a remnant of the snake he had killed. The feel of its slimy corpse sent a shock through his body and, without any conscious direction on his part, Jason's arm jerked in the air, flinging the remains far away. He gagged from the thought of the dead snake, gagged from the memory of crushing it, of bringing the Resurrection Stone down on it again and again until he had smashed the life out of the serpent, gagged from the realization that he had used the sacred artifact to wish for a blowjob and kill a snake. He wondered if he would be damned, wondered if he had already been damned to spend eternity on the edge of a hurricane, living this moment over and over, forever searching in the mud for the treasure he had thrown away and forever finding the rotting carcasses of dead snakes.

"Jason!" His mother's voice brought him back to reality. Jason shook the rain out of his eyes and started to search once more, sweeping his hands over the grass, feeling for the pieces of the stone.

The fire alarm howled, piercing the storm's furious roar with a long, eerie wail.

"Jason! The boat!!"

His fingers touched something hard, jagged on one side. Jason laughed as he picked up half of the stone. Its blood red color, accented by wetness, seemed darker than he remembered and Jason trembled. But not from the cold and the rain, rather from a power that emanated from the relic. A power he had not felt earlier. An incredible power.

Jason stuffed the half Resurrection Stone into a pocket and hunted for the other piece, scrabbling in the muddy grass. Jason by now was soaked through with rain and covered with mud, and resembled the Swamp Thing more than a teenager.

"Jason!!!"

"Coming!!" he screamed back, not sure if he could be heard over the wind and the siren. From above came a ripping, tearing sound and Jason saw a tree branch crash down into a power line, tearing it from its pole. The line fell in a slow lazy loop that landed right in front of him and began a wild jerky dance, an electric cobra hissing and spitting sparks as it twisted and turned on the grass.

Jason kept an eye on the line as he swept the ground with his hands again, certain that the other piece of the Stone was close by. But it was not and Jason wound up scuttling in the mud like a crab, moving from side to side, searching, searching, searching.

A hand touched his shoulder.

"Jason! Watch out for that line! Do you want to get killed?" It was Aunt Lee.

His tears mixed with the rain on his face. "I've got to find something!"

"It's too dangerous. And there's no more time. Get up."

She grabbed Jason by the shoulders and pulled him to his feet. He sobbed and Aunt Lee hugged him protectively, leading him to the house.

"You're soaked. What's so important out here?"

"Something I lost," Jason blubbered. "I have to find it."

"Not now," his aunt said. "Your mother's very upset. I made her go on ahead with one of the wagons. I'll get you towels from the house to wrap yourself in."

Jason was too weak to resist. His body trembled from the beating the storm had given him and he let his aunt drag him along, hopeless at ever finding what he had once had.

Then he cried out as something sharp dug into the heel of his sneaker. He lifted his foot and saw the second half of the Heart Stone.

Jason grabbed it and held it up for his aunt to see.

"Yes!!!" he crowed in triumph. "Yesss!!!"

"That's what you've been looking for?" Aunt Lee said in disbelief. "An old rock?"

"It's special to me," he said. "Let's go. Forget about the towels. I'm fine."

Jason and his aunt struggled across the rain-soaked grass to the board-walk where the remaining wagon waited to be hauled to the ferry. The luggage was protected by a garbage bag whose loose corners snapped and fluttered in the wind like tethered bats. Jason grabbed the wagon's handle and started for the dock with his aunt.

The wind whipped them from the ocean side of the island with a sting-ing salt spray, while the rain pelted them from above without mercy. As they walked, they saw other stragglers leaving, luggage wrapped in plastic, bodies encased in slickers or trash bags, pets soggy, wagons waterlogged. Jason's feet squished in his rain-filled sneakers. He laughed.

He had the Stone!

The scene at the dock was chaos. The ferry, ominously named the *Island Ghost*, rocked as the storm lashed at it. People were hardly recogniz-able in their rain gear, although Jason saw George Wensel and his family along with a few other familiar faces. Jason had never paid much attention to the Wensel family and only vaguely recognized them now. George's wife clung to a boy of about twelve and to a girl of nine or ten with glasses.

Jason saw Carol with her parents, her father tall and stern, her mother tentative and afraid. Carol looked small and vulnerable, a wet bird lost and alone. Jason wanted to comfort her, wanted to hold her, wanted to make everything all right for her. Then he heard a loud argument coming from the direction of the ferry. It was Greg and two of the *Ghost*'s crew. Jason asked a kid next to him what was happening.

"They won't let that guy take his dogs on the boat," the kid said.

"Why not?" Jason asked. "People have dogs."

Indeed, there were many dogs waiting to board, their owners carrying the small ones or holding umbrellas over the larger ones to protect them from the rain, sometimes seeming to care more about their canines than their families.

"Not like those dogs," the kid said. "They're killers."

"Killed that small dog on the beach," a man volunteered.

"Some nut kid turned them loose," said another.

"Can't have vicious dogs on the boat," a woman said.

"Storm's bad. They say it's going to hit full force," someone else put in.

"There wasn't much warning." The crowd seemed to Jason on the edge of panic.

"It's been on the weather for days."

"Yesterday was so nice."

"Too hot. You could tell something was coming."

"Lookit that boat."

"They ever lose any of 'em?"

"Nineteen thirty-eight. The big one."

"Nothing to worry about."

"Jason."

"Yeah, ma."

"Are you okay?"

"They're not letting Greg's dogs on."

Jason saw Aunt Lee talking to the ferry people while Greg stood nearby, patting Castor and Pollux on their flanks to quiet them. Aunt Lee was talking loud and gesturing but the ferry people seemed unmoved. She turned away from them to speak with Greg.

Jason saw Carol look his way and waved to her. She waved back. A sharp gust of wind smacked the ferry hard against the dock, sounding a noise like a thunderclap and making the lines from the boat to the dock stretch and creak.

Aunt Lee returned.

"What's happening with the dogs?" Jason asked.

"He's going to try to hire a boat."

Jason saw Greg leading Castor and Pollux toward a small motor boat tied up at the dock, tossing in the violent water. A man in a yellow slicker stood on the dock near the boat.

"At least there'll be more room for the people," Annabelle said as she watched the scene. "Jason, did you go to the bathroom before we left?"

"For god's sake, Anna, leave him alone," said Lee.

"I'm his mother, not you. Jason?"

"Yeah, ma."

"Good. Who knows when we'll get another chance."

"On the other side," Lee said. "That's where."

Jason saw Greg shake hands with the man in the slicker, who then got into the boat. Greg followed him and pulled at the dogs' leashes but Castor and Pollux held back.

"He's crazy to go in that boat," said Lee. "It's too small for this storm. I can't believe Hopper's doing it."

"Hopper?" Jason asked.

"Ed Hopper. Fisherman. Been here forever. Probably thinks he's seen it all and it can't hurt him."

Jason watched Greg trying to coax the dogs on board. Castor put a tentative paw on the boat's railing. The storm raged around them. Everyone on the dock watched the boarding.

"Looks dangerous," Jason said.

"It is," said his aunt. "Very dangerous."

Greg pulled Castor into the boat and now talked to Pollux, tugging his leash and coaxing him forward. As the big dog stepped down to the railing, a wave smashed into the boat, tilting it and throwing the dog off balance. His foot slipped and was crushed between the boat and the dock as they struck together. Pollux let out a horrible yelp and Greg pulled him into the boat. Then the *Island Ghost*'s fog horn sounded and a crewman yelled "All aboard! All Aboard!!" The crowd surged forward.

"Stay close."

"Yeah, ma."

It was easier said than done. Everybody wanted to be first, and the drenched mass was not in a good humor. Jason's mother stood next to him, inseparable as a hawk from her brood. She turned a vicious eye on anyone who tried to get between them and used her elbows to back up her expression. Lee tried to keep close but was separated from them.

The boat rocked as Jason boarded. The swaying almost knocked him off his feet but he steadied himself on a railing. The stairway to the upper deck had been closed off to keep the rain out of the lower areas, so the passengers that would ordinarily have spread out over both decks of the boat was jammed onto one. And, in spite of the crew's efforts, water leaked in from everywhere as the fierce storm slammed into them. People fought over small things.

"Jesus, get your foot off…"

"…can't breathe."

"Don't they know…"

"…water everywhere."

"…really going to take this boat out?"

Jason's mother clutched him to her breast.

"Are you all right?"

"I'm okay, ma. Really. Okay." He wasn't, but he wanted to calm her.

"Where's Lee?"

"Here somewhere."

"Where?"

"I don't know. She's all right. We're all going to be all right. Ma, let go. You're crushing me." Reluctantly, Annabelle let him go.

The boat swayed to one side and Jason, his mother, and everyone else would have lost their footing if they hadn't been packed together. The boat pushed off from the dock with a horrible grating noise. Jason got a look at the dock and saw it bob crazily, then realized that it was the ferry that was bobbing, struggling in the water's pounding currents.

He saw Greg's small boat about fifty feet away, with Greg, Ed Hopper, and even the dogs hunkered down in life jackets. They bumped through the choppy swells like a toy boat being swamped in a bathtub by a laughing three-year old. The little boat lifted almost out of the water as a big wave hit it and appeared about to capsize, then miraculously righted itself at the last second. A sheet of rain blew across the window, obscuring Jason's view.

From under the ferry's deck the engines clanked and roared as they worked to move the laden boat through the rough water. The acrid stench of oil, diesel fuel, and exhaust filled the passenger space and, because all the windows had been shut to keep out the storm, soon had everyone choking and gasping for air.

Jason looked at his mother, her face distorted with terror. He had never seen her so frightened in his life. If he still thought of her as God, as children usually regarded their parents, that thought would have ended now. But his mother had lost her divinity years before. Jason wanted to comfort her.

"Ma, don't worry. It's going to be all right."

She stood motionless, not replying, her eyes seeing a horrifying abyss, an abyss that seemed to be coming closer and closer with an intention as inevitable and final as the setting of the sun.

Music played in Jason's mind.

love

love for everyone

Across the boat he saw Aunt Lee wave to them.

"Look, ma, Aunt Lee. Over there. Look!"

His mother turned in the direction he pointed, not seeing.

"It's going to be all right," Jason repeated. He wondered if she heard him.

oh oh oh oh

i promise

They motored across the bay for what seemed like hours but was in fact only five minutes when the crew started passing out life jackets. An announcement over the crackling PA system made it official.

"As a safety precaution, the crew is distributing life jackets. This does not mean we are in any danger. Make sure your children's jackets are in place before putting on your own. Thank you."

"Oh, God," his mother sobbed. "We're going to drown."

The music left his mind and Jason shivered at his mother's words. He touched the pieces of the Heart Stone, one in each pocket of his jeans. They warmed his hands. Jason tried to stay calm by soothing his mother.

"Ma, nobody's going to drown. He said it's a precaution. Just in case."

Too late he knew he had said too much.

"In case of what?" his mother asked. "In case the boat goes down, that's what they mean."

"The boat's not going down," he said.

As if to mock his words, a blast of wind pushed the boat to one side. People screamed, his mother among them. Water leaked through whatever cracks it found and the waves rolled the boat back and forth.

A hideous, desperate scream shocked the air. Everywhere heads turned, necks craned to find the source of the frightening sound. It came again, the shriek of a damned soul being thrust through the gates of Hell into an eternity of unspeakable horror, and all eyes were drawn by that ghastly cry to the staircase leading to the top deck. There, George Wensel, clad in a blue slicker, struggled on his hands and knees up the wet, slippery stairs, bellowing like an animal in its death throes. His wife cried out.

"Oh my God! Stop him somebody, stop him!"

His son and others reached for him but it was too late. George stood at the top of the stairs and braced his back against the closed hatchway door. He pushed up with a strength available only to the heroic or the mad and the hatch flew open, letting rain and sea water pour in and cascade down the stairs like Niagara. He scrambled the last few feet to the top deck, disappearing into the storm. The hatchway was thrown shut behind him by the wind with a sound like the gate of a tomb closing.

"Claustrophobic," Jason heard someone say.

"Had to get out."

"Can't blame him."

"Feel that way myself."

"He'll drown."

"Poor man."

"Not him, he's got millions."

"Prices he charges."

"Bastard."

"Fucker."

"Let him drown."

George's wife tried to get up the stairs but her fellow passengers held her back. She cried out for the life of her man.

"Oh, God, don't let him drown! Somebody save him. Don't let him drown!!"

The boat lurched and Jason staggered into the people next to him, then saw a blue form plummet past a window. George's wife also saw it. Her cry pierced the tumult of storm, engines, and shouted conversations.

"He's overboard, ohmygod, he's in the water, overboard, help him, help him, please!!"

Jason's stomach turned as he thought of George Wensel floundering in the stormy bay, water filling his nose, his mouth, pouring down his throat and into his stomach, his lungs. A dark cold salty death. He thought he would vomit.

what a life

The boat shuddered from a powerful blow to its prow. Jason lost his balance and slammed his head into a pole, almost losing consciousness. His mother grabbed him. Jason heard fragments.

"…hit something!"

"A small boat!"

"…man with the dogs!"

"…going down!"

"Water's coming in!"

"…sinking!!!"

The words startled Jason back to awareness. He squinted through the rain splattered window and saw Greg and the fisherman Hopper bobbing helpless in the heaving water, hanging onto splinters of their boat. The dogs were nowhere to be seen.

The PA crackled. "Secure your life jackets. If you should find yourself in the water, stay calm. We have radioed for help."

"We're going to die!" Jason's mother shrieked. "We're all going to die!!"

It was like yelling fire in a theater. Everyone went crazy, thrashing around, trying to see what was happening, trying to determine whether the boat was going down, looking for water lapping at their feet, securing their vests. Children cried, men cursed, women screamed. Jason saw Carol far across the boat. He wanted to call to her but she wasn't looking his way and there would be no chance of getting her attention in the uproar.

"You're bleeding."

An old man stood next to Jason, a man with piercing blue eyes.

Jason touched his hand to his temple and saw blood. He realized that he must have cut himself when he hit his head. In the ocean that would bring sharks. He hoped there were no sharks in the bay.

what a life

    what a life

        what a life

The boat listed to one side and everyone slid screaming in the direction of the tilt. Jason's heart froze. This was the end. His time had come. His head spun and he started to gag. Time elongated like a stretched elastic band. Sweat broke out on his brow and his heart palpitated. He couldn't breathe. The old man spoke again.

"It's going to be all right. I promise."

"Who are you?" Jason asked.

"Just another traveler," the man said. "Going home."

For Jason, time stopped.

His mind opened like a Chinese puzzle box coming apart at warp speed.

In the center of the box floated a universe the size of a pea.

Our universe.

Jason stood outside of it and within it at the same time.

Seeing all of it. Knowing all of it. Being all of it.

Freedom and power flowed through him. Exhilarated him.

Terrified him. Transformed him.

A loving warmth, a light, filled the center of his chest.

Jason *Knew*.

Tears filled his eyes.

Knew, not believed. *Knew*. As fact.

Immutable Fact.

Unquestionable Certainty.

Jason pushed toward the stairs that led to the upper deck, the stairs George Wensel had climbed just minutes before.

"Where're you going?" his mother called. He didn't answer.

"Jason, stop! Come back!!"

Jason kept going, the crowd separating before him like the Red Sea before Moses. As he climbed the stairs, the boat lurched but Jason held his balance. When he reached the top, he lifted one hand and thrust it against the hatch. The heavy wooden door swung straight up, opening for him and letting the rain pour in. The people below shouted in anger and fear. Jason climbed out onto the upper deck and faced the storm.

Around him was a dark wind, blowing sheets of heavy cold rain, shrouds of rain that made it almost impossible to see. In the pilot house, men in slickers waved at him to get below. The sound of the wind was as the sound at the center of a star, a cataclysm of energy, raging uncontrolled, limitless, the sound of life and death, birth and rebirth, chaos and creation, being and nonbeing.

Jason stood on the deck like a mountain, unmoved by the power of the storm. His hands steady and his nerves calm, Jason took the pieces of the Resurrection Stone from his pockets and lifted them above his head, fitting them together.

The pieces fused into one and glowed.

The wind howled in agony and a loose plank ripped from the deck, smashing into Jason's side. It shattered against him, cracking half his rib cage, but he did not feel it, did not move. A maelstrom of water leapt over the boat, pulling at Jason, sucking at him, trying to drag him down. A funnel cloud appeared from nowhere and tore across the deck, snapping up planks and hurling them at Jason, splintering them against his body and his head, tearing his flesh, but still he did not move, the Stone blazing like the sun but with a light that didn't burn.

"CEASE!!!" Jason shouted.

For a fraction of time, all was still. The wind did not blow, the rain did not fall, the water did not surge, the boat did not sway, the people did not shout. Then a bolt of blue-white lightning flashed from the highest point in the sky and washed over Jason, lighting him up like a star and lifting the Stone from his hands.

The Stone vanished as the lighting enveloped the boat in a soft radiance before slowly dissipating. The wind blew one last time, the tired breath of the defeated. Jason dropped to his knees.

And the rain ceased. And the waves calmed. And the clouds cleared. And the people quieted. And the sun came out as if the storm had never been.

And Jason looked into the clear heavens and cried.

And laughed.

And fell to the deck unconscious.

Clippings

Hurricane Eric Mysteriously Dissipates
Unexplained Phenomenon in Maryland
by Robert Lunt

FT. HAMILTON, Maryland—In an event that meteorologists have only been able to describe with words such as "unbelievable," "fantastic," and "miraculous" the passengers and crew of the ferry boat *Island Ghost* were saved from drowning off the coast of Cranberry Island yesterday when Hurricane Eric, with winds of up to 90 miles per hour, suddenly and rapidly dissipated at 11:06 in the morning.

Not only did Eric mysteriously leave Cranberry Island, but the storm, which had covered a 75.000 square mile area, broke up in only a matter of minutes everywhere, leaving a bright, clear day behind. According to Dr. William Frazer of the Naval Meteorological Center in Annapolis, storms of this magnitude "cannot possibly lose their force so quickly." It was, he went on to say, an "incredible phenomenon, unprecedented, one that we shall probably never see again."

Robert "Sandy" Sanderson, Pilot of the *Island Ghost*, was eyewitness to an event seemingly connected to the end of the storm. His story, however, only deepens the mystery. Sanderson reported that a boy, later identified as Jason Stern of New York City, came on deck in the violent weather and held his hands over his head. After that, events took place rapidly. Several planks tore up from the deck and smashed into the boy, yet he remained unmoved. Then a bolt of lightning burst from the sky, striking the boy and enveloping the boat. When the lightning passed, the storm cleared, and the boy collapsed on the deck.

"I've never seen anything like it," said Sanderson. "A man had already been washed overboard but the boy just stood there in the storm and got hit by lightning." The man Sanderson referred to was George Wensel, a Cranberry Island businessman later rescued from the bay. Two other men in a small boat that went down in the storm were also pulled from the water by the Coast Guard. The only fatalities were two dogs lost from the small boat.

It was after the lightning that the storm dissipated in a matter of seconds. Sanderson couldn't believe his eyes. "Suddenly the rain stopped, the wind died down, the clouds parted, and the sun came out. All in less than a minute."

Coast Guard rescuers soon reached the ferry and medivacked the Stern boy to Mercy Hospital in Ft. Hamilton along with the men pulled from the bay. Meteorologists are waiting to question the boy who has yet to recover consciousness and remains in guarded condition at the hospital with serious injuries to his head, face, and body as a result of being hit by flying debris during the storm. His mother, Annabelle Stern, was hospitalized for shock. The only family member available for comment was an aunt, Ms. Lee Henderson, a Baltimore sculptor.

Ms. Henderson reported that her sister and the boy had spent a week at her house on Cranberry Island. Nothing remarkable had happened and the boy had shown no signs of recklessness. He was, in fact, afraid of the water and his aunt could think of no reason why he would have gone to the top deck of the boat during a dangerous storm. No one had an explanation for his behavior.

Further south on Cranberry Island, Eric's fury vent itself in full force on the huge Colony condominium and caused the death of Kenneth Rose, a local entrepreneur responsible for the development of the resort property. Residents who did not evacuate took refuge on the upper stories while flood waters swept through the basement and first two floors of the Colony. Mr. Rose, who maintained that the Colony was "hurricane and flood proof," was discovered by rescue workers drowned in his second floor office.

*   *   *

Hurricane Boy Still In Coma
by Robert Lunt

FT. HAMILTON, Maryland—One week after an event that continues to astound and puzzle meteorologists, the boy at the center of the mystery remains in a coma in Mercy Hospital. The youth, fourteen-year old Jason Stern of New York City, is in serious condition with no signs of improvement. He is not on life support but is unable to move or speak and has not opened his eyes since being hospitalized.

His attending physician, Dr. Steve Gordon, a specialist in brain injuries, is confounded by the case. "The boy has no brain damage we can detect, there is no edema, no bleeding in the skull, no swelling. His MRI and CAT scans are clear, yet he can't regain consciousness." Dr. Gordon is waiting for a second opinion from a team of New York doctors arriving later this week to examine the youth.

The mystery surrounding the boy only intensifies the parallel mystery regarding the sudden dissipation of Hurricane Eric on Labor Day. The storm, with 90 mile per hour winds, had unleashed its fury on the coast of Maryland when, at 11:06 in the morning, it rapidly cleared. A spokesman for the Naval Meteorological Center in Annapolis, Dr. William Frazer, said that it is impossible for a storm of this magnitude to act in such a manner. Dr. Frazer went on to say it was "totally unprecedented" behavior for a storm and that its clearing was "like something out of the Ten Commandments, a miracle of Moses." The storm "literally disappeared" in a matter of minutes.

Meteorologists from around the world have flocked to Ft. Hamilton and its neighboring barrier reef and popular summer resort Cranberry Island to study the area and examine the storm data. At the time of the storm's clearing, the Stern youth was on the deck of a ferry boat evacuating vacationers from the island. Dr. Frazer said that a weather satellite had picked up an "unusual electrical disturbance" surrounding the ferry boat just prior to the hurricane's dissipation. Further investigation remains to be done, but there is conjecture that the boy and the clearing of the storm are linked. However, Prof. David Armstrong of the Naval Observatory, says that it is "preposterous" to think that the boy could have affected the storm. "It is not possible," he went on to say, "for a human being, and certainly not a fourteen-year old boy, to exert any influence over even a rain shower much less a hurricane." A multitude of questions remain but many of the answers lie locked inside the mind of a comatose boy.

        *   *   *

Hurricane Boy's Aunt To Wed
by Robert Lunt

FT. HAMILTON, Maryland—Six months after the still unexplained dissipation of Hurricane Eric off the coast of Maryland, the aunt of the comatose boy at the center of the mystery, Jason Stern, is to wed on Cranberry Island.

Ms. Lee Henderson, a sculptor and teacher who works in Baltimore and summers on Cranberry Island, is to marry Mr. Greg Lugan of Pittsburgh. The wedding is scheduled for Labor Day, according to Ms. Henderson, "as a tribute to my nephew."

The boy remains in a coma at New York Hospital, where he was transferred after a month in Mercy Hospital in Ft. Hamilton. The boy's mother, Mrs. Annabelle Stern, wanted her son closer to home, where arrangements are being made for his long-term care. Doctors have been unable to determine the cause of his coma nor have they been able to shake its death-like grip.

Ms. Henderson and Mr. Lugan will become year-round residents of Cranberry Island after the wedding. Ms. Henderson is relinquishing her Baltimore teaching position to work full time at her art. "I'm drawn to my sculpture more and more these days," she said. "I don't want to do anything else." Mr. Lugan, a writer, is working on a novel.

Both Ms. Henderson and Mr. Lugan were present when Hurricane Eric mysteriously vanished. Neither has an explanation for what happened nor can either shed any light on how young Jason Stern might have been involved in the event. A popular belief is that the boy somehow released or focused an electric charge into the atmosphere that calmed the storm, although scientists are quick to dispute such theories. Nevertheless, no scientific explanation has been given for the phenomenon.

Mrs. Stern, the boy's mother and Ms. Henderson's sister, is in seclusion in New York and would not respond to this reporter's questions. Her husband, Friedreich Stern, was not available for comment.

*   *   *

Condominium Condemned
by Robert Lunt

FT. HAMILTON, Maryland—The Colony condominium on Cranberry Island, severely damaged last Labor Day by Hurricane Eric, was judged today to be "unsuitable for occupancy" because of structural damage caused by flood waters and was designated a condemned property by the Board of Supervisors of the town of Ft. Hamilton, which has jurisdiction over the island.

The luxury condominium, erected in 1992 by real estate and investment speculator Kenneth Rose, was attacked from the beginning by environmentalists who claimed that the construction of the ten-story tower would be an insult to Cranberry Island's delicate ecostructure. Opponents had argued against the project in court for several years until a ruling in Mr. Rose's favor in 1990 cleared the way for construction.

Work on the Colony was hampered by the fact that all materials and workers had to be ferried in, as no land route or connection exists between Cranberry island and the mainland. Nevertheless, the tower went up quickly and the resort residence had its first occupants in late 1992. Mr. Rose was hailed by his peers as a visionary and attacked by his opponents as an opportunist who had raped the environment and was putting lives at risk because the structure would not stand up to a major storm.

Hurricane Eric, whose mysterious conclusion has been the subject of widespread speculation, seemed to prove the environmentalists right. Most of the residents were evacuated before the storm hit, but Mr. Rose and a number of his supporters remained in the Colony during the storm. When flood waters threatened, all the residents except for Mr. Rose fled to the upper floors. Mr. Rose, whose last words reportedly were "I'll show those bastards who's right," remained in his second floor office and was subsequently drowned.

No plans are yet in place to demolish the structure. Because of the high cost of transporting labor and equipment to Cranberry Island, the Colony may be left to stand, a monument to man's will to dominate nature and to nature's simple determination to be.

*   *   *

Hurricane Boy One Year Later
by Carl Walter

NEW YORK—(Special to the New York Times) One year after a remarkable occurrence in Maryland, Jason Stern, the boy at the center of the mystery surrounding the sudden dissipation of Hurricane Eric, remains in a coma at New York Hospital where doctors do not expect him to regain consciousness. The events of the past year have been as much of a puzzle as the precipitating incident.

Here is what is known. First, Hurricane Eric formed off the coast of South Carolina last year during the latter part of the week just prior to Labor Day. Second, the storm, with winds reaching 90 miles per hour, made a sudden northwesterly move on the Sunday before Labor Day and traveled 300 miles to the Ft. Hamilton, Maryland area in about 15 hours. Third, at the height of the storm, the Stern boy climbed onto the deck of a ferry boat evacuating vacationers to Ft. Hamilton and was enveloped in a blaze of lightning. Moments later, the hurricane cleared.

Scientists from around the world still have no explanation for the event, nor do doctors have an explanation as to why the Stern boy has not recovered. Popular theories abound, ranging from UFOs to secret government weather control experiments to an Act of God. No one theory, however, with the possible exception of the miraculous, has gained any widespread acceptance.

The boy's mother, Mrs. Annabelle Stern, in the only public appearance or interview she has consented to, discounted ideas of divine intervention and told Larry King that her boy Jason "was never interested in God." He was "a practical boy, good in math and science. I wanted him to be a scientist." She is as much puzzled by what happened as anyone.

Mrs. Stern is preparing to take her son out of the hospital and care for him at home. She recently celebrated his fifteenth birthday with a few of his friends and her sister and brother-in-law, Mr. and Mrs. Greg Lugan of Cranberry Island, Maryland. Mrs. Lugan (nee Henderson), a sculptor, recently completed a set of pieces commemorating the events surrounding the Hurricane Eric mystery. She is the mother of a three-month old son.

This reporter was allowed to visit Jason Stern in the hospital. The enigma involving his coma and of the events of last year is only deepened upon seeing the boy. His face and body, which had been hit with planks torn from the ferryboat deck by the storm, show no mark, scar, or evidence of any injury. His face is calm, his breathing deep and regular, his color healthy. His expression is one of complete peace and in his presence there is the remarkable feeling of great serenity, joy, and love. Perhaps the theories of the miraculous are not far from the truth.

*   *   *

Epilog

phil

phil

jason

                              yes

        jason

                              it s me

i m dreaming

        you were now I m here

what s going on

       not sure

it s like we re thinking together

       like telepathy

consciousness without the net

we ve gone beyond the net crossed it

transcyberspace

has a nice ring to it

where are you

floating

you ve been in a coma

how long

over a year what happened on that boat

i don t know

it was big news you stopped the storm

i remember   with the stone

the resurrection stone

yes   used it to stop the storm

impossible

so how do they explain it

they can t

it was a miracle

so now you believe in god

why not

you never did

that changed   everything changed
it all became clear on the ferry

be careful   things are clear only to nuts

i m not crazy   my mind opened up

you drop acid

no i just saw things differently
how

that we re god experiencing not-god like that website says
         the one you told me about
god chose to find out what it was like not to be god   *in*   *that*
choice
      god extended itself big bang created
a   *world in*   *which to forget*   *who it was*
     who we   *are*
       the world   *of opposites*

opposite to god

finite instead of infinite mortal instead of   *eternal god*
      experiencing not-god
we must remember our godhood
             that we are one

that was quite a ferry ride

i guess i woke up

what do you mean

you said once that every now and then one of us
     wakes up to the truth

and that s you

i think so   *you know what else*

what

we are stars

i know their atoms make our bodies

that s only the physical part   they
hold our souls between lives on earth

plato said something like that

he was right

i visited you

thank you

i met your mother your aunt   she got married

to who

greg

what do I look like

i don t know

right

yeah

                sometime

what s happening

        i don t know

you okay

                  i think I m coming to

what are you going to do

i don t know

everybody s going to want to know what happened

then I ll tell them

what will you say

i

　　　　　　am

　　　　　　　　　　　　God

　　　is

　　　　　　　　a

　　　　　multitude

　　　we

　　　　　　　　　　are

the

infinite

e

x

p e

ri

encing

the finite

Web Pages

fright.crossing.com

File: Frightful Stories
Author: Unk <unkxxx@duosep.com>
Date: 25 May 1993 17:12:04 GMT
Local-ID: <3b4dp7$nm1@duosep.com>
Title: Bugs

Lydia watched the ladybug walk across the page of her book. The spotted red insect looked like a dot of punctuation searching for its place on top of a lower-case i or at the end of a sentence.

Lydia closed the book with a slam, crushing the little bug.

"Why'd you do that?" asked Mark, who sat in the beach chair next to Lydia. "Ladybugs are harmless and they say it's bad luck to kill one."

"I like squashing bugs," Lydia said.

"Well, honey," said Ann from her spot on the bright yellow beach blanket, "you sure came to the right place. If there's one thing this island has it's bugs. Bugs on the beach, bugs in the restaurants, bugs at the hotel, bugs everywhere."

"Yeah," said Mark. "And you know what? I think Lydia's perfume attracts them."

Lydia smiled and played with one of her long gold earrings. A white moth fluttered past her face. Lydia's hands moved like cat paws to clap the moth between them. When she opened her hands, the moth's dead body and broken wings blew away in the light breeze.

"Ugh," said Ann.

"One less bug in the world," said Lydia. "You should thank me."

"Excuse me," said Mark. He got up from his chair and went into the ocean for a swim.

Lydia spent the rest of the day at the beach, reading and talking and taking the sun. When the black flies came, as they always did to bother the sunbathers around four in the afternoon, Lydia used her towel to swat as many as she could and was happy to see her friends join her in killing the annoying biters.

"See," she said, after the last of the flies had been killed or had flown off, "it's them or us."

"You make it sound like war," said Mark.

"It is," said Lydia.

On the way back to her hotel, Lydia killed a butterfly, mashed a spider and tore down its web, and stepped on a praying mantis. As a fat bee flew past her, Lydia reached out with unusual speed and caught it in her hand.

She held the furry buzzing creature between her finger and thumb. After glancing around to make sure no one was looking, she popped the bee into her mouth and swallowed it. A perfect day, she thought.

That night after dinner, Lydia went for a walk on the beach. Stars filled the sky and their reflections shivered like ghosts in the ocean. She gazed up at a distant blue sun.

Then Lydia heard the sound of thunder.

She cocked her head to one side to hear better and realized it wasn't thunder. It was a buzzing, fluttering, whirring, flapping, scratching noise that blended into a threatening chorus.

Something bit her cheek.

Lydia slapped the bug dead and examined its little body in the starlight. A black fly. It was unusually late at night for black flies.

Something bit her leg, then her neck. She killed two more flies, then a mosquito and a moth that appeared from nowhere. The thunder was almost upon her.

Lydia started back to the hotel.

Suddenly insects swarmed over her, stabbing through her light summer dress, tearing at her flesh. Lydia ran, swatting at the air to drive off the bugs and slapping at herself to stop the biting but it did no good. For every insect she killed, a dozen more, a hundred more, a thousand more took its place.

A cloud of insects descended over her and Lydia could no longer see the stars.

Lydia stumbled in the sand and fell as bees stung her face and flies tore at her skin. She opened her mouth to scream but moths flew in, their soft wings and bodies smothering her cry. Lydia tried to get up but tripped again and went down. The insects covered her like a blanket. She thrashed for several minutes, then her movements slowed and finally stopped.

The cloud around her thinned and faded like dissolving fog.

The next morning a crowd gathered to stare, unbelieving, at the skeleton on the beach.

A skeleton with long gold earrings lying next to it.

A skeleton surrounded by the small bodies of hundreds of dead bees, flies, crickets, gnats, mosquitoes, flying ants, and bugs no one could name. A skeleton whose mouth was filled with dead moths.

A skeleton staring without eyes into the merciless sky.

A skeleton whose sharp black bones gleamed in the sunlight like the remains of a giant alien insect.

fright.crossing.com

File: Frightful Stories
Author: Unk <unkxxx@duosep.com>
Date: 25 May 1993 17:12:04 GMT
Local-ID: <3b4dp7$nm1@duosep.com>
Title: The Makinaw

"Good morning, Mr. Croner. Welcome to Makinaw."

Henry Croner smiled and followed the manager into the inn. Behind Henry and the manager walked two bellhops, ready to provide any assistance Henry might need.

The Makinaw was nice, he thought, pleasant and charming in a contemporary style. Modern but cozy. The manager led Henry to his room.

"This will be yours," the manager said. "You can change here."

Henry took off his dirty street clothes and put on the freshly pressed leisure clothing one of the bellhops was holding. The crisp light green outfit suited him, he thought, even though he could find no mirror in which to admire himself.

The room, decorated with delicate blue and white flowered wallpaper, could have used more furniture, Henry thought. All he saw was a bed with a fluffy white comforter.

"Good," said the manager after Henry changed. "Now let's get you something to eat."

Henry went with the manager and the bellhops downstairs to a big dining hall. As they entered, a waitress gave Henry two pills and a paper cup of water.

"Vitamins," said the manager.

Henry took the pills and smiled at the waitress. She didn't smile back and Henry asked why.

"Don't worry about it," said the manager. "It's just the way she is."

But Henry did worry about it. He liked people to smile at him. It made him nervous when they didn't. He told that to the manager and they sat down.

"Look, Henry," said the manager, "you're going to be all right here, even if some people don't smile at you. You're going to be fine. Your vitamins will help you worry less."

Henry ate with some of the other guests, all of whom wore the same light green suits and all of whom were quiet. When the man across from him didn't return his smile, Henry got up and reached for him but a waiter pulled Henry away.

Later, two exercise instructors took Henry outside for a walk. The grounds of the Makinaw were well kept, with the grass closely cut and the bushes neatly trimmed. Henry admired the tall handsome fence that surrounded the Makinaw and served to keep out anyone but the guests.

The next few days went quickly. Henry liked the routine and the games and most everybody smiled at him. The only thing missing was the news. The television showed only movies. There were no radios, only tape players for music. Soft music.

Henry enjoyed his talks every afternoon with the manager, who always wanted to know how Henry was doing. Fine, Henry would say. Just fine.

And he was fine. Just fine. Until he found the newspaper.

Someone had dropped it behind a bush on the grounds. Henry spotted it and stuffed it under his shirt before anyone saw him. That night he looked at it in his room.

His picture was on the front page.

"CRONER TO UNDERGO TESTS" the headline read.

"Henry Croner, the Mad Postman, will undergo testing at the Makinaw State Mental Hospital this week. The tests will determine his sanity during the ten years in which he killed 75 people, hacked them up, and mailed the pieces around the country."

Henry stared at his picture and remembered.

The next day Henry got rid of the newspaper without anyone seeing him. When they gave him his pills, he held them under his tongue without swallowing, then spit them out later. He smiled at everybody and did everything they asked him to, without any fuss.

After a week of not taking his pills, Henry began to think clearer. He felt stronger and better than he had since arriving at the Makinaw. He was ready to leave.

Henry planned it carefully. The next time he went for a walk on the grounds, Henry asked his guards if they wanted to play tag. They went along with him and Henry was it. He chased one guard behind some bushes and killed him with a single blow to the head.

Henry strangled the second guard with shoelaces he had taken from the first, then dragged him behind the bushes. There Henry bit off the guard's nose.

Henry changed clothes with one of the guards then ran for the fence and climbed over it. No one saw him go and that, thought Henry, was good.

He didn't want anyone to stop him.

Henry squeezed the warm, moist lump of flesh and cartilage he had taken form the guard's face.

He had to get to a post office.

www.TheSecretofLifeRevealed.com

"We are God in human form experiencing not-being-God."

GOD AND THE UNIVERSE

God is and has been and will be all that is and was and ever can be. God is eternal, infinite, and one. At some "time" it was God's "thought" to experience not-being-God. This "thought" was what we call the Big Bang from which the tangible universe was created. The universe and all life and things in it are the opposite of God: limited, separate, and subject to change, aging, and death. This is what is meant when we say we live in a world of opposites. It is through the universe that God experiences not-being-God.

We are spiritual beings having a human experience. We are the *infinite in the finite*. Each of us is part of God and it is that spirit that is our true self. We live in the dream we have created, believing in our limited, mortal forms and not knowing our true eternal selves. It is only by the gradual awakening of our spirits that we eventually rise to knowledge of our divine nature. As Shakespeare said, the world is but a stage. We never die, only assume different roles. When the play is over, we will know who we truly are.

Fear and the Belief in Separateness

God is one while we appear to be many. In our material forms we believe in our separateness from each other. This belief in separateness is essential to the experience of not-being-God and is the foundation of life on Earth.

Belief in separateness gives rise to fear which in turn gives rise to the wrongs we do. The seven deadly sins (a word taken from the Greek that means "missing the mark") are good examples of how the belief in separateness influences our actions. The underlying purpose of these sins is to control fear by assuming power. Three of these sins assume power over people:

Pride: "I am better than you and have the right to control you."
Anger: "I can hate you and have the right to kill you."
Envy: "I deserve what you have and have the right to take from you."

Three of these sins assume power over the appetites of self:

Greed: "I can have as much as I want."
Gluttony (addictions): "I can consume as much as I want."
Lust: "I can have as much sensual pleasure as I want."

The first of these two groups of sins fills the emptiness that comes with the feeling of separation by taking in the self-esteem, lives, and property of others. The second group attempts to fill this emptiness by taking in possessions, substances, and sensual experience. The remaining sin, sloth, assumes power over God by denying action. However, the feeling of emptiness cannot be denied and cannot be remedied by anything other than the realization of the truth of our connectedness and collective God-hood.

Fear and the Need to Control
Taking control of a situation, which generally means taking control of people, reduces fear by providing the illusion of being in command and of being strong and unassailable. However, when people are controlled they eventually rise up to overthrow their oppressors, thus bringing about the very thing that the oppressors feared. The need to be free is a manifestation of our Godliness and can never be denied. God is free, as we are meant to be.

Individual Fear and Collective Fear
To overcome feelings of separateness and the resultant fear, individuals form and join groups for mutual protection and for the advancement of common interests. This is what builds cities, states, nations, religions, and other collective associations. Such institutions, when they focus on the

good, have done much to advance humanity and provide people with the opportunity to find their true selves. It is easy, however, for the fears of the group's members to transform into a collective fear in which the group itself feels threatened by other groups and then becomes oppressive or war-like. This is the pattern of dictatorships and restrictive societies everywhere.

Fear and Evil
Evil is a manifestation of fear. Because fear is generated by the belief in and feelings of separateness from others and from God, the evil done by an individual or group is directly proportional to the degree of that belief in separateness. The leaders of Nazi ("not-see") Germany were so blinded by their belief in separation that they institutionalized it with a Final Solution of government sanctioned death camps for all who were different. This evil is the ultimate expression of collective fear.

EVOLUTION
Evolution is the process by which we (the universe in conscious form) becomes aware first of itself (ourselves) and then of God and finally of the fact that we are that God. Darwinian Theory has evolution upside down in the sense that our evolving physical and mental forms do not give rise to higher states of consciousness, rather it is our emerging God-conscious-ness that creates more and more sophisticated physical forms in which to dwell. The highest expression of consciousness is that of the God-person: spirit in form fully aware of its spiritual nature.

RELIGION
God is to organized religion as the elephant was to the blind men. Each blind man, according to the story, touched a different part of the elephant and judged the elephant to be that part, as when touching a leg and describing the elephant as a column, or touching the tail and describing the elephant as a rope. In this manner organized religions touch a part of God and make the mistake of taking that part for the whole. When the

collective fear of a religious group is added into the mix, there is the basis for crusades, inquisitions, and holy wars.

"AS WE UNDERSTOOD HIM"

The Twelve Stop programs that began with Alcoholics Anonymous in the 1930's have as part of their philosophic and therapeutic basis the idea that each individual can regard God in his or her own way and that this belief will be sufficient to energize the recovery process. The Twelve Steps themselves have only 200 words, yet one phrase is considered so important that it is repeated twice and underlined on each occasion:

- Step 3: Made a decision to turn our will and our lives over to the care of God *as we understood Him*.
- Step 11: Sought through prayer and mediation to improve our conscious contact with God *as we understood Him*, praying only for knowledge of His will for us and the power to carry that out.

This is one of the most revolutionary and liberating phrases in all of religions and spiritual thought. It frees us from the burden of having to prove and protect our faith by destroying those who believe differently.

KARMA, REINCARNATION, AND DNA

As we act in our lives we create patterns of thought and action that persist after the death of our earthly bodies. This karma (a form of cause and effect) manifests in the location and circumstances of our rebirth and in the DNA that directs the construction of our bodies. This process of birth, death, and rebirth is the fundamental mechanism of human life. It is the mechanism we, as God, have created to support the illusion that we are not-God.

Cause and Effect

The world we experience is not ultimate reality, yet we believe that it is. Our belief is reinforced by what seem to be immutable laws of life: the passage of time and cause and effect. However, because we are spiritual beings, we do not in fact exist in time nor are we subject to cause and effect. Our bodies and the world we see exist as they do only because we believe they should exist that way. Our infinite creative power is controlled by our belief systems to project the world we believe we should experience. As we free ourselves from limited beliefs, we will create worlds in which time, aging, and death do not exist.

PAIN AND SUFFERING

Pain and suffering are the inevitable result of our belief in separation and provide a direct path to finding the truth of our existence. No one seeks the truth in times of happiness, joy, fulfillment, and success for it is in those times that we feel we are right, that our picture of the universe is correct, and that we are in control of our lives and the world around us.

It is only when we are beaten down like Job that we ask the important questions and are prepared to find the answers. This is why the Twelve Step programs have the success they have. It is only by "bottoming out" that people will admit that they are not in control of their lives and then turn to a solution. Only when we have exhausted a particular belief system are we ready to accept a new one. Only when we have taken a belief to its limit are we ready to move on. Only when we are too miserable to continue on a path will we look for a new one. And even then, resistance to the process of change will still be great because we are "programmed" to believe in false ways in order to experience our humanity.

THE PURPOSE OF LIFE

The purpose of life is to experience it and to become aware of our true selves (God). The highest expression of that purpose is to act with love, which means to help another grow physically, mentally, and spiritually. Love is God in action. As we *evolve* we wake to that love.

FURTHER READINGS

A Course in Miracles, Foundation for Inner Peace, Tiburon, California
Alcoholics Anonymous, Alcoholics Anonymous World Services, Inc., New York
God Speaks, Meher Baba, Dodd, Mead & Company, New York

we dream
countless stars
whose number
i know
and souls
as many as tears
    we dream
    to know joy
    without truth
    and pain
    in place
    of our light
we dream
to know life
not eternal
and death
unknown
without birth
for i
cannot die
or be born
    we dream
    in my heart
    to know all
    we are not
    for all we are not
    must be known
we sleep
and we dream
yet soon
will awake
    to KNOW
    that we are
    what i am

About the Author

Frank Hertle is a published poet and produced playwright. He studied fiction writing with Doris Betts and Andre Dubus, and screenwriting with Richard Walter (of UCLA). He has written nearly two dozen stage plays, from 10 minutes to full length, and a number of screenplays. His plays for stage include MONSTER, a two-act thriller that ran for eight weeks off-Broadway at the Jose Quintero Theater in the winter of 2000. While his film scripts create worlds of spectacle, his plays focus on the intimate moments when people face each other in life-affirming or life-threatening situations.

His novel THE RESURRECTION STONE is an irreverent coming-of-age adventure in which love, death, sex, violence, poetry, philosophy, God, and the Internet are all part of a boy's journey to a profound revelatory experience.

Printed in the United States
209361BV00001B/328-333/A

9 780595 208081